VENGEANCE

Stuart M. Kaminsky

Vengeance

COMPASS PRESS

AN IMPRINT OF WHEELER PUBLISHING, INC.

Published in Large Print by arrangement with
Tom Doherty Associates, LLC, in the United States and Canada.

Compass Press Large Print book series;
an imprint of Wheeler Publishing Inc., USA

Set in 16 pt Plantin.

Library of Congress Cataloging-in-Publication Data

Kaminsky, Stuart M.
    Vengeance / Stuart M. Kaminsky.
        p. (large print) cm.(Compass Press large print book series)
    ISBN 1-56895-870-6 (hardcover)
    1. Private investigators—Florida—Fiction. 2. Sarasota (Fla.)—Fiction.
3. Large type books.
I. Title. II. Series

[PS3561.A43V46   2000]
813'.54—dc21   00-024179
                                                                      CIP

To Francis and King Stuzman,
With Fond Memories of the Midway

In tasks so bold can little men engage,
And in soft bosoms dwells such mighty rage?

—Alexander Pope
The Rape of the Lock

THERE WERE THREE reasons I was staying a few miles over the speed limit on 301 heading toward Bradenton.

First, Sarasota is full of the very old, to whom the State of Florida will grant a driver's license even if the person is blind or too short to see over the dashboard. Old people and tourists are treated with dignity in the Sunshine State. They have the dollars. Many of them drive not in the State of Florida, but in a state of complete oblivion, leaving accidents in their wake, driving on in the certainty that they are doing no evil. A second group of drivers in abundance is the smiling and soused teens and their parents. They are not outsiders. Their pickup trucks proudly bear decals of the Confederate flag and bumper sticks with comments like WE DON'T GIVE A SHIT HOW YOU DID IT UP NORTH and YOU CAN HAVE MY WIFE BEFORE I'LL GIVE UP MY GUN.

These two groups seem miraculously to miss each other in the highway bumper-car game and cause only misery, mayhem and death to the majority of people who drive and live normally beneath the sun and in the wake of hurricanes.

I said there were three reasons.

The second is that my wife died in a car crash in Chicago a little over three years ago. Six months and five days more than three years. It wasn't her fault. Someone had sideswiped her, probably an accident, sent her into a low concrete wall on Lake Shore Drive, and driven away fast. Never found. I've driven as little as I could since then, but sometimes I have no choice if I'm going to make a living. I drive carefully, always aware of the upcoming driveway hidden by shrubs, the white Nissan with no visible driver, the maroon Ford Futura that may or may not be weaving just a little two blocks back in my rearview mirror. Until a few months ago, I used to sweat whenever I drove, even with the automobile air conditioner dialed to high.

The third reason I was only a few miles over the speed limit letting cars, vans and trucks whip past me was that I was reasonably sure I was too late. I didn't know if I wanted to get where I was going in time to stop a murder.

The radio was on. I seldom listened to music, I liked a voice, almost any voice, a southern Baptist preacher, G. Gordon Liddy, Rush Limbaugh, Dr. Laura, an abusive local talk-show host on WFLA out of Tampa using words I thought were prohibited by the FCC. If I were lucky, I'd catch NPR and listen to *All Things Considered* or *Fresh Air* but really, any voice would do and I didn't always listen to the words.

I wasn't alone in the car. Ames McKinney sat erect, seat-belted next to me, riding shotgun. Literally. He had an old Remington M-10 twelve gauge pump-action shotgun lying across the lap of his yellow slicker. Ames seldom spoke. He had said almost all he had to say in his seventy-four years of life. Ames looked like an aged Gary Cooper with long white hair and a face of sunned leather.

He knew how to use a gun, though he was not supposed to have one. Ames had come to Sarasota three years earlier in search of his business partner, who had run off with all the money from the sale of their business back in Arizona. Ames and his partner had gone out to the white sand behind the trees on South Lido Beach and had an old-fashioned shoot-out. Ames won. The judge called it justifiable homicide and gave Ames a suspended sentence for carrying an illegal firearm. There are actually laws about dueling in Florida, but the judge wasn't about to invoke them. The partner fired first. Actually, the partner fired four times before Ames shot him. I was there. I testified on his behalf. Ames thinks I saved him from Old Sparky.

I made a turn off the highway at Ellenton, saw the huge shopping mall I've never been to flash by me and headed west toward Palmetto.

Past the Gamble Mansion, preserved as it had been when slaves lived in shacks and the second floor was reached by ladders that could be pulled up in case the Seminoles attacked. Past the tomato-packing plants, tiendas and pawnshops where the migrant Hispanic laborers worked and shopped.

By the time I had made a turn and headed north on Tamiami Trail, I was sure we were going to be too late.

It began to rain. It began to rain hard. Summer was the time for rain on the Gulf Coast. But weather truths, like human ones, had begun to change here long before I arrived.

My windshield wipers worked. I was driving a newly rented white Geo Metro, which wanted to leave the road with every blast of wind.

I had an address and only a general idea of where I was going, but with a turn again I knew I was in Palmetto. Palm trees went wild in the wind. The streets began to flood. Traffic slowed to a crawl. People, all black, ran for cover or home. I drove trying to see street signs and passed the one I was looking for. I went to the next corner and turned left around a battered green Chevy that was stalled in a deep puddle. The driver was an old black woman with gray hair. I caught just a glimpse of her but I could see that she was sitting in a state of near-perfect calm. She had been through this before. She had been through much worse before. So had I. She would endure. I probably would too.

I found the house whose address I had been carrying around for three days. It was dark. The morning was almost as dark, with black, driving rain. A pickup truck with a tow winch was parked in the driveway. The house was a one-story cinder-block bunker. There was no grass on the place where a lawn should be. There was just a thin lake of rainwater with bits of debris, dirt, beer bottles and rocks peeking out.

I turned off Dr. Laura in midsentence as she

4

told a weeping young woman to stop crying and take charge of her life. She could have been talking to me.

Ames and I got out of the car and I was soaked deep as I hurried to the front door of the house. Ames, yellow slicker protecting him, walked cradling the shotgun, right hand at the trigger. Lightning crackled and struck somewhere on the other side of the nearby Manatee River.

I knocked. Thunder above. The noise of pelting rain. My feet were getting soaked through my shoes. I knocked louder. No answer. I didn't expect one. I tried the doorknob. Since the rain was knocking at the door too, I didn't think any fingerprints remained on the knob. I was breaking the law. I should have called the police hours ago, but the police were not happy with me at the moment.

The door wasn't locked.

I started in but Ames put out a long, lean arm to hold me back so he could enter first. This was the home—well, the house—of a dangerous man, a man who had...Later, I'll talk about it later. Now, I followed Ames inside. There were no lights on, but it was still day and in spite of the storm, there was enough light so that I could see faintly.

The rain pounded on the roof demanding to be let in, demanding to carry away this concrete hell.

A sofa and unmatched cushioned chair and a metal folding chair were covered with dirty clothes, full ashtrays and empty Dr Pepper cans and amber beer bottles.

Maybe he hadn't been here when the knock had come, even though his truck was. Maybe he was away somewhere. A friend, if he had one, had picked him up and they were out looking for trouble or for me.

"Here," said Ames in his raspy voice as he stepped over the debris and through an open door.

I followed him into a kitchen that smelled like a Port-o-Let at a county fair. Dishes, food in the sink, an overflowing bag of garbage and a body on the floor.

I turned on the light. A large roach scurried out of the garbage bag and headed for the darkness.

There was blood, damp, fresh. Ames looked down at the body, around the room and shook his head. The shake was hardly more than a tick but I knew Ames McKinney. He hated filth, human and otherwise.

"Let's go," I said, turning off the light.

There was a telephone in the living room but I couldn't bring myself to stay here any longer and I didn't want to report finding my third corpse in four days. I didn't search the place. I didn't go into the bedrooms. I knew what I would see. I just wanted to get out. Maybe I would call the police from my office when I was dry and I wasn't shaking. Maybe I would call and tell them a story. It wouldn't be the truth, so I needed time to make it up.

The rain was heavier.

I had to move slowly going back to the car where the rising water was now up to mid-hubcap. I wondered if any neighbors had seen us go into the house. I wondered if any neighbors had seen someone go in an hour or two before us. I wondered if anyone in this neighborhood would tell even if they had seen the murder on their front lawn.

Ames and I got in the car and I drove slowly through heavy rain that would move the waste but not wash it away.

My name is Lew Fonesca.

The crumbs of Gretel that had led me to that house had begun to drop four days earlier when...

1

"HOT IN HERE."

She looked around my tiny office, trying not to show uncertainty and disapproval.

"Air conditioner doesn't work," I said.

"Then why do you leave it on?"

"Fan makes the air move a little. Your daughter is missing?"

She nodded.

So far all I had from her was that her daughter, Adele, was missing and that the woman's name was Beryl. She hadn't given a last name yet. She was holding that back till she decided if she was going to trust me with it. Beryl was about forty, with dark hair cut short, on the thin side, and she was wearing a serious but slightly shabby loose-fitting blue dress with a belt and no style. She kept her purse on her knees and her knees tight and together. She had nice blue eyes and had probably once been very pretty. She also had a blue-yellow bruise on her cheek the size of a large peach.

I had somewhere I had to be in a little over an hour, but I couldn't bring myself to hurry this woman. She needed to take her time. She needed someone to listen to her story.

"I have a picture," she said, opening her purse.

I waited. The air conditioner buzzed and I pretended it wasn't hot.

"Here."

She handed me a little photograph that looked as if it were taken in one of those automatic camera booths you find in malls.

The girl was definitely pretty. She had blond, straight hair, was wearing a green sweater and showed a fine set of white teeth. She looked grade-school young.

"Adele," Beryl said, looking toward the window as if her daughter might suddenly appear.

It was my turn to nod.

"How'd you get hurt?"

She touched the bruise on her check and said, "Fell in the bathroom of the motel."

"Tell your story, Miss..."

"Mrs.," she corrected looking down at her purse. "Husband moved out when Adele was little. Driver."

"His name is Driver?"

"No," she said with a sigh. "His name was Dwight. Tow truck driver."

"He was a tow truck driver," I prompted.

"Still is, I think. Few minutes back, I lied."

"You lied?"

"To you. Said I fell in the motel."

She started to raise her hand to the bruise on her face and changed her mind.

"He did it."

"Your husband?"

She nodded and sighed, lips tightly together.

"You live in Sarasota?"

"No, but it looks like he does. Not sure."

I glanced at my watch, pretending to be considering the situation. I now had less than half an hour to get where I had to be.

"Adele and I live in Brisbane, Kansas. Dwight left when Adele was seven. I can't say I was all that unhappy to see him go. He sent a letter two months back," she said. "To Adele. Don't know what it said. She didn't show it to me, but I did see the return address. Don't remember the address, but it was from here."

I nodded.

"I think she ran off to be with him. I raised Adele alone. Not much to do for a child in Brisbane after school. I worked days and a lot of nights at the restaurant, Jim and Ella's Good Food. Truckers welcome. Most nights Adele would watch the TV, look out the window of the apartment at the oil rigs in the field. At least till she got older and got in with the crowd."

"Bad crowd?" I asked.

"Only crowd in Brisbane, if you count four or five kids as a crowd."

"Go on."

"Not much more to tell. She's smart. Good grades, always good grades, but she got into a little trouble once in a while. She's got a temper like Dwight."

"Her father," I said.

"Got on the junior cheerleaders but didn't go to practice and they cut her," said Beryl with a sigh. "In a couple of school plays. One she had a lot of things to say. How do they remember all those things to say?"

I ignored the sweat on my scalp.

"I don't know," I said.

"Well," Beryl went on. "Life is a puzzle."

"Yes," I said.

"She ran away a little over three months ago. No note. Just packed up and left a message taped to the TV saying she was going and she would call. I told Josh Hamilton, the sheriff, that she had run and he took a picture just like the one you're holding and said he'd follow up and maybe get her on milk cartons and paper bags if she didn't show up in a few weeks. I told him about the letter from her father."

"And you...?"

"Worked, waited. She didn't show up. Josh suggested I get one of those things you put on your phone that shows the number someone is calling you from in case she called. I did—couldn't really afford it—but...but no call from Adele till two weeks ago. I wrote down the number. Adele sounded bad, scared. Wouldn't tell me why. I told her to come home. She said she couldn't, that she'd be all right."

Beryl reached into her purse and came up with a sheet of paper. She handed it to me. It had an 941-area-code number.

"I called her back," Beryl said, fingering the little silver latch on her purse. "Called back maybe fifteen times. No answer. Little over a week ago a man answered, said I was calling a pay phone outside a motel on Tamiami Trail in Sarasota, Florida. I got a ride from Ellis to Wichita, bus here. Adele is fourteen, just barely. She's pretty, smart and in trouble. I've been wandering around for the last week

11

looking for her, but I don't know how to do it or what to ask."

"Did you go to the police?"

"Yes," she said. "First thing. They took a picture of Adele and the phone-booth number and said they'd look into it. Nice man, a sergeant, said it would get it posted and go in the computer. I got the feeling Adele was going in a big box with a thousand or more other lost children."

"I think you're right."

I placed the phone number right next to the photograph of the smiling girl on my desk.

"How did you find me?" I asked.

"Motel I'm staying at, the Best Western, is just down the street. Came here for a Dairy Queen fish sandwich just maybe fifteen, twenty minutes back. I showed the man who served me the sandwich Adele's picture. Told him my story. He said maybe you could help."

"Anything else?" I asked.

"Yes," she said, looked down and then straightened up. "Who are you?"

"My name is Lewis Fonesca. I used to work for the state attorney's office in Cook County, Illinois. Investigations. One morning my wife took the car to work. She died in a car accident on Lake Shore Drive. It was winter. I wasn't going any further up in my job and I'm not ambitious. I was cold and too many places and people reminded me of my wife. Am I telling you too much?"

"No."

There was more but I didn't see the need

12

to share it with Beryl. I had come to Sarasota a little over three years earlier, just drove till my car gave out and I felt safe in the sunshine after spending my life in the gray of Chicago. I drove away from the dead-end investigator's job with the State's Attorney's office. Now I made a sort of living finding people, asking questions, answering to nobody. I had a growing number of Sarasota lawyers using me to deliver a summons or find a local resident who hadn't turned up for court or a divorce hearing. I had a county process server's license, complete with a full-color card with my photograph on it. It was the same face I saw in the mirror: sad, balding. A short, thin man who definitely looked Italian.

Occasionally, I would turn up some street trade, a referral like Beryl from Dave at the Dairy Queen. I lived in and worked out of a second-floor office in a two-story office building behind the DQ parking lot. Entrance to each of the offices was through a door to the outside. My door, like the others, needed a coat of paint. The metal railing on the balcony was starting to rust seriously.

I had a deal with the building manager. The landlord lived in Seattle. By giving the manager a few extra dollars a month beyond the reasonable rent for a seedy two rooms he referred to as a "suite," he ignored the fact that I was living in the "suite." The outer room where I now sat with Beryl was designed as a reception room. I had turned it into an office. The room behind it was a small windowed office, which I had turned into a living space. I had fixed it up to my satisfaction. The clothes I had brought with me from Chicago would hold out for another year or two. I had a narrow bed, an old dresser, a small closet, a television set—with a VCR picked up at a nearby pawnshop—and a low bookcase, which stood next to the dresser and was overflowing with paperbacks and videotapes. To get to the bathroom, which had no bath, I had to walk outside past five offices, accepting whatever the weather had to offer. I showered at the downtown YMCA every morning after I worked out there. Normally, I bicycle to the Y. My bike was standing in the corner behind my new client.

There was nothing but my name printed on the white-on-black plastic plate that slid into the slot on my outer door. The plate didn't indicate what service I provided.

"Man at the Dairy Queen," she said, nodding at the door, beyond which was the concrete landing overlooking the Dairy Queen on Route 301, which was also Washington Street, though in my two years in town I never heard anyone call it anything but 301. They also called Bahia Vista "Baya Vista," and Honore Avenue was usually referred to as Honor Avenue,

"He said you had feelings."

She looked at me for about the third time and saw a sad-looking forty-two-year-old man with rapidly thinning hair and reasonable dark looks wearing a short-sleeved button-down blue shirt and gray jeans.

14

"You're a detective, like on television," she said. "Rockford."

"More like Harry Orwell," I said. "I'm not a detective. The only license I have in this state is a card with my picture on it that says I'm a process server. But any citizen can make inquiries. That's what I do. I make inquiries."

"You ask questions."

"I ask questions."

"What do you charge?"

"Fifty dollars a day, plus expenses."

"Expenses?"

"Phone calls. Gas. Rental car. Things like that. I report to you every night if you want me to. You can stop my services anytime before the next day. My guess is I'll find Adele in two or three days or tell you she's not in Sarasota."

"Okay," she said, opening her purse once again and pulling out a wallet, from which she extracted five tens. "I will need a receipt."

I took the money, found a pad of yellow legal-sized paper and wrote out a receipt. She took it and said, "I told you I'm staying at the Best Western. I'm in Room Two-o-four."

"Well," I said, handing her my card. There was nothing on it but my name, address and phone number. "You can call me here day or night."

Beryl took my card, looked at it, put it in her purse, and snapped her purse closed.

"I am not a warm woman," she said. "I do not show my affections. I did not do so with Adele, but I do love her and I think she knows that. Please find her."

15

"I'll do my best to find her." I said. "A few more questions. What's your last name?"

"Tree. My name is Beryl Tree. My daughter is Adele Tree. Took my maiden name back when Dwight walked out, took it back and gave it to my daughter. His name is Handford, Dwight Handford."

"And he knows you're in town and where you're staying."

"Didn't tell him where I was stayin'. Just ran into him on the street, coming out of the Waffle House across from the motel. He looked scared, then mad. I asked him where Adele was. He hit me, told me to get back to Kansas or the next time he saw me he'd..."

She stood looking at the humming air conditioner. She had something more to say. I waited.

"He, Dwight, was married before me. Said he divorced her. Had a daughter before he married me. Josh, he's the sheriff..."

"I know."

"Josh came checking on him once. Didn't know what it was about till Adele ran off. Then Josh told me. Dwight spent prison time for...for doing his first daughter when she was twelve."

I knew what "doing" meant.

"Adele's a pretty girl," she said. "Too pretty maybe."

"I'll find her," I said.

And she was gone.

I pulled some Kleenex from my drawer, wiped my head, face and neck, and threw the used tissues into my Tampa Bay Bucs waste-basket. My shirt was sweat-blotched and clinging wet to my back. It was a hot December day in Sarasota, probably about eighty-four degrees and humid—hot for winter, but not unheard of. It was the middle of the snowbird season. Tourists and winter residents rented or owned overpriced houses and apartments on the mainland in Bradenton, Sarasota and all the way up the coast to Pensacola and down the coast to Naples. The winter crowd with real money were in the resorts and condos on the beaches of Longboat and Siesta Keys. All in all, there were about 200,000 people in Manatee and Sarasota Counties combined during The Season.

In Sarasota, south of the airport, there is a strip of low-cost motels on Tamiami Trail. The strip stretches for a couple of miles to down-town and stops just before the theater district. The primary residents of the motels are small-time pimps and prostitutes, mostly runaways like Adele, though in the winter unknowing French and German tourists wander into these motels with their families, swimsuits and cameras. This was where I'd start looking for Adele's phone booth. If that failed, I'd go south of Bay Front Park and downtown and start my search among the malls, restaurants and shops.

Sarasota has hundreds of restaurants catering to retirees, tourists and full-time working residents. It could be a long day or two of work. If she was still in town, I didn't think Adele would be that

17

tough to find, and I needed the fifty dollars. My backup was to find Dwight Handford. From what little Beryl had told me about her husband, I had the feeling he wouldn't be found by simply looking in the phone book. I was right. I'd find him if I had to, but I'd go for that phone booth first. How long it would take to find Adele Tree depended on what happened at my meeting in less than half an hour.

I had gone three weeks with no work but serving papers twice, thirty-five dollars for each job. Both servings had been easy. They're not always easy. People who took the court order I handed them tended to see me as the enemy, the messenger for the system, the first step in doing them in. I've been slapped, threatened and hit a few times. Usually, though, the recipient was stunned. I always dressed casually, spoke politely and asked if I was speaking to the person I was looking for. If I was, I handed the papers to him or her. If I wasn't and the person admitted that I had come to the right place, I gave that person the papers. It was legal. I could simply drop the papers on a table or on the floor.

There are servers who simply tear up the papers they are supposed to serve and swear that the deliveries were made. There are others who carry guns and push through doors and face a knife or a rifle to get the job done. Pride, not money, for these people.

I carried no gun. If things looked really bad on a job, I turned the papers back in and said I couldn't find the person I was looking for. That didn't happen much.

The money was running out and I needed Beryl Tree's fifty or a hundred dollars, and there was a good chance I was on my way to another job.

I knew Sarasota and Bradenton reasonably well now. They were still small towns where a pretty young girl might be remembered. There was also that chance that Adele had used a phone near where she was staying.

I put Adele's photo and the phone-booth number in my wallet and changed into a clean white shirt and my only sport jacket, a solid navy blue a little too heavy for Florida. My gray jeans didn't look too bad with the shirt and jacket. This was a casual town. I went down to the Dairy Queen with my bike.

It was a few minutes before noon. I was hungry. I bought a large chocolate-covered-cherry Blizzard and a deluxe burger and thanked Dave for sending me a client.

"Lady needs help," he said. "Kid running away like that. I see a lot of those kids."

Dave was probably around my age, but years in the sun working on boats in the bay had tanned his skin dark. His body was hard and strong, but his face had gone to sun-fried hell.

"I think I can find her," I said while he prepared the burger and shake.

"Kids," Dave said with a shake of the head.

When my order came up I showed Adele's photograph to Dave. He looked at it for a while and squinted in thought.

"Yeah, the lady showed it to me. I don't think I've seen her," he said, "but who knows? She cuts her hair, maybe dyes it, puts on a lot of makeup, orders a Dilly Bar and off she goes. I could have her picture right in front of me and not recognize her. Who knows?"

"Thanks, Dave," I said, taking my Blizzard and burger.

"Who knows?" he repeated. "You know what I mean?"

"I know," I said. "You know anything about a guy named Carl Sebastian?"

"Know of him," said Dave. "Big money, property, real estate, all over the *Herald-Tribune* society pages, always in Marjorie North's column with his wife, a real looker."

"You read the society pages?"

Dave shrugged.

"What can I say? I'm a reader. I read the Wheaties box in the morning. Read an article in some magazine this morning about the history of cod fishing. You know the Basques used to be great cod fishermen. Read the label on the jar of Dundee marmalade while I was having breakfast this morning. You know, the white jar?"

"Yeah."

"History of the company right there on the little jar. I read."

I ate fast and figured that if I took some short-cuts I could pedal the mile or so to the high-rise, high-priced condominium on a quiet street a few hundred yards from Sarasota Bay and maybe be there on time.

I made it with about three minutes to spare. A woman with white hair and a white dog looked at me while I chained my bike to a tree. She looked and then turned her attention back to the dog, who watched me as I walked past and then, assured that he was safe, lifted one leg and aimed for a thin tree with round green fruit that might be oranges.

I stepped into the blue polished granite-floored lobby, pressed the button next to Carl Sebastian's name and was buzzed in almost instantly. A quiet elevator with well-polished dark-wood panels brought me up seventeen floors, to the penthouse.

The door to the only apartment on the floor was wide open. I stepped in and a man's voice called, "Out here."

The living room was big, light but tasteful, with neutral, luxuriously textured furniture as a foil for colorful abstract paintings on the walls. I crossed the room and headed for the man standing at the railing of the balcony beyond. He turned to me.

"How old would you say I am?"

I looked at the dark handsome man standing next to the railing of the balcony overlooking the bay. He was bigger than I am, about six feet and somewhere in the range of one hundred and ninety pounds. His open blue shirt, which may have been silk, showed a well-muscled body with a chest of gray-brown hair. The hair on his head was the same color, plentiful, neat. And he was carefully and gently tanned. He had a glass of something that looked like tomato juice in his hand.

"V8," he said. "Great drink."

He offered me the same. I settled for water.

There was a slight accent, very slight, when he spoke. He reminded me of Ricardo Montalban.

"Just guess."

"What?"

"How old you think I am."

He looked away from the boats bobbing in the bay and the cars going over the bridge to Bird Key and beyond to Lido and Longboat Keys. He was giving me his profile.

Answering a question like the one he asked could lose me a job, but I hadn't come to this town to go back to saying "Yes, boss" to people I liked and didn't like. All I wanted was to make as much money as I needed to stay alive and well supplied with used videotapes. Besides, I had a sure fifty dollars coming from Beryl Tree.

"Sixty," I guessed, standing a few feet away from him and looking him in the eyes when he turned his head and smiled.

"Closer to seventy," he said with satisfaction. "I was blessed by the Lord in many ways. My genes are excellent. My mother is ninety-two and still lives in good health. My father died two years ago at the age of ninety-four. I have uncles, aunts...you wouldn't believe."

"Not without seeing them," I said.

Sebastian laughed. There wasn't much joy in his laugh. He looked at his now empty V8 glass and set it on a glass-topped table.

"Lawrence told you my problem?" he asked,

facing me, his gray-blue eyes unblinking, sincere.

"Your wife left. You want to find her. That's all."

Lawrence Werring was a lawyer, civil cases, injury lawsuits primarily, an ambulance chaser and proud of it. It had bought him a beautiful wife, a leather-appointed office and a four-bedroom house on the water on Longboat Key. If I knew which one it was, I could probably have seen it from where Sebastian and I were standing.

"My wife's name is Melanie," Sebastian said, handing me a folder that lay next to the empty V8 glass. "She is considerably younger than I—thirty-six—but I believed she loves...loved me. I was vain enough to think it was true and for some time it seemed true. And then one afternoon four days ago to be exact, she..."

He looked around as if she might suddenly rematerialize.

"...she was gone. I came home and clothes, jewelry, gone. No note, nothing. That was, let me see, last Thursday. I kept expecting to hear from her or a kidnapper or something, but—"

"The police," I said, holding the unopened folder in front of me.

He shook his head.

"I'd like to keep this quiet for now," he said. "There is the distinct possibility that my wife has left me for...She may not want to be found."

I opened the folder. There was a description of the missing jewelry, a list of credit cards, and the names, addresses and phone numbers of two people. And then there was a neatly typed one-page summary of Melanie Sebastian's life. I skimmed the biography as Carl Sebastian stood watching and drinking a fresh glass of V8.

Melanie Lennell Sebastian was born in Ogden, Utah, earned an undergraduate degree in social science at the University of Florida and moved with her parents, now both dead, to Sarasota, where she worked for a Catholic services agency as a caseworker till she married Sebastian four years earlier. There was a photograph of Melanie Sebastian in the folder. She was wearing red shorts, a white blouse and a great smile. Her dark hair was long and blowing in the breeze. She had her arm lovingly around her husband, who stood tall, tanned and shirtless in a pair of white trunks, looking at the camera. They were standing on the white sands of a Gulf Coast beach, probably a few miles from where we were standing.

"Pretty," I said, closing the folder.

"Beautiful," he corrected. "Exquisite, charming."

"Any guesses?" I said. "About what happened?"

He shrugged and moved from the balcony into the living room. I followed, folder in hand. We stopped in front of a painting of his wife on the wall over a big comfortable-looking pale suede sofa. In spite of the sofa and the tasteful contemporary look about the place, it wasn't my kind of home, but I could appreciate what it cost—which, I think, was the point.

"Another man perhaps, but I doubt it," he said. "At least I hope it isn't, but...We have had no major quarrels. I denied her nothing, nothing. I am far from a poor man, Mr. Fonesca and..."

He paused and sighed deeply.

"And," he continued, composing himself, "I have checked our joint checking and savings accounts. Most of the money has been removed. A little is left. I have my corporate attorney checking other holdings, which Melanie might have had access to. I find it impossible to believe she would simply take as much money as she could and just walk out on me."

"You ever done any acting, Mr. Sebastian?"

The look on his face changed and there seemed to be a definite tinge of pink in the perfect tan.

"What the hell do you mean?" he said.

"There was a little hitch in your voice when you mentioned another man," I said, having decided that none of the chairs in the room were designed for sitting in, at least not by me. "I thought you might want me to pick up on that."

"Maybe I made a mistake in calling you," he said.

"Maybe," I said.

I didn't like the Carl Sebastian I had seen so far. Maybe there was a real Carl Sebastian under the Ricardo Montalban imitation. I might lose the job, but I didn't need the money that badly, not with a bit of Beryl Tree's life savings about to go into my wallet.

"What's your fucking problem here, Fonesca?"

This was much better. He was in my face now.

"I want to talk to whoever Carl Sebastian was before he became Carl Sebastian in capital letters," I said. "You want the folder back?"

I stood waiting. I didn't smile. I don't smile much. He was making a decision.

"Okay," he said, his shoulders dropping a little, the blissful all-white-toothed smile fading. "I came out of the army, poor family back in Dayton. My father worked as a bagger in a supermarket. My mother was home with a bad heart and diabetes. I never went to college. Got a job with a construction company. Union apprentice. Worked up, into the office. Look at my hands."

He held out his hands, palms up. I looked.

"The cuts, the calluses, don't go away, not ones like this. I used these hands to climb over the backs of men and a few women to get where I am. Some of those backs had razors growing out of them. I've been cut, but I haven't fallen. Melanie is smarter than I am, not street smart, but smart. And she wasn't for sale. I didn't buy her to show her off like

26

some of the people I know who say they're my friends. There are razors under those thousand-dollar sports jackets and regret under the beautiful faces of their wives. Melanie is real."

"The hitch in your voice," I said.

"You don't give up."

"You want me to."

"No, no." He shook his head and smiled. "I want someone who doesn't give up. I...She has a good friend. This is very difficult for me."

"A good friend?"

"For about the last year, Melanie has been seeing a psychiatrist, nothing major, problems to be worked out about her childhood, her relationship to her parents. The psychiatrist's name is Geoffrey Green. That's Geoffrey with a 'G,' but I'll bet my ass he started off with a 'J,' and I know that there was a 'berg' at the end of that 'Green' a couple of decades ago. I checked. He's got an office over one of those antique shops on Palm Avenue. I'm not a young man. I'm not immune to jealousy. Green is both young and good-looking. There were times when I couldn't make up my mind whether my suspicions were simply that of an older man afraid of losing his beautiful young wife or they were reasonable worries."

He looked up at the painting of his wife.

"I'll check it out," I said. "If I'm still on the job."

"You're on the job," he said, his voice low as he turned away from me.

"Melanie is a bit of a loner," he went on. "But

27

because of business connections we belong to a wide variety of organizations. Selby Gardens. Asolo Theater Angels, Opera Guild, charity groups, and we're seen at balls and dances. Melanie said that in the past two years we have been on the *Herald-Tribune*'s society page eleven times. In spite of this, Melanie had no really close friends, with the possible exception of Caroline Wilkerson, the widow of my late partner. Her address and number are in the folder along with Green's."

"And what do you want me to do?"

"Do? Find my wife, of course," Sebastian said, turning from the painting to look at me again.

"Has she committed a crime? Stolen money from you, money she doesn't have the right to take?"

"I don't know. I don't think so. The money in the accounts was both of ours. The jewels are hers."

"So she's free to go where she wants to go, even free to leave her husband, take money out of your joint accounts and wander away. It may be a boyfriend. It may be a lot of things."

"I just want you to find her," he said. "I just want to talk to her. I just want to know what happened and if there's anything I can do to get her back."

"She could be halfway to Singapore by now," I said.

"Your expense account is unlimited," he answered. "I just want you to keep me informed if you leave town in search of Melanie and I would expect you, as a professional, will keep expenses to a minimum and give me a full accounting of all expenditures when you find her."

"If I find her," I said. "I'll do my best to find out why she left. If I find her, I'll have to ask her if she's willing to talk to you. I'll tell you where she is if she gives me permission to tell you."

"I understand," he said. "Come with me."

I followed him into an office, where he moved to a desk and picked up something that lay next to a computer. The office was bright, with large windows and another angle on the bay, going north. The walls were "decorated" with about a dozen large, framed photographs, black-and-whites: Dust Bowl, toothless men with caps and overalls, scrawny women with their arms draped over the shoulders of scrawny children standing in front of clapboard shacks.

"If I find she's left the area, it'll have to wait till I finish a job I've got," I said.

"How long will this other work take you?"

He had a checkbook in his hand, a red leather checkbook.

"Few days, no more, probably. Can't be sure, but not long."

"Would a bonus persuade you to put this other work aside?" he asked, tapping the checkbook against his side.

"No."

"Anything could have happened to Melanie," he said. "Doesn't that mean something to you?"

"I can recommend someone else you can contact about the job," I said. "There are about eight licensed private investigators in Sarasota. Another handful in Bradenton. A few in Venice. Maybe three of them are reasonably good."

"Are you independently wealthy, Mr. Fonesca?"

"No, but I don't have to be wealthy to be independent."

"Do you have any idea of what it's like to lose a wife?" he asked with a catch in his voice.

"Yes," I said.

"Okay," he said without pursuing the loss of my wife. "I'll give you a chance. Larry said you're good. He also said your fee is negotiable. I'll write out a check. If it's acceptable, you have the job. If not, hand it back, give me the folder and the name of a reliable private detective and we'll shake hands and go on about our business."

He put the checkbook on the desk, opened it, pulled a glistening gold pen from his pocket and wrote. He wrote fast, tore out the check and handed it to me.

I looked at it. Five hundred dollars.

"Consider that is for your fee and expenses. If anything is left, you can apply it to a daily payment of one hundred and twenty dollars a day. Of course I'll want an itemized bill before final payment. If you run out of money, come back to me and we'll work it out."

I nodded to show that I agreed and put the check in the folder.

"How long do I keep on looking? I can probably find her but it might be hard and it might be easy and it might even be impossible if she's really smart."

He touched my arm fleetingly and directed me back into the living room.

"Let's say we reevaluate after three days if it goes that long," he said. "But I want her back if it's at all possible. I want to find her soon. I'm too old to start again. I don't want to be alone and I love Melanie. You understand?"

I nodded, tucked the folder under my arm and let him lead me to the front door. Usually in a situation like this I would have to ask for some information, numbers of any credit cards they shared, the tag number and make of her car and various other things to make my job easier. But Carl Sebastian, or maybe his friend and attorney Lawrence Werring, had anticipated well and the information was in the folder.

"My card is in the folder," he said, opening the front door. "My office phone and cell phone numbers are on the front. My home number is written on the back. Keep me informed. Call anytime. As often as you like."

He waited with me at the elevator.

"Anything else I can tell you?" he asked.

"Your wife have any living relatives?"

"No, it's all in the folder. Her background. All she has is me. And I don't think she's gone far. We've traveled all around the world, but she considers the Gulf Coast her home. I could be wrong. Where will you start?"

31

The elevator hummed to a stop and the doors opened silently.

"Her friend Mrs. Wilkerson or maybe the psychiatrist, Green."

"Good," he said, putting out a hand to keep the door open while I got on. I don't know what Caroline can tell you that I haven't. Yet, maybe there was something said, some...I don't know."

I stepped into the elevator, turned to face him and did my best to smile confidently at Carl Sebastian as the doors closed. He looked a little older than he had when I first saw him on the balcony.

2

"TELL ME SOMETHING important and ask me a question."

Ann Horowitz, Ph.D., sat forward in her upright chair to reach for her white foam cup of coffee and the chocolate biscotti I had brought her from Sarasota News and Books a block away.

Ann was almost eighty. A small woman with a tolerant smile, she was given to bright dresses. Her hair was gray, straight and short enough to show off her colorful bright yellow and red stone earrings.

Her office was small, neat, a desk on one side, another desk across from it and three chairs, blue and comfortable. There were two windows to let in light but they were high on the wall. From where I sat I could see blue skies and white clouds and in the past I had seen an occassional gull.

Ann had retired to Sarasota with her husband, Melvin, a sculptor, ten years ago. She had left her writing and her practice as an analyst and devoted herself to her son and his two young children, who lived in town. She also devoted herself to a passion for history. She had grown bored after five years and opened a small office practice.

Every time I came to see her she handed me a magazine or a book and told me about a fascinating chapter or article on how the Seminoles had won the war against the United States or how a small town of immigrant Mayans in Texas was thriving economically because they had retained the knowledge and the lessons of their history.

"I have enough money to pay you what I owe you for today and last session," I said.

"Good. Pay after we talk. You've told me something. Now the question."

"You know a psychiatrist named Geoffrey Green?"

She nodded her head as she chewed a reasonable piece of biscotti.

"I've met him a few times. Have a few of his former patients."

"What can you tell me about him?"

"That is a second question and is part of your hour," she said, "in spite of the coffee-and-biscotti bribe."

I held out my hands to show that I accepted her condition.

"He's good. He's expensive. He is young. But then, to me almost everyone is young."

"Even in Sarasota?"

"Less so here, but the world is vast. My favorite opening of a book is Douglas Adams' *Hitchhiker's Guide to the Galaxy*. It's something like 'The universe is very, very big.' I am amused by understatement."

"He mess around with his female patients?"

She paused mid-drink and put down her cup. She folded her hands in her lap and gave me her full attention.

"You have reason to believe he does?" she asked.

"Maybe," I said.

"Well, I will answer you enigmatically. You may be half right."

"I don't understand."

"When you do, let me know. I can say no more. Subject is dropped. Now, to you."

"You don't want to talk about some lost tribe in the wilds of Indonesia?"

"I do not. What are you doing for fun?"

"Watching movies, videotapes."

"And?"

"Working, eating, trying not to think, dreaming."

"You have a good dream for me, Lewis?"

"Maybe."

"Every time you come to see me you have a dream the night before. Tell me."

She reached for the coffee.

"Worms in my ear," I said.

"In your ear?"

"You sure you want to hear this while you're eating?"

"I could make you violently ill with stories I have heard and continue to eat," she said, working on the remaining crumbs of biscotti.

"White worm, right ear. My wife is in the dream. I feel something funny, a tickle in my ear. She says there's a worm crawling into my ear. I panic, tell her to get it out. She tries. I feel her fingernails gently going for the worm. She says she is having trouble getting a grip on it. It's crawling deeper. I tell her to get a tweezer, fast. She runs into the bathroom, comes back with a tweezer, probes for the worm. I feel the metal, cold, touching the inside of my ear, jabbing. She is having trouble. Finally, she lets out a sound. I know she has it. She does, but she has to struggle. It comes apart. She digs it out of my ear in pieces while I keep asking 'Is it out? Is it out?' When she says it is, I run into the bathroom, turn on the shower, brush away real and imagined worms."

"You are nude? You don't have to take off your clothes?"

"Nude."

"Your wife. She is also nude?"

"Yes, no, I'm not sure. Now she's wearing something flimsy, white."

"And you were in bed with her when you discovered this worm?"

"I...yes."

"You see where this is going?"

35

She finished her coffee, shook the cup to be sure she hadn't missed a drop or two and placed the cup on her desk next to the photographs of her grandchildren.

"Yeah, at least part of the way."

"Tell me."

"Sex," I said.

"When is the last time you had sex? I mean with a woman or a man other than yourself?"

The phone rang. She was like an answering machine. She couldn't bring herself to turn it off or let it ring. I had asked her once to put on her answering machine when we talked. She had gone into a brief explanation about how she could do it, but in doing so she would wonder who was calling and not give sufficient attention to our session. In addition, she worried about her husband. Melvin had a bad heart. So I sat quietly, welcoming the opportunity to think not about my next answer but the possible ones after that.

"I'm sorry. I can't talk now. I'll call you tomorrow morning....You have my diagnosis. I am not changing it....I am being reasonable. Good-bye."

She hung up and said to herself and me, "HMOs." Then to me, "So, last sex?"

"The night before my wife died."

"With your wife?"

"Certainly, with my wife. We've been through this."

"Why aren't you angry with me? You should be at least a little angry," she said. "I was angrier at the HMO clerk than you are at me for suggesting you might have had sex with someone other than your wife the night before she died."

The chair I was sitting in was a recliner. I reclined and clasped my fingers together on my stomach.

"I don't get angry anymore," I said.

"Nothing makes you angry?"

"I don't know. I think I'm looking for something to make me angry and I don't want to find it. Does that make sense?"

"Perfect sense. Next question: Why do you always say 'my wife' instead of using her name? You have never spoken her name to me. You want to answer or you want to spend a week thinking about it?"

"It hurts."

"To say her name?"

"Yes."

"Pain sometimes just sits there waiting. If you confront it, perhaps it will get smaller. Do you want that pain to grow smaller?"

"I don't know. No, I don't want it to get smaller. I want it right there where I can find it."

"And feel sorry for yourself?"

"Yes, there's a great comfort in feeling sorry for myself."

"When you're ready, you'll be able to say her name. It will hurt, but it will feel right."

"I don't want it to feel right."

"We'll see."

"Her mother was overweight. Nice face, but overweight. I..."

"Yes?"

"Nothing."

"Your wife was a lawyer."

"Yes. I don't want to talk about my wife today."

She leaned forward, pursed her lips, raised her eyebrows and said,

"Then we'll put that aside for now. You are working? You plan to pay me so I assume you are working. What are you working on? Besides your dreams."

"A runaway wife. A runaway girl."

"This is one person or two? A runaway girl who is also a wife?"

I leaned farther back in the recliner and looked up at the ceiling.

"Two people."

"And you are engaged, interested in finding them. It's more than a job, a way to make money?"

"I don't know."

"Your wife ran away," she said.

I remained calm and said,

"She died."

"And you never had children."

"You know that."

"Are you angry yet?"

"Not even close."

I didn't look, but I was aware of her rising.

"Enough for today. Go look for your missing females. We'll talk about them next week. A missing wife. A missing daughter. And that dream. One thing I think it might be telling you is to stop punishing yourself. You know the Italian ice shop on Seventeenth Street?"

It was my turn to sit up. The recliner slid back and I felt slightly dizzy as I opened my eyes.

"I know it."

"Stop there. I recommend the banana chocolate. Melvin likes watermelon. Be good to yourself, Lewis."

Ann Horowitz is a good six inches shorter than I am, and I'm touching the lower edge of average. I took out my wallet and handed her two twenty-dollar bills. I had first met her when I served papers on her to appear in court to testify in a case involving one of her patients. She had taken the papers at her door, dropped them on the table inside her apartment and invited me in. No one had ever invited me into their home after I served them papers.

She was fascinated by process serving, wanted to know all about it, told me that serving papers for appearances before tribunals went back to biblical times. I was a member of a historically important profession. That wasn't the way I saw it. For me it was anywhere from twenty-five to fifty dollars for a few hours of work.

Ann Horowitz had said she saw pain in my eyes and asked if I wanted to talk about it. I said I didn't and she asked, "How long can a person enjoy their pain?"

"Till they die, if they're lucky."

She gave me her card and said that she wanted to talk to me even if I didn't want to talk to her. She planned to do more research on my honorable profession and fill me with history if not pride. She also said that she would charge me only ten dollars for each session. After our first session, I gave her twenty dollars and that became the fixed rate for our meetings. There had been a few times when I was behind on my payments, but I always caught up. I learned from a lawyer whose daughter was seeing Ann Horowitz that he was paying her an even one hundred per session, most of which was covered by his expensive health-care plan.

She handed me a copy of an article from *Smithsonian* magazine about John Marshall, the first chief justice of the Supreme Court.

"Jefferson hated him," she said. "America was formed as much or more by Marshall than Washington or Jefferson. Great man. Read it. Tell me what you think. No hurry."

There was a couple sitting in the outer office when I left holding my article. They looked embarrassed and familiar. The woman looked down, pretending to read a recent office copy of *People*. The man smiled and adjusted his glasses.

Ann told them to go into her office. Before she followed them, she whispered to me, "Someday you will be able to say her name and we can really begin."

"I thought we began months ago," I said.

"No, I've just been softening you up."

She followed the couple through the office door and closed it behind her.

The wife's voice came through to the reception room. I couldn't make out the words, didn't want to, but there was immediate pain, immediate anger.

I went in search of someone who might know how to find Adele Tree. I had someone in mind. My bicycle was locked to a No Parking sign. I had made up my mind. I had to rent a car. Carl Sebastian had to pay for it.

The EZ Economy Car Rental Agency was six doors north of Dave's Dairy Queen on 301. EZ was located in a former gas station. There were cars parked in front, cars behind the lot. The bigger rental agencies were out at the airport. EZ claimed that they offered lower rates by being in a low-rent neighborhood and catering to those who wanted anything from a banged-up semi-wreck with 80,000 miles on it to a new Jaguar with a few thousand miles on it.

I had rented from EZ before when I had a job that required it. I preferred the bicycle.

The two men in rumpled suits inside the office of EZ were leaning back against the desk, arms folded, waiting for the phone to ring or me to walk in.

"The detective," said the younger one with a smile that seemed sincere. He was no more than thirty and quickly growing as round as his older partner.

"Process server," I corrected.

We had gone through this routine the last

41

four or five times I had rented a car. It seemed to amuse both of the men.

"What can we do ya for?" said the older man.

They had introduced themselves when I first met them. One was Alan. The other was Fred. I couldn't remember which was which.

"Compact."

"We've got a Corolla," said the young one.

"A Geo Prizm," said the older one.

"Same difference," said the younger.

The older man chuckled.

"How long?" asked the young one.

"What's the weekly rate now?" I asked.

"For you?" asked the older man. "A hundred and eight-five plus insurance. The usual. You get it gas full. You return it gas full."

"What have you got for a hundred and forty including insurance?"

"An Amish three-wheel bicycle," said the young one.

They both laughed. The older one turned red and started to choke. The younger one patted him on the back till he returned to semi-normal.

"Oh God," said the older one, wiping away tears.

"Geo Metro," said the young one. "It's clean. It's this year. It's white. It's small and it runs. You just have to play the radio a little loud if you want to hear it. Air conditioner is great. We'll throw in an air freshener, a green one shaped like a pine tree."

"Will I need it?" I asked.

Alan and Fred shrugged.

"One thirty, and we're losing money," the older said.

"We like you," said the younger one.

"You're a regular. You send us business." This amused the hell out of the younger one.

"I'll take it," I said.

"You want to give him the keys and papers, Fred?" asked the young one.

I had them now. Fred was the older one. He had stopped crying.

I not only had their names straight, I also had a car that smelled as if a heavy smoker had lived in it. The car also had 34,000 miles on it. I could have probably negotiated a deal to buy it from them for about three weeks' worth of rental fees, but I didn't want a car. I tore open the plastic bag, took out the pine tree, set it on the dashboard, turned on the air-conditioning and opened the windows.

I drove the half-block to the DQ parking lot, which was less than half full—not bad for late afternoon. There was a line and people were seated at the two umbrella-covered tables, eating and laughing. At least the three teenaged boys at one table were laughing. A pair of thin women in their fifties wearing thin sweaters, which they didn't need, sat at the other table eating silently.

I was suddenly hungry, very hungry. I got in line, ordered two burgers and a Coke from Dave and gave him the article on John Marshall. He thanked me and said he would read it as soon as he had a break.

The teens were laughing louder and throwing

43

bread from their burgers at each other. One of the boys heaved a chunk of sandwich. It sailed into the back of one of the two women.

"Sorry," said the kid who had thrown the burger. He was grinning.

The thin woman didn't turn.

"Give me a second, Lew," Dave said when I got to the window.

He moved back into the DQ, past the sink and out the side door, throwing his white apron on a table as the door closed. He appeared in front of the table where the teens were still hurling food. At first they didn't see him. The boys were big. Football types.

"Pick up what you threw and give the lady a real good apology," Dave said. "Then leave and don't come back for at least a week. And if you come back, come back docile. You know what that means?"

All three boys stood up. Dave didn't back down.

The boys were no longer laughing.

"We didn't mean nothing," the biggest boy said.

There was defiance in his chunky face.

Another boy stepped in front of his friend and put a hand on his chest.

"We're sorry," said the second boy with some sincerity. "We was just celebrating. My friend Jason here, he just found out that he doesn't have HIV. Just got the report from the hospital. He was sure he—"

"None of this guy's business," said Jason.

"Let's just go, Jace," said the mediator,

looking at the third boy, who nodded in agreement.

"Clean up first and apologize," said Dave.

"No way," said Jason, looking my way to be sure it would be three against one if it came to throwing punches.

"Any of you know a girl named Adele Tree?" I asked.

"No," said the mediator. The answer was wary. Something about the name had hit home.

"How about Adele Handford?"

All three of them turned toward me. The name Adele had hit home. They looked at each other. The thin women got up and left, carrying what remained of their meal.

"Her friend Ellen. I almost got the HIV from Ellen," said Jason.

"Easy Adele," said the mediator. "Must be talkin' about Easy Adele."

"Where can I find her?"

They looked at each other again.

"I'll clean up the mess you made. It's too late for the apology."

"They'll clean it up," Dave said. "It's their mess, Lew."

I shrugged.

"Then how about I give you each five bucks."

"Why not?" said the mediator, moving between Dave and Jason and heading for me.

I pulled out my wallet and give him five singles. I would charge the payoff to Carl Sebastian. There was no point in asking them about

45

Melanie Sebastian. She was in a different league.

"Sarasota High," said the kid, who was blond and reasonably good-looking except for some much-needed dental work.

"She goes to Sarasota High School?"

"She did," he said. "I haven't seen her around the last three, four weeks, somethin', you know?"

"Not enough," I said, though it was a start.

"That's what I know. You guys know what happened to Easy Adele?" he asked.

Jason smirked. The third kid said, "She said she was living with her father. I don't know where. She was whorin' on North Trail. I seen her. By the motels, you know?"

"I know," I said.

The kid in front of me backed away and Dave repeated calmly,

"Pick up your mess."

Jason was the last to bend over and start the job.

After the three had driven off, taking time to screech the brakes and throw Dave and me the finger, I got a fish sandwich, a burger and a cherry Blizzard. There was no one waiting in line behind me. A couple with a small girl had disappeared when Dave came out of the DQ.

"They're not bad," he said. "Just stupid. I don't like that kind of stupid."

Dave got my sandwiches and cherry Blizzard and started to read the article.

I went across the parking lot and up the stairs

to my laundry basket-sized two rooms with a view of 301 from each.

I turned on the lights, looked at the whirling air conditioner and sat down at the desk in the outer office to check the Sarasota and Bradenton phone book for Dwight Handford. There was nothing. I didn't expect there would be. I tried Dwight Tree. Nothing.

While I worked on my dinner and watched the ice cream melt in my float, I called the Best Western and asked for Beryl Tree's room, 204. She answered on the second ring.

"Yes," she said.

I could hear a television in the background. I thought I recognized the *Hollywood Squares* music.

"Lew Fonesca," I said.

"Yes?"

"I haven't found her yet but I have a lead. It looks like you might be right. I think she was is or was staying with her father."

"Oh."

"She did go to a high school here, at least for a while. I'll go over there in the morning. They may not want to give me any information so I might have to get you to talk to them."

"I'll be here all day," she said. "I'll just get something to eat and bring it back to the room."

"I'll call tomorrow," I said. "Good night."

I took off my clothes, touched the stubble on my face, put on my YMCA shorts and a University of Illinois T-shirt and moved into my back room. I had what was left of my food and my Blizzard. I had the folder on Melanie Sebastian and I had a tape of *Charade* I'd bought two days before for two dollars at Vic's Pawn Shop on Main Street.

While I watched Cary Grant searching for Carson Dyle, I started a folder on Adele Tree. So far there wasn't much in it, a photograph and the few notes I was now writing. I had a feeling the folder would grow.

I was working. Two cases. Lots of questions. My grandfather, my mother's father, played the mandolin. He used to say that the mandolin held the answers. He never made it clear what the questions were. I liked listening to him play old Italian folk songs, songs he made up, even an Elvis tune. He particularly liked "Love Me Tender." He lost himself in the mandolin. Closed his eyes and listened to the answers.

"It all ties together," he would say, eyes closed, mind who knows where.

I heard the mandolin in my head. It asked questions. I had two clients who had lost someone close to them. Carl Sebastian, who had chosen me on a chance recommendation, had lost his wife. I had lost my wife. Maybe I could find his. Beryl Tree had lost a daughter. My wife hadn't lived long enough to have a daughter. So, I had lost a daughter or son.

Fonesca, I told myself, you can be a morbid son-of-a-bitch. Think of something you like, something that makes you happy, or at least content. Think of movies with William Powell and Cary Grant and Jean Arthur. Think of an order of ribs from Luny's back on Division Street in Chicago. Think of mountains with white caps. You like mountains with white caps.

Think of getting back to work and finding people. Worry about finding yourself later.

3

SARASOTA HIGH SCHOOL was within walking distance of my office-home. I took the car. There were places to go, people to see, things to do and concentrate on.

After I had shaved, washed myself and brushed my teeth in the second-floor rest room six doors down from my office, I put on clean tan slacks and a short-sleeved white shirt and one of my basic bland ties. I've got one brown, one blue and one gray with Mickey Mouse embroidered on it (a gift from a client with a sense of something he thought was humor) and a Salvador Dali tie with melting clocks and distant rocks. This morning I wore the basic brown. I wore my glasses. The only time I normally wore my glasses was when I was driving, but sometimes I wore them in the belief, mistaken or not, that they made me look more like a professional something.

Before I left, I called the office of Geoffrey Green, M.D., psychiatrist to the well-to-do. I wondered what a conversation between Green and Ann Horowitz would sound like.

The receptionist who answered was pleasantly sympathetic when I said I had a problem. She asked me who had referred me to Dr. Green and I said Melanie Sebastian. I told her I needed only a few minutes of his time.

"One moment, please," she said.

I stood at my window waiting and watching the morning traffic on 301. Across the street was a bar called the Crisp Dollar Bill. It was in a sagging building and the once bright-red sign, according to Dave, had long ago faded to a sickly pink. Next to the bar was a small two-story building with a dance studio on the second floor. The studio had large glass windows. Once in a while I would stand on the balcony, maybe lean on the railing and watch people waltz.

South of the bar there was a consignment shop and a few other stores. Behind these businesses were the last vestiges of the wall of the old White Sox spring-training stadium.

The Sox had moved to Ed Smith Stadium on Twelfth Street before I broke down in Sarasota. In the summer, the Minor League Sarasota White Sox had played at Ed Smith and the town had boasted that Michael Jordan had briefly lived in town, a one-season drawing card. The Sox had moved out and the Cincinnati Reds had moved in. I still hadn't gone to a baseball game.

"Mr. Fonesca?" the receptionist chimed.

"Yes."

"Dr. Green can see you for a few minutes at one o'clock today. Can you make that?"

"Yes."

"Come about ten minutes early to fill out some forms."

"Okay. I'll be there."

I hung up. I'd let her hold on to the illusion that I was a potential patient until it got to the point where I might be billed. I couldn't afford that bill. If I had a leg and one arm in the door, I knew how to squeeze my way in.

The DQ was closed. Too early. I walked to Gwen's Diner at the corner. Gwen had retired four years ago. Her daughter Sheila had taken over. Regulars started calling her Gwen Two. After a while they dropped the "Two." Sheila had a teenage daughter who waited tables after school. Her name was Althea. I wondered if she would become Gwen Three. Maybe it would become a tradition, like the Phantom, the Ghost Who Walks. There would be a Gwen to replace the last Gwen until some developer like Carl Sebastian decided to have a giant step on Gwen's Diner, sweep it away and build an office building or more high-cost and high-rise apartments.

The place was crowded with people who stopped by on the way to work and the marginal and long retired who had their daily ritual breakfast to be near people and be recognized.

I was becoming a more-or-less regular. I came when I had to get up early. If I got up late, I picked up something at Dave's DQ. Gwen's opened at five in the morning, before sunrise.

There was an opening at the counter between

a guy who looked like a truck driver and an old man who looked like a gray stick.

Gwen, who wore a morning smile, an apron and a minimum of makeup on her pink round face, placed a white mug of coffee before me.

"Eggs scrambled soft, two strips and rye toast?"

I nodded. She nodded too and hurried off, coffee decanter in hand.

People at the five tables behind us talked softly, respecting the morning, slowly waking up.

"Seen you here before," said the old man on my right.

I nodded and drank.

"You from the North?"

I nodded again. Drank some more coffee.

"New York?"

"Chicago."

"I'm from Steubenville, near Cleveland. Dean Martin was from Steubenville. I knew some of his people."

"That a fact?"

"Fact," he said. "Been down here fifteen years. Thinking of going back but...nothing up there for me anymore. Wife died six years back. Know what I mean?"

"Yeah."

"You don't feel like engaging in the art of conversation," he said.

I smiled. It wasn't much of a smile, but it was something.

"Sorry," I said as Gwen who had been Sheila returned with my plate. "I've been here about three years. My wife died too."

"Sorry to hear that," he said. "She must have been young. Caroline was seventy-two, not so old anymore, with the medicines and all, you know?"

"Yeah," I said, starting to eat.

"So, my name is Tim and you're...?"

"Lew."

"What do you do, Lew?"

I gave him a small shrug. What did I do? I got through each day. I watched movies. I took work when it came my way or I had to eat, drink and survive.

"I'm a process server."

"That a fact?"

"No brag, just fact," I said.

The eggs were fine, not quite raw. The bacon was crisp. I was feeling a little more human. The coffee was helping.

"Dangerous?" Tim asked.

He had swiveled toward me on the round blue counter seat.

"Not usually."

"No offense, but I don't think I'd be able to handle a job that made people mad at me."

"The hours are good," I said.

"I'm a welder," said Tim. "I mean I was a welder. Don't do it anymore. I liked it."

"Corky Flynn," came a voice from my left.

I glanced at the trucker type on my left. He was bulky, probably a few years younger than me. He was looking at me now, chewing something.

"Corky Flynn," he repeated. "You remember? Wasn't that fuckin' long ago."

I looked at him as I ate. The face and name didn't ring a bell.

"You served papers on me. Divorce. You came to my garage, handed it to me right in front of Earl and Spence."

"I don't think so," I said.

I kept a folder with the names of every person I served papers to and the time I served the papers, and I made a note about where I had served the papers.

"Never served papers on you, Mr. Flynn," I said.

"It wasn't you?"

"Nope. Maybe someone who looks a little like me. Lots of people look like me. When was it?"

"Right after New Year's."

"This year?"

I ate while I talked. Tim the welder was listening, waiting for some violence he could talk about with his friends over an open campfire.

"I only served papers on two people in January," I said. "Both women."

That was true.

"I could swear..." Corky Flynn said, examining me closely.

"Ever make a mistake before, Corky?" I asked.

He sighed.

"Too many times. I married three of 'em. That's why I work a double-hour day. Got to pay them off. Used to drive trucks, big rigs, but my back...never mind. Sorry. I'll pay for your breakfast."

"I accept," I said.

He got up and pulled two tens out of the pocket of his jeans. He dropped the bills on the counter, patted my back and said, "Sorry. Been having a bad week."

"You happen to know a driver named Dwight?" I asked, looking up at Corky Flynn.

"Driver of what?"

"Delivery or tow truck, don't know."

"Dwight, Dwight. Yeah, Dwight, don't know his last name. Don't want to. He's trouble. Mean. Works out of a station somewhere off Cattlemen or McIntosh. Triple-A jobs I think. Has a chip of steel on his shoulder, looking for trouble. Mean son of a bitch. He comes to me with that attitude and I'll knock that steel chip into his neck. My advice, stay away from him."

"Can't. Know how I can find him?"

"You know what I know. See you around."

I held up a hand to acknowledge his departure.

"Thought he was going to hit you," said Tim with a touch of disappointment in his voice.

"Sorry," I said.

"You would have shot him, put him away with a kick to his balls or a karate chop," he said.

"No," I said. "Corky Flynn would have beat the hell out of me. Corky left enough to cover your breakfast too. Be my guest."

Tim smiled. His teeth were false and white but his smile was real. I touched his shoulder and went out into the morning sun. The high school was about two blocks away, across 301, past the McDonald's, the *Sarasota Herald-Tribune* office, a motel, a fried-chicken franchise and a discount eyeglass shop.

I drove the Metro to the school parking lot, took a space for visitors and left the windows open. Maybe it would help the pine tree get rid of that smell of stale tobacco.

Kids were heading toward the old red-brick three-story building and the newer one-story blocks behind it.

The girls were dressed in the latest costume they thought would make them look sexy and the boys were looking at the latest costume that made them look cool. Grunge was back in for both groups. I preferred preppy. Most of the book-toting kids, who looked too young to be in high school, walked in zombie-like steps, eyes hooded from lack of sleep, talking in hoarse voices. I wondered what it would be like to teach a classroom of the teens I was walking through, especially a class in the morning. I'd rather face Corky Flynn in a dark doorway.

A girl with nothing pierced, at least nothing on her face or tongue, and looking more awake than her peers, directed me to the office of Mr. Kwan, the associate principal and disciplinary officer. He was in one of the older one-story buildings.

There were four green plastic and aluminum chairs to the right of the door. In front of the chairs was a desk behind which sat a pretty, thin, black woman talking on the phone. Behind her were other desks, file cabinets and a pair of women bustling with papers. To the left were two windowed offices with doors closed. In the first office, a heavyset, gray-haired woman was leaning forward over a desk pointing a yellow pencil at a sullen-looking, overly made-up girl with blue hair. The girl's arms were folded over her flat chest. She didn't like what she was hearing. She didn't like the heavyset woman. I wondered what she did like.

In the second office, an Asian man of no particular age stood next to a desk. His arms were folded like those of the girl in the next room. The man, who I assumed was Mr. Kwan, was wearing a short-sleeved white shirt, a solid blue tie, tan slacks and a lot of muscle. He was talking to a fat boy, who met Kwan's eyes. The fat boy had a definitely dense look. He was either stupid, or suffering—or enjoying—the aftereffects of some drug. I'd seen that look.

The black woman hung up the phone. Before I could speak, she held up a hand with long, red-painted fingernails, indicating to me that I should hold my complaint, thought or request.

She picked up the phone again and said, "Yes, Mrs. Stanley. I know. But Mr. Kwan says it's important that you see him today....I understand, but if you can just get away from work for half an hour....Yes, William is in trouble again. Yes, it is very serious....Noon? Fine."

The woman looked up at me and hung up the phone.

"Yes?"

"I'd like to see Mr. Kwan," I said.

"About...?"

"Adele Tree, or she might be using her father's name, Handford."

"You are...?"

"A friend of Adele's mother," I said, looking over my glasses.

"Well..."

The phone rang. She reached for it and pointed to the lineup of plastic and aluminum chairs. I sat next to a kid in overalls who had slouched so far down that he seemed to be in serious danger of slipping onto the floor and into oblivion. The boy was young, black and bored.

"What're you in for?" I asked.

He looked up at me.

"Who're you?"

"I'm nobody. Who are you? Are you nobody too?"

"What ya talking about?"

"Just talking," I said, looking down the line at three other waiting students in the seats next to us. Two girls were whispering. The third kid was big. He was white. He had short hair. A tattoo showed dark through his white T-shirt. He seemed to be sleeping.

"You know a girl named Adele Tree or Handford?"

"Maybe. You a cop? You don't look like a cop."

"No, a friend of her mother. What do you know about Adele?"

"Nothin'."

He looked at the busy secretary.

"Nothing? What would five bucks do for your memory?"

"Nothing," he said. "I don't know what I don't know. But I'll tell ya somethin'. I only know one Adele. She's not as dumb as she makes out. She plays dumb to get close to the football players, basketball players, like that."

"Adele?"

"Yeah," he said.

"How do you know she's not dumb?" I asked.

He looked over at the woman behind the desk, who was still on the phone. She had a pencil and was taking notes as she nodded. She pointed the pencil at the kid I was talking to and made a motion with it. He sat up. Pencils seemed to be the weapon of choice in this office.

"She was in my math class," the kid said, still looking at the woman behind the desk. "In there only maybe, let's see, a week, two weeks. This is advanced math, man. Honors. I don't know how she got in, but she tested in or some such and she was hard to figure. Too much makeup. You know, like a whore, but she was smart. Nothing Mr. W. could throw at her she couldn't come back with. I mean just like that. Same in English."

"You said 'was,' not 'is.'"

"Haven't seen her for three or four weeks."

59

"You're an honor student?"

"Yeah, surprised?"

"Yeah," I answered.

" 'Cause of..."

"What are you in trouble for?" I asked.

"Nothing."

"Then why are you here?"

"My mother wanted to talk to me," he said, nodding at the black woman behind the desk. "She's workin' on a scholarship for me to Howard."

"Howard?"

"Damn straight. I wanna be a city planner. I wanna come back here with one of those real sharp suits in six, seven years and tell them to rip this whole fuckin' city down, startin' with Newtown, and start a new one."

The door to Kwan's office opened and the fat boy slouched out, a yellow card in his hand. Maybe Kwan had given him a penalty for kicking someone in the face in a soccer game.

Kwan looked at the woman behind the desk, who was still on the phone. She pointed her pencil at the two girls and the big sleeping kid and then at me. Kwan nodded and moved in front of me.

"Good morning, Ty," he said to the kid waiting to change the world.

"Morning," answered Ty.

"You are?"

"Lewis Fonesca. Friend of Adele Handford's mother, Beryl, family friend."

"Come on," said Kwan, heading for his office and looking at his watch.

We went in the office. He closed the door and looked through the window into the bustling morning staff and waiting students.

"Not much privacy," I said.

"Not supposed to be," said Kwan, motioning to a chair in front of his desk.

The chair was the brother of the ones in which the kids outside the office sat waiting. Kwan sank back in a slightly more comfortable chair behind his desk. The office was tiny. The desktop was empty except for a neat file of manila folders, a full but not overflowing wooden in-box and an out-box with one sheet of paper in it. A pile of yellow penalty cards rested in the middle of the desk. Through the window to the outside, Kwan had a pretty good view of the white wall of the building next door.

"Adele Handford," I said. "A student here. Pretty. Blond. Smart. Gets in trouble easily. I've heard her called Easy Adele. Her mother is looking for her."

"You her...?"

"I'm a family friend," I said.

"We have almost two thousand students here, Mr...."

"Fonesca, Lewis Fonesca."

"I know you from somewhere," he said, studying my face.

"Gwen's Diner," I said. "I eat there sometimes, early, like you."

A look of recognition came into his eyes and he nodded with some satisfaction after having scratched the itch of recognition.

61

"I think I know the girl. Can't tell you much about her," he said. "Off the top, she's a smart kid. She was sent to me two or three times because she talked back to a teacher and she was caught with a boy in the storage room behind the gym. I'm probably not authorized to tell you that much but I think the girl might be in trouble."

"What kind of trouble?"

Kwan bit his lower lip and looked at the building next door. He made a decision, turned his head, pulled a pen out of his pants pocket and wrote something on the back of one of the yellow cards. I was getting a penalty. He handed the card to me. I looked at it:

"Sally Porovsky, Children's Services of Sarasota."

"You have an address for Adele?"

"I have an address, but it wouldn't do you any good. I drove by it on the way home one night. It's a golf shop. I stopped and asked for her father. Of course they had never heard of him."

"But she's living with her father somewhere?"

"She was. Somewhere."

"And?"

"You have the name of someone who can give you answers. I talked to the father once. I had asked the girl to have him call me when she got her first disciplinary referral. He was calm. He was polite. He said he couldn't come in because he had to work. He told me his daughter knew how to take care of herself."

"That's it?"

Kwan looked at the office window, leaned forward and said softly,

"Between you and me, there was something about the guy that scared the hell out of me."

Children's Services of Sarasota was in Building C of a three-story office building in a complex of red office buildings on Fruitville Road just off of Tuttle. Building A, according to the board, housed an accountant, a physical therapist, two psychologists, an accountant and a dermatologist. Building B was home to a dentist, a podiatrist, a gynecologist, a hair-removal office and a hypnotist.

Inside the small lobby was a receptionist stuffing envelopes. He was probably about thirty, lean, clean, wearing glasses and a tieless blue shirt, obviously gay and not trying to hide it.

"Sally Porovsky," I said.

"Nice to meet you, Sally. I'm Mary Ellen," he answered with a smile, continuing to stuff envelopes.

I looked down at him, saying nothing. He kept stuffing, stopped and looked up at me.

"It was just a joke," he said.

"I got it."

"You're going to report me to Sorensen, aren't you?" he said. "I can't keep my mouth shut."

"I'm not going to report you to Sorensen,

63

Mary Ellen. I just want to see Sally Porovsky."

"My name isn't really...Oh, my name is John Detchon."

"Mine is Lew Fonesca. Can you...?"

"Oh, sure. Up the elevator. Second floor. Straight ahead. Her name's on her cubicle. You're lucky she's in. They're usually out on the road, house visits, school visits, court. You know?"

"I don't, John," I said, moving to the open elevator.

"You're sure you're not going to tell Sorenson?"

"Joke stays between us girls," I said.

"You're straight, aren't you?"

"Yes."

"That's all right. You're not my type."

The doors closed and I rose slowly up to the second floor. The elevator smelled of mold. When the doors opened I found myself facing a door marked CHILDREN'S SERVICES OF SARASOTA. I went through and found myself looking down a lane of ten cubicles, each surrounded on three sides by glass. Beyond the cubicles were offices with nameplates. There were no windows facing in. Four-foot-high piles of cardboard boxes lined the faded pink walls. Inside the cubicles, the small desks with computers on each were covered with papers, manila folders, green files and coffee cups. There were people at only two of the cubicles. Sally Porovsky's Dilbert niche was easy to spot. It had her name on the glass.

Her back was to me as I approached. Her

eyes were fixed on the computer screen and she kept adjusting her glasses and talking to herself.

"Sally Porovsky?" I asked.

She let out a gasp and did a small bounce in her chair. Then she turned and said. "You scared the hell out of me."

"Sorry."

She was about my age, maybe forty, maybe a little younger. She was solid, ample and pretty with clear skin, short, wavy dark hair and a voice that could give Lauren Bacall's a run for the roses. She was wearing a black skirt and jacket over a white blouse. A string of heavy, colorful beads hung around her neck.

"Can I help you?" she asked.

"I hope so," I said. "My name is Fonesca, Lew Fonesca. I'm a friend of Beryl Tree. I'm representing her. She's looking for her daughter, Adele Tree, but she's using the name—"

"Oh Lord," said Sally Porovsky, swiveling to face me. "Adele's mother is dead. At least the Adele I know."

I shook my head.

"Alive and reasonably well and worried. She's at the Best Western on Forty-one."

"And you can prove that?" she asked. "Prove she's the mother of the girl we have an open case on?"

"I can bring her mother here, complete with identification and tears."

Sally thought for a moment, bit her lower lip, glanced at the computer screen and said, "Bring her."

"I've got a one o'clock appointment," I said. "I can have her here by three."

"Make it four," she said. "I've got to finish a report now and then go out on a home visit. How did you find me?"

"Mr. Kwan at Sarasota High."

She nodded.

"Bring Mrs..."

"Tree."

"Tree, at four-thirty and we'll talk," she said. "I'm afraid I have to get back to my report now. I'm about two months behind on paperwork. So, if you'll excuse me."

"Two minutes more," I said. "You can time me. It might be a lot less, depending on your answer to one question."

"I can't talk about Adele until I'm reassured—"

"Not about Adele," I said. "About you."

"About me?"

She took off her glasses and squinted at me.

"Are you married?" I asked.

"What?"

"Are you married?"

"My husband's dead, but I don't see—"

"I'm forty-two years old. I live in Sarasota and work as a process server and finder of lost people. My wife died in a car crash in Chicago a little over three years ago. She was a lawyer. I did research and served papers for the district attorney's office. I have an undergraduate degree from the University of Illinois in political science. When my wife died, I quit my job, got in my car and drove as far as it would take me. It died in Sarasota. I have no children. We were going to but...I'm healthy, work out almost every morning and I bicycle a lot. My background is Italian, but I'm not Catholic. I'm not much of anything, but my mother and sister are Episcopalian. That's less than two minutes."

"Why are you telling this to me, Mr. Fonesca?"

"You think I'm crazy," I said.

"That depends on the answer to my question," she said.

"I want to know if you'd go to dinner with me tonight, tomorrow night, any night."

"You do this a lot?"

"I've never done anything like this before," I said.

"Never?"

"I swear," I said. "I'm not completely sure why I'm doing it now. Say no and that's it, back to business. I've got references who will swear under oath that I don't do things like this."

She looked up at me for what seemed like a very long time.

"You seem harmless, but...we can talk about it after you bring Adele's mother to see me," she said. "I really have work to do."

I wanted to keep listening to her voice and looking at her. I thought she was probably right if she thought I had gone crazy. Maybe my session with Ann Horowitz had pushed me over the top.

She swiveled around to face her computer again and I headed for the elevator.

"All done?" asked John Detchon, who was still stuffing envelopes.

"For now," I said. "I'll be back at four-thirty."

"I'll call out the color guard," he said.

I pushed through the door to the street and wondered why I had done what I had just done. Was I trying to please Ann Horowitz? Maybe. Did Sally Porovsky remind me of my wife? No. Maybe a little. Of my mother? No. Was it her voice? Partly. Was I coming back to life? Hardly. I'd return with Beryl and act as if I had never gone mad in front of Sally Porovsky. I'd walk away and forget the moment of insanity and she would adjust her glasses and, I hoped, do the same.

When I got to the Best Western hotel and found Beryl Tree's room, I knocked.

"Who is it?"

"Lew Fonesca," I said.

The door opened. A man stood before me with a gun in his hand.

4

THE MAN WITH the gun was Ames McKinney. I've already told you about Ames. Tall, long white hair, grizzled, lean, brown and seventy-four years old. Ames was not supposed to bear arms. It was a right he had lost after using an ancient Remington Model 1895 revolver to kill his ex-partner in a duel.

The first time I met Ames was an hour

after he called me the first week I moved into town. His Sam Elliott gruff voice had simply said, "You know a place called The Round-up. On 301, just up from Fruitville."

"Yes," I had said.

"Be there in half hour?"

"Yes."

"Names McKinney. Lean, old, can't miss me."

The Round-Up was one of the many odd-ball restaurants in Sarasota, a town known more for its well-heeled tourists and wealthy retirees who lived on the offshore Keys than its cuisine. There are some good restaurants, and there is a hell of a lot of variety, including the Round-Up, which boasted on a red-on-white sign in the window, "The Best Chinese Tex-Mex in Florida." Few challenged this claim, especially not the homeless who wandered past every day.

The Round-Up is gone now. Owner Round Harry was carrying too much weight. He died and the place was boarded up. Six months later it was and still is a shoe-repair and tailor shop run by a couple from Colombia who speak almost no English.

Restaurants come and go fast in this town. So does money.

Sarasota is rich, but even the rich need maids, supermarkets, police, firemen, tailor shops and shoestores. There is a middle class and a lower class in Sarasota and everyone, even the snowbirds, the well-to-do who came down only in the winter from as far north as Canada and as far east as Germany, knew it.

Parking was not rough in front of the Round-Up, not in the summer. Parking isn't rough anywhere in Sarasota in the summer. There's plenty of parking and no lines at the restaurants or movies.

The Round-Up wasn't packed but it wasn't empty and there was good reason. The food was cheap and spicy, the service fast, and no one hurried you out. You could nurse a beer or even an iced tea with a pitcher in front of you while you watched the Atlanta Braves on cable. The Round-Up was not a quiet place. Harry wheezed when he walked; the Braves game bellowed; drunks poured drinks for each other with shaking hands; and a pride of lawyers, sales managers, real estate dealers and knowing locals talked deals loud enough to be heard.

I spotted Ames McKinney in ten seconds, the time it took my eyes to adjust from the sun to the near darkness. The place wasn't big but the tables weren't jammed together. There was leg and elbow room and the smell of beer and something frying. The Round-Up had the universal look of a run-down bar and grill. The grizzled old man sat at a two-chair table in the corner, his back to the wall—Wild Bill covering himself from a sneak attack after drawing Aces and Eights.

He looked up at me from what looked like a plate of chop suey over nachos. I pegged his age at about ten degrees below the temperature outside. His hair was white and cut short. His eyes were light, probably blue-gray, and

70

as I walked toward him I saw none of the telltale red or yellow in the whites that gave away the lifetime drinker.

"Fonesca," I had said stopping in front of him.

He pushed his chair back and got up holding out his hand. His shirt was a red flannel with the sleeves rolled up and his jeans were faded but clean. I couldn't see his feet but I was sure he was wearing boots.

"Ames McKinney," he said, sounding more like George C. Scott than he had on the phone. "Anyone every tell you you look like that guy in the movies?"

"Charles Bronson," I tried.

"Other guy," he said. "Skinny sad guy. Don't remember his name. Have a seat."

I sat.

"Order something," he said. "On me, no strings, no obligations. Foods kinda nuts but it's not bad."

I nodded at Round Harry, who was sweating in spite of the almost cool air. He wiped his hands on his apron and shouted, "What'll it be?"

"I'll have what he's having," I shouted, pointing at Ames McKinney.

"Suit yourself," Harry shouted and went about his business.

Ames McKinney wiped his mouth with a paper napkin and looked at me.

"I know people," he said. "Mostly. Get it wrong sometimes."

"Who doesn't?"

"Got your name from a lawyer in a bar," he said ignoring me. "Not much choice. Small town. Could have had more choice in Bradenton, but I'm on one of those mopeds so I decided to stay cheap and local. Your listing was the smallest."

"I appreciate your confidence," I said.

"Don't joke on me, Mr. Fonesca," he said gently. "I'm country, but I'm no dolt. We can laugh together but not at each other. You can't stop yourself then we can just have us a lunch, talk about the gators and the blue water and white sand and say good-bye."

"I'm sorry," I said. "I'm big city. Sometimes I don't know when I'm doing it."

"Apology accepted," said McKinney, taking a bite of whatever it was Harry now placed in front of me in a steaming blue metal bowl along with a glass of dark beer.

"Special," said Harry. "Mandarin Nacho Supreme."

He departed and I looked at McKinney.

"You in a hurry?" he asked.

"No," I said.

"You gonna talk to me straight?"

"I'll try," I said, drinking some beer and looking down at the brown stuff in the bowl.

"How's business?"

The Braves must have done something interesting. Harry and some of the customers groaned, and one shouted, "You see that?"

"Business is bad," I said.

McKinney nodded.

"Then you got time to concentrate on what I'm gonna give you."

"Depends on what it is," I said.

"How old you, Mr. Fonesca?"

"Call me Lew," I said. "I'm forty-one."

"Your people? Italian? Mex?"

"Italian."

He nodded and ate some more.

"You a good man?"

I shrugged.

"No, but I'm an honest one. I can prove it. You can see my office."

"Lots of crooks are broke," he said. "They just don't know how to do thievin' right. But I believe you," he said, wiping the bottom of his plate with a wad of sourdough bread.

"Thanks," I said. "What is it you want me to do?"

What he wanted was for me to find his former partner, a man named Amos Sprague, who Ames had tracked to Sarasota.

"I tracked him slow through a sister of his in Yuma, a dentist he went to in Truckee, a car dealer he bought a Dodge pickup from in Texarkana," Ames had explained. "Got him down to here. Lost him. Need some help."

"Can I ask why you've spent a year looking for Amos Sprague?"

Some business guys at the table behind me let out a whoop of laughter. One of them started to choke.

"We were partners, cattle. Hard work, but it pays if you know what you're doin'," said McKinney. "Amos took the money out of our joint account on a Saturday afternoon and took off in the company truck."

"How much did he take off with?"

"A million and four hundred thousand dollars even. He left eighteen hundred in the bank. Bought a motor scooter and been livin' on the rest since."

"And you want your money back?" I asked.

"I want Amos Sprague dead," he said. "I can't live dignified or die justified with this unfinished between us."

"So I find Amos Sprague and tell him to give you your money back or..."

"Tell me where he is and I shoot him between the eyes."

"Seems simple enough," I said. "My fee is..."

"Contingency and some cash out flat," said McKinney.

"I don't..."

"I've got a little over five hundred to my name. I'll give you half and a week. You can't find him in a week I get me a job and raise enough to find someone who can. You find him and get the money back and I give you twenty thousand. Simple as that."

"Fair enough," I said toasting him with what remained of my beer. "What can you give me on Sprague?"

He had given me enough to find Sprague, who had a new name, new wife, new teeth and a reputation for philanthropy. I found him and made the mistake of telling Ames. The two old men had an old-fashioned duel on the beach. I had arrived in time to watch it and testify later that Sprague had pulled his gun and fired first.

Ames had decided to stay in Sarasota. I guess he was my best friend.

I stepped in and Ames closed and locked the door behind me.

Beryl Tree was sitting in the straight-backed chair that went with the small desk near the window. The chair was beyond the bed near the bathroom. The window drapes were closed and only one small lamp over the bed was on.

Beryl Tree had her hands folded in her lap.

"He called," she said.

"Ames called you?"

"No, Dwight. Called. Said if I didn't get out and stop lookin' for Adele, he'd come and kill me. He knows you're lookin' for him too. Told me to tell you to stop."

She touched the bruise on her face.

I moved over to the bed, sat and faced her. She was holding on, sitting straight, but there was a catch in her voice and her eyes were focused on some distant thought on a far-away planet. If she started rocking, I knew she would be in real trouble.

"How did he know where you were?" I asked, reaching over to touch her hand.

When she felt my fingers, she came back to earth, almost, and looked at me as if she were trying to remember who I was.

"Remember I told you I saw him at the Waffle House across the street? He followed me, watched me go into this room. After he called, I called your number. Mr. McKinney answered. I guess I sounded...he asked what

75

was wrong, said he was your friend. I told him and..."

"I was fixing your air conditioner," Ames said, holding the gun at his side. It looked like the one with which he had shot his partner, a gun right out of a Randolph Scott western. "Tryin' to anyway."

"They could send you back for carrying that gun," I said.

"Not much choice, was there," he said.

"Maybe not," I agreed.

"Borrowed it from Ed. He's got a collection," said Ames.

Ed Fairing owned the Texas Bar and Grill on Second Street off of downtown. The Texas was not a place where you'd find snowbirds, retirees and people with money. You would find great hot chili and good thick burgers, both with enough fat to kill a long-distance runner and enough taste to lure a vegetarian. Ames had a small room behind the kitchen. In exchange for room and board and a minimal salary, Ames kept the Texas clean and swept. Ames had once been more than a millionaire, but he was content with his job. It gave him plenty of time to think, read the Bible and do odd jobs for me from time to time on his motor scooter. Ames had also become a great source of information. People liked to talk to the tall, quiet man, and the people who came into the Texas often had interesting things to talk about.

"Ever hear of Dwight Handford?" I asked Ames.

Ames thought for a moment and then said,

"From Ms. Tree's description, I think maybe he came into the Texas about three or four months back. Drunk. Tried to start a fight with a tomato picker named Seranas, skinny little fella minding his business. Ed threw this guy out who mighta been Handford."

When Ed threw someone out, it wasn't figurative. Ed Fairing had played two years for the Dallas Cowboys. Never a starter. Popped a knee. Gained some weight. Lost some weight and moved to Sarasota, where he had relatives. With the few thousand dollars he had left, Ed had bought the bar and made a living serving as his own cook and bartender. Ed still topped 300 pounds and never lost his temper.

"Think you could ask some questions?" I asked.

Ames nodded.

"Think you can get that gun back to Ed fast?"

Ames nodded again.

"I'm not goin'," said Beryl Tree.

"And I'm not going to stop looking for Adele. But we can get you somewhere safer."

"That'll be fine," she said.

"Okay. Pack your things."

"They're packed."

"Pay your bill."

"Already did. I knew I couldn't stay here."

"Good. Then I'll take you to the place Ames lives and works, the Texas Grill. You'll be safe there. I've got a stop to make then. After that I'll pick you up and we we'll go see a lady who might be able to tell us how to find your daughter."

I got up and put a hand on her shoulder. She looked up at me.

"I'm not going without Adele."

"I know."

"Be careful of Dwight."

"I will."

I looked at Ames, who nodded in understanding, tucked the gun into the pocket of his loose-fitting faded jeans, draped his blue, equally loose shirt over the weapon and moved to the window. He pulled the drapes open just enough so he could see outside and said, "Looks okay."

Ames went first. I was sure that if Dwight Handford appeared he would get the surprise of his less-than-savory life. I hoped he didn't appear. I didn't want Ames ending his life in prison.

I picked up Beryl Tree's suitcase. It wasn't heavy. She got up from the chair and followed Ames through the door with me behind. Ames stood watch while I pulled opened the door of the Metro for Beryl Tree and dropped the suitcase on the backseat.

"See you at the Texas," I told Ames. "You fix the air conditioner?"

"Got to get some parts. Might be cheaper to buy an old one or a used one," he said.

"Might be," I agreed. "Meet you at the Texas in a few minutes."

Beryl and I didn't talk as I drove up 301, turned left on Main and then made a right on Lemon to Second Street. We got to the Texas before Ames, but he wasn't far behind. He parked his scooter next to me. There were plenty of spaces. Parking was no problem in Sarasota, even in tourist season.

"Ames'll take care of you," I said, handing him her suitcase.

"I've taken care of myself my whole life," she said. "I don't see that changing."

"You like chili, good burgers?" I asked.

"I've served enough of 'em to know the good from the bad."

"Try Ed's and we'll talk later."

I got back in the Metro but before I could close the door Beryl Tree said, "You need more money?"

"I'm fine," I said. "You're way ahead on retainer."

"And I get an itemized bill when you find Adele."

"To the last penny," I said.

I left them standing on the sidewalk and drove the five blocks to the office of Geoffrey Green, Psychiatrist. I made it with ten minutes to spare.

There was a space in front of Carigulo's Restaurant between a green Saab and a blue Rolls-Royce. The Rolls had a For Sale sign in the window.

The narrow passageway between Golden Fleece Antiques and Robintine's Fine Oriental Rugs and Carpets led to a brightly tiled, small, open courtyard with a bubbling fountain in the center. To the right of the fountain was a large wooden door with a golden handle. The sign next to the door said FERGUS & SONS. I wondered what Fergus and his sons did and how they paid the rent. To the left of the fountain was a similar door marked GEOFFREY GREEN, M.D., PH.D. I opened the door and found myself in a carpeted waiting room twice the size of the two rooms I worked and lived in. A sliding glass window stood open in front of me. I told the matronly receptionist who I was and she asked me to have a seat. The only other person in the large green-carpeted waiting room was a nervous young woman, about twenty, who hadn't done much to look her best. Her hair was short and dark. Her brown skirt didn't really go with her gray blouse. She ruffled through a magazine, looked up at the clock on the wall and over at a tank of colorful tropical fish and then back at her magazine. I was halfway through an article about Clint Eastwood in *Entertainment* magazine when Green's office door opened and he stepped out. There was no one with him. If he had a patient, the patient had gone discreetly out another door.

Geoffrey Green was in his late thirties. He wore a dark suit, had dark hair and was ruggedly good-looking. I'd bet he climbed mountains or skied when he wasn't tending to his patients.

"I'll be with you in a few minutes, Dorothy," he said to the nervous woman, who nodded, frowning.

"Mr. Fonesca?" he said, looking at me. "Please come in."

I followed him into his office. He opened his

drapes and let in the sun and a view of a very small, lush garden and a colorful tiled wall.

The office wasn't large compared to the waiting room, but it would do. There was a desk, a chair, a small sofa and two armchairs. The colors were all subdued blues with a touch of gold. A painting on the wall showed a woman standing on a hill looking into a valley beyond the ruins of a castle. Her face wasn't visible.

"Like it?" Green asked, sitting behind his desk and offering me the choice of coach or one of the chairs. I took a chair.

"The painting? Yes," I said.

"One of my patients did it," he said. "An artist. A man. We spent a lot of time talking about that painting."

"It's..." I said.

"Gothic, haunting," he said. "Yes."

"I was going to say melancholy."

"Yes. I'm sorry, Mr. Fonesca, but I'm going to have to get right to your questions. I have a patient waiting."

"I understand. Melanie Lennell Sebastian..."

"I can't give you any information about why she was seeing me or what was said," he said softly.

"What can you tell me about her?"

He sat back, picked up a well-sharpened pencil, put it down, looked out the window and made a decision.

"Melanie Sebastian is a remarkable woman,"

he said, choosing his words carefully. "She's been through a great deal in her life. The town where she grew up—"

"Ogden, Utah," I said.

"Ogden, Utah," he repeated. "Her mother was sick, recurrent brain tumors from what I understand. Melanie took care of her. Every day from the time she was about ten she came home and relieved her father, who worked evenings. I think he was a carpenter. Melanie just took care of her mother, didn't play with other children much, just read and took care of her bedridden mother. When she was fourteen, her father had a heart attack and had to retire. Melanie went to work in a restaurant waiting tables after school till ten at night. No boyfriends. No close friends. It was Melanie's idea to move to Florida with her father and mother. They moved to Gainesville while she earned her degree while continuing to work. Then, about four years ago, just after her parents died within a week of each other, she met Carl Sebastian."

"And what's she like?"

"Complicated," he said, playing with his pencil. "Dedicated herself to her husband and to helping children. She worked long hours for not much pay at a Catholic agency. She fought the system, the courts, the psychiatrists, to save children. When Melanie Sebastian gives her love, she gives it with a conviction, compassion and ferocity I've never seen before."

"You know this from experience?"

"I know it from observation. I've told you more than I probably should."

"You haven't told me why she was seeing you and what you make of the story of Melanie Sebastian you just told me," I said.

"And I won't," he said, putting down the pencil and looking at me.

"Do you know where Mrs. Sebastian is?"

"No."

The answer had come slowly.

"Any ideas?"

"Maybe."

"Want to share them with me?"

He didn't answer.

"This one may get me kicked out, but we're both in a hurry," I said. "Mr. Sebastian thinks you and his wife were having an affair."

Green cocked his head and looked interested.

"You've already more than hinted at that. And if we were having an affair?"

"Or are," I amended. "Well, it might suggest that she would come to you. Her husband just wants to talk to her."

"And you just want to find her for him?"

"That's it," I said.

"First," he said, getting up from his desk chair, "I am not and have not been having an affair with Melanie, Mrs. Sebastian. In fact, Mr. Fonesca, I can offer more than ample evidence that I am gay. It's a relatively open secret, which, in fact, hasn't hurt my practice at all. I get the gay clients, men and women, and I get women who feel more comfortable talking to me than they would a straight male or female. I don't get many straight men."

"You can somehow prove that?" I asked. "Or do I just take your word?"

"The truth is," he said, looking at his watch, "I don't have the time to prove it nor the desire, but I'm sure if you ask in the right circles, you'll get the confirmation you need."

The chair was comfortable. I was tempted to lean back.

"Okay, let's say you're gay."

"Let's say."

"You could still be a friend of Melanie Sebastian. She was, or still is, a patient. She might be inclined to confide in you."

"She might," he said, standing up and smiling. "In which case, I couldn't tell you."

"Dilemma," I said.

"It would appear."

"I told Sebastian that when I found her I wouldn't tell him where she was if she didn't want to be found. When I find her, I'll do my best to persuade her to talk to her husband or tell me why she won't."

"When," he said. "Not if. You don't look like a terribly confident man, Mr. Fonesca."

"About most things I'm not. About finding people, I am."

"You'll have to excuse me," he said, checking his watch again.

"If she gets in touch with you, please give her my card or my number. I just want to talk."

He took the card and gave me a sympathetic smile.

"May I ask a somewhat personal question, Mr. Fonesca?"

"I don't think I'm your type, Doctor."

He chuckled. It sounded sincere.

"No, I've seen a great many people with severe depression. I've learned to recognize some of the signs, and—"

"I've already got a shrink," I said. "And I couldn't afford your rates."

"How do you know?"

"Friend told me," I said. "Besides, I'm straight. You don't take straight males."

"I said I don't get many of them. I didn't say I turned them away. Normally when a patient leaves I ask them to go out that door so patients don't run into each other, but since Dorothy has already seen you—"

"And I'm not a patient."

"And you're not a patient. You can go out the front through the waiting room."

He ushered me to the office door and opened it, saying,

"I'm sorry I couldn't have been more help."

"I'm used to it," I said. "I'm patient. Time is one thing I have too much of. Too much time and so little to do."

"Spoken like a true depressive," he said. "I don't expect to be talking to or seeing Mrs. Sebastian, but if I do I'll give her your message. I don't think she'll talk to you."

"I'll be in touch," I said.

"Take one of my cards on the way out," he

said, and then, looking past me, addressed the nervous young woman with "Come right in, Dorothy."

Dorothy waited till I was clear of the door, pressed her lips together and entered the inner sanctum. The door closed.

I stood for a few seconds watching the fountain in the small courtyard.

With two hours till I had to pick up Beryl Tree for our appointment with Sally Porovsky, I headed for the legal offices of Tycinker, Oliver and Schwartz. I had served papers for all three of the partners in the past and had gotten to know Harvey. Harvey did the computer work for the trio and was well paid for his expert services. He had a small, well-equipped room down a corridor near the washrooms where the secretaries could watch him. Harvey had a drinking problem. The secretaries were under orders to report all of his arrivals and departures. Harvey knew this, agreed to it and wanted it. It seemed to help him cut back on his drinking. Harvey did not want to lose this job. The question was whether he needed computers or alcohol more.

Harvey's drinking, which had slowed considerably since I first met him, was tolerated because Harvey was a genius. I was on a straight retainer with the firm of T,O & S. I served papers at no fee. My retainer came in the form of access to Harvey whenever I needed him, provided I didn't abuse the privilege.

Some of what Harvey did bordered on the

illegal. Part of his unwritten and unspoken agreement with T,O & S was that he would solemnly swear that all the information he obtained on the Net was legally obtained.

Harvey could access information from the police—any police with a computer—credit agencies, banks, hotels, almost every major corporation, the Pentagon, the FBI and probably even the shopping lists of the wives of every member of the Israeli intelligence community.

I found Harvey in his windowless office drinking club soda and studying something on the computer screen in front of him.

Harvey looks more like an ex–movie star than a computer hacker. Harvey is tall, dark, wears a suit and tie, and sports short hair of gold. He's MIT but you wouldn't know it from his looks.

"Harvey," I said.

He grunted something and then made an effort to pull his attention from the screen.

"Lewis Fonesca," he said. "Looking as happy as ever. Here for work or a sports tip for the week? If it's a sports tip, go with Duke over North Carolina if you can get three–two or an even bet with a six-point spread. The screen tells me."

"Work," I said, handing him the folder on Melanie Sebastian. He opened it and went through the documents slowly.

"Who prepared this?"

"Her husband."

"Good job. You want the Tuesday special or..."

"She left, pulled the money out of their joint accounts. You have the numbers of the accounts, the list of credit cards and numbers, GTE calling card, whatever else you can turn up. He wants her found."

"Take me about ten minutes if I don't hit any problems. You want to wait?"

I said I did and took a seat while Harvey hit keys, moved a mouse, moved to another computer, hummed something that sounded like a busy signal and said things to himself like "Uh-uh-uh-uh" and "Here I come. Here I come." Fifteen minutes after he started, Harvey turned to me and said.

"She hasn't used any of her credit cards for the last week. She hasn't rented a car or taken a plane out of Sarasota, Tampa, Fort Myers, Orlando, St. Pete, Miami in the last four days, at least not under her own name. She did come into Sarasota from Raleigh-Durham Airport last Monday. Early morning arrival. Can't do much if she's using cash and a different name, but I can run all kinds of variations on her name or any others she might use. People tend to stay with something they can remember."

"Middle name is Lennell," I said.

"Yep, see it right here. Mother's maiden name was Fallmont. Let's see...plenty to go on. Take some time. Bank accounts are cleared out. She doesn't have any others in her own name."

"How much did she pull out?"

He turned to the screen, moved the mouse,

pressed a button and said: "Forty-three thousand, six hundred and fifty. Took cash. Left three dollars in that one. Another twenty-eight-two in cash from this one. Left fifty dollars and nine cents."

"See the description of that jewelry?" I asked.

"Nice list."

"Can you see if she sold any of it?"

"I can play a would-be buyer, go on-line offering more than market, but jewelry...It's hard to market price. Still, the descriptions are good. I've got her Social Security number. I'll get the numbers of her relatives, friends—if you can give me names and..."

"Can you see if Geoffrey Green, the shrink, has rented a car, bought an airline ticket. The works."

"Yep," said Harvey. "I saw Green three or four times when I came here and, let's say, recuperating."

"And...?"

Harvey shrugged. "Didn't hurt. Didn't help."

"Why'd you stop seeing him? Big fees? No help?"

"Sometimes a shrink who charges a lot of money is good. Green is good, but I think he started to come on to me," said Harvey. "Hard to tell. I know what computers are thinking but I have a problem with people. He was careful. I wasn't interested. Got uneasy. You know. Rapport between shrink and neurotic was deleted."

"Any way you can talk to your computer to find out if...?"

Harvey nodded.

"Credit-card use. Organizations. Magazines he subscribes to. I can look. I'll be a little curious myself."

He took a drink of club soda. The bubbles were long gone. What I was asking him to do was illegal, not just on the border. I was more interested in what was right than what was legal. If I got caught, I would take what came. Ann Horowitz, who charged considerably less than Geoff Green said I wanted to be punished, to be righteous and punished. A short, tarnished Lancelot in recycled Levi's jeans.

"I'll call you," Harvey said. "I've got something else to finish, take me an hour and then I'll go back on the trail of the missing Melanie. I'll check every day to see if I can find anything till you tell me to stop."

"Thanks, Harvey," I said.

"My pleasure," he said. "My meditation. My therapy. My answer to AA. My work. Anything else?"

"Are all the computers going to crash and the world to face disaster when the millennium begins?"

"You hoping yes or no? I get the feeling that, if you don't mind my saying, you're a little suicidal."

"I don't know."

"A few minor glitches," he said. "No planes falling out of the sky, blackouts, nothing like that. If you have friends thinking of loading up on gas, water and automatic weapons and heading for cabins back up in the Georgia hills, don't try to talk them out of it. The Net tells me that they won't listen."

"I'm reassured," I said. "And I'm late."

Harvey had already returned to his screen.

I was back at the Texas Bar and Grill ten minutes later.

The windows of the Texas are painted black with only a neon Budweiser sign to serve as a beacon. The name of the bar is printed in big white letters on the blackened window. Inside, the Texas, which had all the comforts of Judge Roy Bean's Jersey Lily, was lit with ceiling bulbs and muted yellow spotlights in the corners. The yellow walls were decorated with steer horns and old firearms. The tables were heavy, round, solid oak and surrounded by hard-hatted construction workers, garbage disposal men, cops, firemen, people on the edge of coming back from oblivion or sinking into it, and a handful of longtime Sarasota businessmen and women who know that the best chili and burgers in town were in the semidarkness of the Texas.

Beryl Tree and Ames were at a table in the back near the bar. Ames was watching the door. Beryl was nibbling at a giant chili burger. Ed Fairing, the proprietor and chef, was talking to Ames. Ed sports a big flowing mustache and wears string ties with turquoise or Petosky stones. Ed probably would have enjoyed pulling unruly customers out into the street for a public execution. Ed, though born and raised in the good part of Sacramento, California, lived the role. He had even developed a Texas accent.

"Fonesca," he said, giving my hand a more than hearty shake. "Happy as ever."

"Happy as ever," I said.

"Burger and chili? Chili or burger? Beer?"

"Burger, thick, cheese, tomato, no onion," I said, sitting. "You pick the beer and put it in a mug."

"Gonna see a lady?" Ed said. "No onion, no chili. You always have onion and chili."

"You should have been a private eye, Big Ed," I said. He loved to be called Big Ed.

Ed left and I turned to Beryl Tree.

"Everything's quiet," said Ames. "I called Flo. She said she'd welcome the company."

I nodded and said, "Mrs. Tree..."

"Beryl," she said.

"Beryl," I continued. "I'm going to eat fast and we're going to see a therapist who might know how we can find Adele. Just tell her who you are, why you want your daughter found, about your husband, everything. If she asks for identification, give it. Her name is Sally Porovsky."

"A therapist? They think Adele is crazy? Dwight's the crazy one," she said, pushing away her half-finished burger.

"Your daughter's been through a lot," I said. "My guess is the police or a court or her school referred her to the counseling service where Ms. Porovsky helps kids. You don't have to be crazy to need help."

She nodded, though I knew she was still not convinced.

"When we finish talking to Ms. Porovsky, Ames and I will take you to a friend's house where your husband won't be able to find you," I said.

"If Dwight comes looking, he'll find me. He's mean, rotten even, but he's not a fool. He's smart in some ways. You know, like a animal, sharp teeth. I think he means what he told me. If I don't go and call you off, he'll do his best to kill me and maybe you, too."

Ed came back with the steaming burger and a mug of beer. The foam curled over the side as it was meant to. I thanked Ed, who ambled over to another table, looking as if he had spent a lifetime in the saddle.

"You want to call it off?" I asked.

"No way on earth or in heaven," she said.

Ames sat quietly watching the door, hands in his lap. I hoped he wasn't carrying the gun I had seen him with earlier.

I ate fast. The burger was great and Ed had topped it with blue cheese and a thick tomato. I drained the mug of beer and got up.

"Let's do it," I said in my best imitation of William Holden in *The Wild Bunch*. Considering the surroundings, it seemed like the right thing to do. Considering who I was and how I probably sounded, it was a bad mistake.

John Detchon was at the reception desk reading and talking on the phone at the same time. He recognized me, smiled and examined Beryl Tree. He had probably seen a lot of Beryl Trees from behind his desk. Ames was waiting in the car. I wondered if it would be worth asking Detchon if he knew Geoffrey Green or anyone who might know him. Sarasota isn't that big and I didn't think the gay community, if it was a community, would be hard to keep track of. I decided against it, at least for now, and led Beryl to the elevator.

She clutched her purse and looked straight ahead.

When the doors opened and we went into the office of Children's Services of Sarasota, I saw more people sitting in the cubicles than I had before. They were making notes, phone calls, faces. Sally Porovsky looked as if she hadn't moved. Whatever it was about her kicked in and I decided to make a call to Ann Horowitz in the hope of finding some way of dealing with a feeling I couldn't deny but wasn't sure I wanted.

"Mr....?"

"Fonesca," I reminded her, disappointed that she hadn't remembered, and annoyed that I was disappointed.

"Fonesca, yes. I'm sorry."

"That's all right. This is Beryl Tree, Adele's mother."

Sally Porovsky's voice was exactly as I remembered it. Musical, a little husky. Sally rose, took Beryl's hand and smiled, guiding her to the extra chair in her cubicle. This time I stood, a step back.

"I'm sorry to ask you this," Sally said gently, leaning toward Beryl and lowering her voice. "But do you have some proof of your relationship to Adele?"

"Got her birth certificate in my purse, photographs, report cards from grade school, health insurance, Social Security card, whatever I could find when I came out here."

She opened her purse and began fishing out folded pieces of paper, cards and photographs of Adele. Sally examined them, returned some and asked Beryl if she could make copies of the ones she had kept.

"Just so I get 'em back," she said.

"I'll do that now and give them right back. Can I get you a coffee, Coke, water?"

"No, thank you."

"Mr. Fonesca?"

"Lew," I said. "No, thanks."

"Be right back."

Sally moved across the room and disappeared to the left behind a pile of cardboard boxes.

"I like her," said Beryl.

"Yes," I said.

"You can tell with some people," Beryl said. "I think she tried to help Adele."

I agreed. Sally returned in less than three minutes carrying a manila folder, handed the original documents to Beryl, who put them in her purse, and sat down.

"Mrs. Tree," she said. "Your daughter said her name was Prescott, Adele Prescott."

"Prescott?"

"Her father's name is Dwight Prescott."

"No, it's Dwight Handford."

"He said it was Prescott. He had a driver's license, Social Security number, Sarasota address," said Sally, putting her hand on Beryl's. "Since Adele confirmed he was her father and...Mrs. Tree, they said you were dead."

"Adele told you I was dead?"

"I'm afraid so."

"He made her," Beryl said. "She was afraid of him."

"She came to Sarasota on her own to look for him, Mrs. Tree," said Sally. "That's a brave thing to do for a sixteen-year-old girl."

"She told you she was sixteen?"

"Yes."

"She's fourteen," said Beryl. "Her birthday was on the fourth of last month."

Sally sat back, sighed, closed her eyes and looked up at me. I nodded to confirm what Beryl had said so far.

"Your daughter got in trouble with the police," Sally said. "They referred her and her father to us. The referral was mandatory, court ordered. That meant they had to work with us."

Someone laughed, a man on a telephone not far away.

"What kind of trouble?"

"She was soliciting," Sally said, taking Beryl's hand again.

Beryl nodded. She knew what that meant and the information didn't seem to surprise her. It hurt, but she wasn't surprised.

"Where is she now?" asked Beryl.

"We don't know," said Sally. "We're looking for her. Her father hasn't been very cooperative and...we're looking. Beryl, Adele said some things to me that...How can I put this? Did your husband ever abuse your daughter?"

"Hit her?"

The pause was long.

"Sexually," said Sally.

This pause was even longer. I turned away.

"I..." Beryl began. "I don't know for sure. He went to prison for..."

"He sexually abused a young relative," I said.

"I thought maybe when Adele was..." Beryl said. "But I couldn't believe it. I didn't want to believe it. Adele never said anything. I can't think."

"I understand. Are you going to be in town for a while?"

"Till Adele and I get on a train, plane or bus out of here," she said.

"Is there anywhere I can reach you?"

Beryl looked up at me. I gave Sally my home-office number.

"Mrs. Tree'll be staying with a friend. I think you should know that she ran into her husband two days ago. He hit her. Then he called her this morning and threatened to kill her if she didn't stop looking for her daughter."

"Did anyone hear the threat?" asked Sally.

"I did," said Beryl.

"Anyone else?"

"No," I said.

We exchanged looks that said we both knew there was nothing the law could do.

"I'll call Mr. Fonesca if we find Adele," Sally said, getting up and helping Beryl to her feet.

"Thank you," said Beryl.

"I'll meet you at the elevator," I said to Beryl. "I've got to ask Ms. Porovsky something."

Beryl nodded and moved toward the elevator.

"The answer is yes," she said.

"Yes?"

"Dinner, remember?"

"I remember," I said. "Tomorrow night. Seven?"

"That's cutting it a little tight," she said. "I've got a home visit in Englewood till five. Make it seven-thirty."

"Dress casual," I said.

"Fonesca, this might be a mistake for both of us."

"Might be," I agreed.

She handed me a card. I turned it over. There was a phone number and address in ink.

"Seven-thirty, then. You like kids?"

"Huh?"

"I have two kids, a boy and girl. Thirteen and nine."

"I like kids," I said.

"Well, be prepared for these two. Dinner only, quick, home and friendly. Agreed?"

"Agreed," I said, looking at Beryl at the elevator. "I'm not dangerous."

"I wouldn't have said yes if I thought you were," she said. "In my work, I see dangerous people all the time."

"Since we're on the subject, think you can give me Handford's address?" I asked.

"No," she said. "But I gave Mrs. Tree his current name. I think you heard it."

"Prescott," I said.

She said nothing.

"Dwight Prescott," I said.

"Got to get back to work," she said. "See you tomorrow night."

John Detchon waved to us from behind his receptionist's desk as we left the building. He seemed to be reasonably happy. I wasn't sure how I was feeling.

5

GUS ZINK HAD DIED more than a year ago. Natural causes. I understand the distinction between murder, manslaughter and accident and natural causes—breakdown of the body, invasion by disease. But it all seems natural in a screwy kind of way. Murder is natural. Usually wrong, but natural.

Gus had come to Sarasota with his wife, Flo, more than a decade ago. He was retired, had money, got elected to the city council as an independent, made enemies and had gone out swinging.

During his campaigns, necessary public

talks, lunches, dinners and various appearances, Gus had done his best to make excuses for the absence of his wife. She was ill or she was touring Europe or visiting one of her brothers or sisters in Alaska, Montana, California or Vermont. The Zinks had no children.

Just before he died, Gus, already more than just sick, was kidnapped to keep him from a key council vote on where to put a branch library. There was big money on the line, big enough to make some landowners and contractors want to insure the location.

I had been hired by the city's only black councilman to find Gus Zink. I had found him. Gus started to fail fast after that last council meeting. He and Flo had gone north, to Vermont, where Gus had been raised. When he died, Flo came back to their house in Sarasota. The house was on the bay but on the mainland, not one of the Keys.

Flo Zink answered the door, a familiar glass of amber liquid in her hand. She looked at me, grinned, winked at Ames, who nodded, and turned her attention to Beryl Tree. A women sang plaintively inside the house. I recognized the voice and the song. It was Patsy Cline.

Flo was in her late sixties. She was dressed in a black silver-studded skirt and vest over a blue denim shirt. She wore boots and looked as if she were on her way to do some line dancing. She was a barrel of a woman, with too much makeup, large earrings, and the distinctly vacant look of a heavy drinker. Even through her generously applied perfume there was a smell of scotch, probably good scotch. Flo, I had learned from personal experience, held her alcohol well, but once in a while there was a scotch overdose and the well-rounded widow Zink turned honest and foul-mouthed.

"I'm Flo," she said to Beryl Tree. "Come on in and let's get friendly. You can tell me your story. I'll tell you mine."

Flo put her free arm around Beryl and guided her into the house. Ames and I followed.

Flo led us into the living room with a view of the bay. The furniture around the room looked as if it belonged on the set of a Clint Eastwood western. Wood, old brown leather, a rough-hewn table made from a thick slice of redwood, and animal skins for rugs. Two paintings on the wall were authentic Remingtons—galloping cowboys, Indians riding bareback.

Flo moved to the double-speakered stereo against the wall and turned Patsy Cline down but not off.

"What are we drinking?" asked Flo. "I know Lew is beer, which I don't consider drinking, and McKinney here is straight whiskey, which he doesn't drink till the sun goes down, so he's having...?"

"You have Dr Pepper?" asked Ames.

"I have every drink known to man or beast," said Flo, holding up her glass to take a drink and purse her heavily painted lips. "Dr Pepper is coming up. And you, Ms. Tree?"

"Beryl," she said. "Just water."

"Suit yourself, my dear," said Flo. "And have a seat. I'll put your bag in your room."

Flo pointed to a leather chair with arms made from the antlers of something from the far north. Beryl sat.

"Something to eat?"

"We ate at the Texas," I said.

"That phony cowboy, Fairing, makes a decent bowl of chili. I'll give the son of a bitch that."

Flo picked up the small suitcase and left us in the living room listening to Patsy Cline sing about how much her lover was hurting her.

Flo wasn't gone long. When she returned, she was carrying a tray with four drinks in tall glasses. The ice in the glasses clinked as she put the tray on the low redwood table.

"This is my special," Flo said. "You can drink Dr Pepper, beer and water and any other piss you want at the Texas. At Flo Zink's you go with the special when the sun sinks its ass into the water, which is what it will be doing in about ten minutes. Now, if you want to sit and hold it while the ice melts and the sun disappears, you go right ahead, McKinney."

We all took a glass.

"Here's to getting through the shit," said Flo, holding out her glass in a toast.

I knew Flo's special. We drank. Ames didn't make a sound and his weathered face didn't change. Beryl Tree choked and caught her breath.

"You get used to it," said Flo.

"I like it," said Beryl, taking another sip.

"I'm gonna love this woman," Flo said to me and Ames.

I took a drink, steeling myself from the memory of the last time I had a special. It burned and tasted like sweet molten plastic. Flo was almost finished with her drink.

"I've got to go," I said after forcing down another small sip.

Beryl continued to drink. Maybe she needed it.

"She'll be safe here," said Flo. "At least from everybody but me."

I was familiar with Flo's arsenal of weapons. They hung on wall racks or were displayed in cabinets in her gun room. I knew some of the guns were loaded. I didn't know which ones.

I turned to go.

"You'll find Adele," said Beryl, fortified with Flo's special, which seethed its way quickly into the nervous system.

"I'll find her," I said. "I'll call you in the morning."

"Not too early," said Flo. "We're going to be talking most of the fuckin' night. Sorry about my language, Beryl."

"I'm a waitress in a truck stop," Beryl said. "I don't think you could come up with anything I haven't heard every day for the last twenty years."

"I can try," said Flo, smiling sweetly.

I dropped Ames back at the Texas and asked him to see if he could get any leads on Adele or Dwight. He nodded, got out and went inside. I headed back to that which passed as home.

It wasn't too late. The DQ parking lot was

busy but not full. I parked toward the back of the lot, locked the Metro and headed toward the concrete stairs.

I didn't see him standing back in the shadows of the building and bushes near the stairway. But I did hear him when my hand touched the railing.

"Where is she?" came the voice from the dark. It was a raspy voice, the voice of a man who might have played an outlaw or a tough sheriff on an old radio show. Or maybe Flo and Ed Fairing had just put me in a western mood.

I stopped and looked toward the voice.

He came out of the shadows. He was big. Boots, badly faded jeans, a short-sleeved button-down white shirt with green stripes. His hair was dark, long, tied back in a small ponytail. My first impression was that he was good-looking and dangerous. Some women, maybe a lot of women, liked that. Most men didn't.

There was nothing in his hands but his fists were clenched tight.

I didn't have to guess who he was.

"Where's Adele?" I asked.

Dwight Handford was no more than three yards away and closing in slowly. I was on the second step. I turned to face him. With me standing on the second step our eyes were almost dead even. Even in the dim light I could see that his eyes were blue-gray and dancing.

"You're a dago, right?" he said.

"And you're a redneck," I answered.

"That sort of sets up how we're gonna have

104

this conversation," he said. He had closed the distance between us to less than a yard. "Dagos understand violence."

"And rednecks know how to come up with it," I said.

"I'm not stupid, dago," he said.

"Can we switch to wop?" I asked.

"Suit yourself," he said with a smile. "I'm planning to hurt you just enough to let you know I'm serious. Then you're gonna tell me where Beryl is. I'm gonna go see her and be sure she leaves town. You're gonna stop looking for Adele and asking questions."

"How did you find out I was looking for you?" I asked.

"You asked a lot of people," he said, inches from my face now. "Where is she?"

"Are you willing to kill me over this?" I asked.

"Maybe, I've...maybe."

"I'm not telling you," I said.

He searched my eyes.

"You're not scared," he said.

"No."

"Why the hell not?"

"You wouldn't understand," I said. "I'm not sure myself. Sometimes I think I came here to sit down in a chair, watch old videos, eat at the DQ and die."

"You're a crazy son of a bitch," said Handford.

"I don't know. I've thought about it. I don't think so. But you may be right. I think it's a lot more complicated than that."

"We'll see," he said, slamming his right fist into my stomach. I started to sink, grabbed the railing. Whatever was in my stomach wanted out. He'd missed the rib cage.

"Where is Beryl?" he asked. "I'm not an unreasonable man. I just want to be left alone. I want Adele to be left alone. She's mine and I full intend to keep her and take care of her."

"You've done a great job so far," I said, sinking back on the steps and letting go of the rail so I could clutch my stomach. "You've got her out selling herself on the Trail."

He stood over me, hands on his hips, and shook his head.

"It's all fuckin' simple for you," he said. "You don't know shit, do you?"

I nodded. I really didn't feel much like talking.

"Then I'll tell," he went on. "It's all about stayin' alive and doing what you feel like doin' without getting caught. You live. You die and there ain't no God watchin'. You understand?"

I nodded again.

"Just because cowards like you say there's somethin' wrong with what I do, don't make it wrong. It's horse shit. If God didn't want me doing what I do, he'd have nailed my ass to the shit house wall long time ago."

"I'm glad I'm being beaten by a brillant, if maniac philosopher," I said, gasping at the end.

"Wop," he said, "for the last time, where is Beryl? Answer me fast. Answer me true or you're goin' to the hospital or worse. You read *Studs Lonigan*?"

"No," I gasped.

"What I'm gonna do to you is in that book. Look for it if you live out the night."

I came up as quickly as I could and rammed my head into his face. He staggered back with a groan and I sank back down on the steps. I had intended to run for the DQ, but my legs weren't on my side. Handford moved back toward me. It didn't take much imagination to know what was about to happen.

But it didn't happen.

A man came out from behind my car. Dwight Handford paused. The man took a few steps toward us. He was built like a wrestler, a short round wrestler. He was almost bald and he looked bored. He wore slacks, a sports jacket and a white shirt with no tie.

"Walk away," Handford said to the man.

The man in the sports jacket moved closer.

"This is between my wop friend and me," Handford said. "A matter of filial responsibility. I heard that word on television. You like that word, wop? Filial."

Handford's nose was bleeding, badly. He didn't bother to hold it or try to stop the bleeding.

"I'm Italian too," said the new man. "And I don't like people calling me names."

"Walk," Handford said between his teeth.

"You walk," said the man. "You walk or I blow your goddamn head off."

There was a gun in his hand now.

"Who the hell are you?" Handford asked.

"I'm a man with a fuckin' big gun in my hand," the man said. "And if you think I won't shoot your pissant balls off, take another step toward Fonesca. Or better yet, take one toward me. The way I figure it you got only one way to go and that's back into the fuckin' night."

"You won't shoot," Handford repeated, but he didn't move.

"It would mess things up," the man said, "but shit, I can make it work. I don't feel like talking anymore. Get the hell out of here, fix your fuckin' nose or die. Those are your choices and I'm real bored here."

Handford looked at me. The look said we were going to meet again. Then Handford looked at the man with the gun. It was the same look.

"Next time I see you," said Handford, pointing a finger at the man, "you may not have that gun."

"Hey," said the man. "If I don't you're in real goddamn trouble 'cause I'll break your neck. Hey, I don't need a show here. Move out."

Handford moved back into the bushes. I could hear him rustling away. I watched the darkness for a few seconds and then turned toward the man with the gun. He was gone.

I groaned my way up the steps, used the rusting handrail and made it to my office. I went inside and locked the door behind me. Light came through the window from the DQ and cars on 301. I leaned my back against the door and tested the spot just below the ribs where Handford had punched me. I was reasonably sure nothing was broken or ruptured. It wasn't that kind of pain.

There was a chance Handford would come back that night. I didn't think so, but you never know. I didn't have a gun but I did have a tire iron in my closet. I had rescued it from my Toyota when it died. The tire iron would remain close to me, and my reasonably sturdy office chair would go under the doorknob. I couldn't count on my guardian angel in a sports coat to return.

I closed the drapes, turned on the lamp on my desk and looked at the air conditioner in the window. It was humming and doing its best to kick out air. Ames had done something to it, but the air coming in was still almost as warm as the night.

I got the tire iron from the closet, brought it back to my desk, reached for the telephone and the folder Carl Sebastian had given me. It was almost nine. It felt like a washed-out midnight. I made my call. An answering machine kicked in with a male voice repeating the number and politely asking me to leave a message.

"My name is Lew Fonesca. I'm working for Carl Sebastian. I'd like to speak to Caroline Wilkerson. When she—"

"This is Caroline Wilkerson," she said, picking up the phone.

Her voice was light, cultured.

"I'd like to talk to you about Melanie Sebastian," I said.

"Are you all right, Mr....?"

"Fonesca," I said. "Aside from suffering from depression and having recently been punched in the stomach by a very big man, I'm fine."

"Have you been drinking?" she asked.

"No," I said. "Forgive me. I'm a little under the weather and the moon is full."

"You have been drinking," she said with irritation.

"No. I'm sober and I'm looking for Melanie Sebastian. Mr. Sebastian suggested that I talk to you."

The pause at her end was long. I tried not to gasp from the pain as I waited.

"Cafe Kaldi, tomorrow morning at nine," she said.

"Sounds fine," I said, fairly sure that I would be in no condition to work out at the Y.

"And Mr. Fonesca, please leave your sense of humor, if that's what it is, at home."

"I'll do that, Mrs. Wilkerson," I said.

We hung up.

I thought of Sally Porovsky at her desk brushing back her hair, adjusting her glasses. I didn't want to think about Sally Porovsky. I had her card. I had her phone number. I thought about calling her and making an excuse and forgetting about seeing her tomorrow for dinner. I pulled the card from my wallet, looked at it, put it down on the desk and knew I was going to go through with it. I made a few notes in my file on Adele. There was a lot to write. I kept it simple.

I watched an old tape of *The Prince and the*

110

Pauper. The tire iron lay next to my bed. A bottle of Advil kept it company. I wondered what happened to the Mauch twins who starred in the movie. I wondered, but not enough to find out.

I wondered about my guardian angel. Who had sent him to protect me? Why? I heard my grandfather's mandolin. He was playing "Darktown Strutter's Ball," one of his favorites.

When the twins stopped smiling at the end of the movie, I leaned back and fell asleep. One of my recurrent dreams came deep but with a new twist. My wife's car was driving in the right-hand lane. Night. She was heading home. The water of Lake Michigan off to her left. I was there. Standing in the median strip, watching her come toward me. A pickup truck suddenly appeared, red, fast, hit her hard crushing her car a few feet in front of me. The pickup sped past. The driver was Dwight Handford. He was smiling at me like the Mauch Twins.

6

PUTTING ON MY JEANS and a loose-fitting black T-shirt was painful now that the punch to my stomach from Dwight Handford had settled in. I've been punched before, usually when I delivered or attempted to deliver a summons to someone who decided that since I was the only one available, he or she would take out their wrath on me.

I had learned that showing a gun wouldn't stop an infuriated recipient from attack. I had tried the gun bit—using an unloaded weapon—once when it looked as if the large Hispanic man standing in his doorway with the summons I had delivered in his hand was going to do something angry, violent and out of control. He had spat at the gun, taken it from me and tried to shoot me. When it didn't fire, he threw it at me, hitting me in the face. He had then run into his apartment shouting in Spanish and looking, I was sure, for something lethal—at the very least a large knife. I picked up the gun and ran like hell to my car. Eight stitches later, I vowed never to try the gun bit again.

I pushed the chair out from under the doorknob and, carrying the tire iron at my side, went outside, where I was greeted by a small lizard on the metal railing. He cocked his head in my direction. Nothing new about lizards in Florida. There were usually three or four scuttling along the concrete and the railing. This one seemed to sense that things were a little different this morning. He looked at me, puffed out the sac under his neck, and watched as I made my way down to the rest room, each step a painful reminder of the reality of the previous night.

The rest room could only be opened by a key, or so I had been told. Once in a while, when the weather really got bad, meaning heavy rain, I found a homeless man curled up under the sink. There was no one in there this morning.

I laid my tire iron across the sink, shaved, washed, brushed my teeth and looked at my face. I am not formidable. I thought about Sally Porovsky and tried out a smile. It wasn't hideous, but it wasn't winning. I'm not ugly. I've been called pleasant, plain, interesting. My wife always said I had hidden appeal, Mediterranean hidden appeal.

My grandparents on my father's side had met in Viareggio, not far from Florence. My grandfather had been a waiter. My grandmother had been a chef's assistant. They came to the United States in 1912 and made their way to Chicago, where they opened a small neighborhood restaurant on the Northwest Side. They were officially retired by the time I was born. My maternal grandparents came from Rome. My mother's father was a reporter for a newspaper. My maternal grandmother worked at a bakery near the newspaper office. When they came to America, she stayed at home and had children and my grandfather split his time between working as a furniture upholsterer and writing for an Italian-language newspaper. He had a political column and a bad temper.

When my parents married, they left the Catholic Church and became Episcopalians. I don't know why. They have never told me, and when I asked, as a child or an adult, they said the equivalent of "Some things are personal, even for parents."

There are times I've thought of becoming a Catholic like my grandparents, but I've never had the religious calling. It just seemed like something I might want to do, which is not a good reason for becoming a Catholic. It is probably a good reason for going to a basketball game or ordering a banana split, but a bad idea for becoming a Catholic.

I tucked my soap, toothbrush and Bic razor in a desk drawer and, tire iron in hand, went down to the Metro. Getting in was painful. Getting out after finding a parking space on Main Street was even more painful. I didn't take the tire iron with me to the Cafe Kaldi.

Caroline Wilkerson was already there. I had no trouble finding her even though the coffeehouse tables were full. She sat alone inside, not at one of the outside tables, an open notebook in front of her, a pair of half-glasses perched on the end of her nose. She was writing in a large notebook. A cup of coffee rested nearby. I recognized her from the society pages of the *Herald-Tribune*. I picked up a cheese and onion croissant and a large coffee and made my way back to her table. I didn't want to bite my lower lip when I sat, but my sore plexus insisted.

When I sat across from her, she looked at me over her glasses, took them off, folded her hands on the table and gave me her attention.

The widow Caroline was a beauty, better in person than in the papers. She was probably in her late forties or early fifties, with short, straight silver hair, a wrinkle-free face with full red lips that reminded me of Joan Fontaine.

If she had spent time with a plastic surgeon, the surgeon had done one hell of a good job.

She wore a pink silky blouse with a pearl necklace and pearl earrings and a lightweight white jacket and no friendly smile.

"Mr. Fonesca?"

"Yes," I said.

She nodded and took a sip of her coffee.

"She didn't. No way," someone said.

A pretty girl with long blond hair and a silver ring through her left nostril had uttered the words of disbelief. The girl began to laugh. So did the girl with short dark hair with her and the boy with a little beard and a baseball cap worn backward.

"Are you in pain, Mr. Fonesca? You look..."

"Minor accident," I said. "I wasn't looking and I ran into something. Do you know that Melanie Sebastian is missing?"

"If I didn't know," she said, lifting her glasses so they rested on top of her head and closing her notebook, "I wouldn't be here talking to you. Carl Sebastian called me. He was frantic. Almost in tears. I couldn't help him. Melanie hasn't contacted me. I would have thought, as Carl did, that if Melanie did something like this, she'd get in touch with me. I told Carl to call the police. Melanie might have been hurt. She could even be..."

I drank some coffee and took a bite of the croissant. It was pretty good. I really wanted an egg.

"Did they fight?" I asked. "Could that be the reason she ran away?"

"Why don't you ask Carl?"

"Spouses sometimes don't want to face certain truths."

"Yes, I know," she said.

The trio at the table next to ours laughed. Caroline Wilkerson looked at them somewhat wistfully for an instant and then back to me.

"Fight? The Sebastians?" I reminded her.

"I don't think so," she said. "But I can't be certain. Carl said nothing about a fight and I don't recall ever seeing them fight or hearing from Melanie that they fought. I'm very worried about her, Mr. Fonesca."

"Any idea of where she might have gone?"

The pause was long. She bit her lower lip and made up her mind and sighed.

"Geoffrey Green," she said softly, meeting my eyes. "He's her analyst and...I think that's all I can say."

"Carl Sebastian thinks his wife and Dr. Green might have had an affair, that she may have left to be with him."

She shrugged.

"I've heard rumors that Geoff Green is..."

"Homosexual," I supplied.

"Bisexual," she amended.

"You can't think of anyplace else she might have gone to, anyone else she might be with?"

"No, but I'll think about it."

I had finished my croissant and coffee and got up slowly. I handed her one of my cards.

"If you hear from Mrs. Sebastian," I said, "would you tell her that her husband just

116

wants to talk to her. If she doesn't want to talk to him, I'd like to talk to her. She can call me at that number. I won't try to talk her into anything she doesn't want to do."

"I hope you find her," Caroline Wilkerson said. "Melanie has had problems recently, depression. One of her relatives, her only close relative, a cousin I think, recently died. That's hardly a reason for...who knows? Frankly, I don't know what to make of all this."

At the moment, that made two of us.

"Are you permitted to let me know if you find out anything about where Melanie is and why she's—"

I must have been shaking my head no, because she stopped.

"I'm sorry," she said with a sad smile, showing perfect white teeth. "That's what I would expect if you were working for me."

When I got to the coffeehouse door, I looked back at Caroline Wilkerson. Her half-glasses were back on and her notebook was open.

Back in the DQ parking lot, I parked the Metro and went to the window for a burger, fries and a chocolate/cherry Blizzard. It was still early. There was no line. Dawn, an almost nothing of a woman, was behind the window, freshly aproned, smiling.

"Dave not in yet?" I asked after she took my order.

"On the boat," she said. "Workin' on it at

least. Said he had the need. And I can use the extra hours."

Dawn was probably in her early thirties and had two small kids, but she looked like a pre-teen. She was sad in the eyes but fresh-faced and never wore makeup. Dave said she had been through a tough time. He let her and her boys live rent free in his one-bedroom rental house off of Orange and north of downtown. With the money she made at the DQ and an additional hundred a month she got from cleaning houses, she got by.

"Ever hear of a guy named Dwight, Dwight Handford or Dwight Prescott?" I asked her over the buzz of the machine as she worked on my Blizzard.

"Know a couple of Dwights," she said. "But not those two."

"It's one guy who uses different names." What's he look like?"

I told her.

She came to the second window, Blizzard in one hand, burger and fries in a bag.

"Rings a cowbell," she said. "I'll think on it."

I nodded, took my food to one of the red picnic tables covered by a gray and red Coca-Cola umbrella and tried to think while I ate and watched the cars and trucks speed down 301. My stomach hurt with the first shock of cold. Dwight had done a very good job with one punch. I was careful from that point on, but I was determined to finish the drink.

Across the street, a man and a boy in his teens

who should have been in school walked into the acupuncture center under the dance studio. On a really quiet day when the traffic was light on this urban stretch of 301, I could even hear the music while I ate at Dave's. My favorites, which they played over and over, were Eydie Gorme singing "La Ultima Noche," an orchestral verson of "The Vienna Waltz," and Tony Bennett singing "I Left My Heart in San Francisco." People were dancing in the window now. One of the instructors, a thin man with a small, well-trimmed beard, was demonstrating something Latin. He had one hand up in the air and the other on his stomach. His eyes were closed and an old couple were holding hands and watching. I couldn't hear the music.

There was a tire shop on one side of the acupuncture building and then to the left as I faced it stood a trailer-supply store and then the bar called the Crisp Dollar Bill. On the other side of the bar was the dance studio I could see from my office window. I had never been in the bar. Dave told me that it had been called the Dugout before the White Sox moved their training camp.

"Mr. F.," Dawn called.

I looked over at her framed in the window.

"Mr. F., I may be nuts or so, but I saw that guy you asked me about, least I think it was him. Could have been. He parked in the lot 'bout an hour back. Pickup truck with one of those things, you know, for hauling cars. Got out and looked around. I remember him

119

'cause he didn't buy anything, just stood around. Morning breakfast was busy. Then he was here, got a coffee, took it off and..."

There was no pickup truck in the parking lot. I took a final bite of my burger, got up as quickly as I could and dumped my early lunch in the garbage can.

"I think I'm wrong, Mr. F.," she said.

I looked toward the back of the lot and up at my office door.

"I think you're right. Thanks, Dawn," I said.

I went past the Geo and headed for the steps, past the spot where Dwight had come out of the bushes. He could have reparked the pickup and waited in his familiar spot. There was no Dwight now. Dawn could have been wrong, but I had a pain in my stomach and a wish for a tire iron that said she wasn't.

The slightly open door to my office made me sure.

Dwight had probably just looked around, seen no one watching and, when Dawn wasn't paying attention, come up the stairs and thrown his shoulder against the door. It was no match for him. I stepped in. The lights were on. Dwight had trashed the place, not that there was much to trash. I pushed the door shut. It stayed in place. Drawers were on the floor. The desktop had been swept away. Papers, an empty glass, business cards and things I didn't remember having were all over the floor. I moved to the other room. Nothing had been touched.

Dwight hadn't been there just to give me a warning. If he had, he would have caved in the front of my TV with the tire iron that now lay on the floor in the doorway. Conclusion: Dwight had been looking for something, something he found. As far as I knew, the only thing I had that Dwight wanted was the file I kept on Adele. It was on the floor with other debris. I had made a note in it that I had taken Beryl to Flo Zink's

I turned my desk chair around, picked the phone off the floor and hit the redial button.

"I'm here," came a familiar voice.

"Flo, it's Lew."

"Bad news for you, Lewis," she said. "Bad news. She's gone."

"She's gone," I repeated.

"Got a phone call about an hour ago. Guy said you'd given him the number. Asked for Beryl. Said he was a lawyer friend of yours, that he was going to get an injunction against her husband, going to get him to tell where Adele was. I asked him if he wanted to talk to Beryl. Said no, asked me the address. That's when it hit me."

"He wasn't a friend," I said.

Dwight had probably called from my office sitting in my chair.

"That's what hit me. You would've called, told me he was gonna get in touch. You would have told him where I live."

"What did you tell him?"

"Beryl had left, gone off to a motel or somewhere. I said she got in a cab and went off,

121

didn't tell me where. The son of a fuckin' bitch hung up. I told Beryl, told her to get her things together, that we were taking her someone safe. While she got ready, I got the car out of the garage, drove around front, went in to get her and—"

"She was gone," I said, seeing if it was worth supergluing a broken little plaster duck I kept on my desk for luck.

"Gone, walked away. I looked for her. Drove all over. Nothing. Lew, I think it's time for the cops. That shit's after her and she's running scared."

"Maybe you're right, Flo."

"I'm sorry, Lew. I fucked up."

"No you didn't," I said, putting the two halves of the duck on my desk. "You figured it out. Flo, I think you might want to get out of there."

"Lewis, I want that bastard to show up here," she said. "I want it so bad I'd pay big dollars for the joy. I'm holding a very large weapon in my hand and if I see him coming to my door, I'm shooting a hole right through the door and him."

"Not a good idea," I said.

"Lewis, I've got money and one hell of a great lawyer. Lord, let him come."

"He's driving a pickup truck—Ford—with a tow winch," I said.

"One more question," she said.

"I'd say 'shoot' but under the circumstances..."

"You've got a sense of humor hiding behind

that sad face, Lewis. Question is, does he have my address? Are you sure? I'm not listed in the phone book."

I looked at my mess of address and business cards on the floor and said, "I think so."

All Dwight Handford had to do after he read my file on Adele and found out I had taken her to Flo's was to get the address out of the address book on my desk.

"How long does it take you to get here from your place?"

"Fifteen minutes, maybe a little more," I said.

"He called a lot more than an hour ago. What's keeping the bastard?"

"Good question, Flo. Maybe you should get out of there for a while."

I knew what her answer would be.

"Beryl was scared, real scared. That man's hurt her. He's sure as hell hurt that kid. He is one dangerous asshole."

That I knew, but I said,

"Lock up tonight. I'll keep calling."

"You going to look for Beryl?"

"I'm going to look."

There was a sound of footsteps coming slowly along the the concrete walk outside my office. I hung up and went for my tire iron. When I had it in hand, I faced the door. Someone pushed it open. I hoped the someone didn't have a gun. He didn't.

"Ames," I said.

He looked at me as unmoved as he always was and said, "I came to work on the air conditioner some more."

He looked at the air conditioner and so did I for the first time since I had come into the office. The front of it was caved in.

"You go berserk?" Ames asked, calmly nodding at the tire iron and then looking around the room.

"No," I said. "Someone came in. Beryl Tree's husband. He was looking for something."

"Find it?"

"Yes."

Ames nodded as if it was all clear to him. Maybe it was.

"Never fix the air conditioner now," he said. "Don't think there was much chance of it yesterday when it was still sort of alive."

"We'll give it a decent burial," I said, sitting at my desk and biting my lower lip.

"Somethin' hurtin'?"

"Beryl's husband. Last night. Told me to stop trying to find his daughter and to get Beryl out of town. He performed euthanasia on the air conditioner and made this mess."

Ames nodded and said,

"I'll have to work out what I owe you some other way than the air conditioner."

I wanted to tell Ames again to forget it, but he couldn't forget what he thought he owed me. He had to pay it off to keep his self-respect.

"I'll think of—"

The phone rang. I had a pretty good idea who it might be. Once again I was wrong. I picked it up.

"Hello."

Ames started to pick things up off the floor. I didn't stop him.

"Fonesca," said Harvey the computer genius. "He tell you? I wanted to be sure you got the message."

"Who? What message?"

"Your partner," said Harvey.

Ames held up a black oblong something. I couldn't figure out what it was for a second. Then I remembered. It was the name plaque that had been on my wife's office door. Ames turned it over, looked at the name, rubbed it gently against the sleeve of his well-worn flannel shirt, placed it faceup on the desk and began to clean up the room.

"My partner?"

"When I called you earlier, he answered, took the message," Harvey said.

"Give it to me again, Harvey. That wasn't my partner. I don't have a partner."

"Then who...forget it. I don't want to know."

"What did you tell him?"

"That I had some information on Melanie Sebastian. Her car was found at the airport. Could have been there for weeks in the long-range parking, but Carl Sebastian reported it missing. Routine check found it. I found the report on the airport computer."

"So she flew away," I said.

"Don't think so," said Harvey. "I went into the records looking for a Melanie Sebastian, or a Melanie Lennell or a Melanie anything who might have flown out anytime between this morning going back to Tuesday. Nothing. Didn't expect to find anything. Then I tried females with the initials M.L. or M.S. Nothing. You have to show ID when you get on a plane, you know."

"I know, but how closely do they look."

"Some do. Some don't. You want the rest?"

Harvey was enjoying himself. I wasn't. But I needed him. I watched Ames and listened to Harvey.

"Then I checked all the women who had paid for their tickets in cash since no credit card of hers showed an airline ticket purchase. Nothing. You know what I did next?"

I was reasonably sure, but I didn't want to spoil Harvey's surprise.

"Taxis from the airport to anywhere with a woman passenger. Town this size with most people getting picked up or having their own cars waiting, business at the airport isn't all that hot for taxis even on the best of nights or days."

I felt like blurting out "car rentals" but I said, "And you found nothing?"

"Nothing. Then rentals cars. I got her, pilgrim. Last Wednesday night. Lady got a red Neon from Budget. Showed an ID, left a cash deposit. You have a pen and something to write on?"

I had a green-and-white push-button pen in my pocket. The word RHINOCORT was in green against the white. I had no recollection of picking it up. Everybody advertises on pens, gives them away. I haven't bought a pen in five years. I found an envelope in the top drawer and said,

"Ready."

"Georgia plates. License number 66884J. Now, you've got three questions, right?"

"Right," I said as Ames, with a handful of junk, stood surveying the room to see what items larger than a paper clip he might have missed.

"Gonna get a broom," he said.

I covered the mouthpiece of the phone and said, "DQ will lend you one."

Ames nodded and left as Harvey said, "Question one: How many days did she rent it for? Answer: Ten days. Question two: Where did she plan to return it? Answer: Back at the airport right here in town. Question three: Whose ID did she show? Answer: Caroline Wilkerson. Driver's license. You ever see a photo of Caroline Wilkerson in the *Herald-Tribune*?"

"I've seen the woman up close, this morning."

"I matched computer images from IDs of the two women," said Harvey. "You'd have to be blind to think it was the same woman."

"So," I said, looking at my watch.

"So, someone with the touch, knowledge and a halfway powerful computer and a color printer could strip in a photograph of Melanie Sebastian over Caroline Wilkerson's and then relaminate."

"You know people who could do it?" I asked.

"I know some and I'm sure there are a lot more out there. I don't think we'll track her that way."

"Thanks, Harvey."

"I'll keep looking," he said.

"You've done enough."

"This is fun. I need fun."

"Then have fun. Call me if you turn anything up."

We hung up and I looked at my wife's nameplate. I remembered it on her door. I remembered her walking out to greet me with a smile, her hair pulled back, her...Question: How did Melanie get Caroline Wilkerson's driver's license?

I did know a lot now. Melanie Sebastian was driving a new red Neon. She was probably still within driving range of Sarasota unless she planned to: (a) drive back from somewhere two or three days away; or (b) return the car to some other Budget office. I was sure Harvey would keep track of that. And (c) was my favorite: She was still in the immediate area. Why?

I reached for the phone and the Melanie Sebastian file, which Dwight had gone through and dumped. It didn't look as if he had taken anything. Why should he? He wasn't looking for Melanie. I was. He was looking for Beryl Tree. I dialed the number for Caroline Wilkerson. It rang six times and the answering machine came on. It was her voice. The message was simple: "Please leave a message." I did. I asked her to call me. Just in case she had tossed my card, I left my number.

Ames returned, broom and dustpan in hand, and went to work. I watched him. Once he had been worth about three million dollars, by his reckoning. Now he was cleaning the floors and tables in a bar and sweeping my floor and he said he was content. I believed him.

"Ames, I've got to find Beryl Tree."

"She's not at Flo's?"

"Ran away. Her husband tracked her down."

I pointed to the mess to indicate how he'd located her.

"We've got to find her," he said as he swept. "I like the lady."

"Then we better start looking for her and her daughter."

"Adele," he said.

"Adele," I repeated.

"Nice name," said Ames. "You feel up to it? You look kind of sickly."

"Dwight came to see me last night."

I got up, rubbed my sore stomach.

"Bad man," said Ames, sweeping the floor.

"Very bad. I've got to get myself in shape fast," I said. "I've got a date tonight."

Ames stopped sweeping and looked at me. Just looked.

"A lady?"

"A lady," I said, tucking the envelope with the tag number of the red Neon Melanie Sebastian had rented into my shirt pocket.

"You sure you're up to it?" he asked.

"No," I said. "But I'm going to try."

I looked at him and he looked at me and then at my wife's name plaque.

"It's worth trying," he said. "You know what trying does?"

"What?"

"Keeps a man alive," he said.

7

BERYL TREE COULD BE in any one of five dozen motels in Sarasota, not to mention more in Bradenton. It would take too long to find her that way. No, the best way to find Beryl was to find Dwight or Adele or both.

I had called Carl Sebastian and told him I had some news.

"Yes?" he said eagerly. "Where is she?"

"I'd like to come by and see you," I said.

"Sure, of course, but I have a dinner meeting tonight. Let's see…It's almost four. Can you be at the bar in Marina Jack in half an hour?"

"Half an hour," I said.

He hung up and I got dressed. I wasn't sure of how I should dress for my date with Sally Porovsky, but considering what I had in mind, I settled for clean blue slacks, a light blue button-down shirt and a red knit tie. Then I headed for Marina Jack's.

It took me a little over five minutes to drive to the parking lot, find a space between a blue Mercedes and a digesting pelican, and head down the pier. The docks jutting off to the right and left of the pier were reasonably full of small to medium pleasure boats that bobbed with the tide. Gulls swooped, cackled and searched for food. A few pelicans sat on the dock or on empty boats, wings tucked into their chests, scanning the water without moving their heads.

A pelican circled above, saw something

and dived awkwardly with a plop into the water just beyond a white boat with the name *Dead Souls* painted on its stern. Someone, I think it was Dave, told me that pelicans keep their eyes open when they dive and the eyes of the bird aren't protected. Eventually, if they live long enough, pelicans go blind.

In front of me, in the circle in front of the restaurant, valets were parking cars, moving around cars that were already parked to wherever cars could be parked. I walked up the steps behind a man, woman and teenage girl. The girl walked the sullen walk of a teen who found neither her parents nor her prospects interesting. The walk said that she planned to keep letting her parents know that she did not plan to enliven dinner with her wit. I read a lot into the walk and when I moved past them while the father checked in at the reservation podium, I got a look at the girl's face and knew I was right. The girl was just about the age of Adele Tree. I wondered where Adele was and who she might be having dinner with.

I wondered how the couple in front of me would react if the sullen girl was missing the next morning. Anguish, yes. Confusion, yes. Denial, yes. And guilt, always guilt. You can tell yourself it wasn't your fault. A thousand shrinks with a thousand mandolins could tell you it wasn't your fault. But it was. You can always think of something you should have done, could have done.

Carl Sebastian blustered and bragged, but a gargoyle called guilt rode on his shoulders, head back, laughing and showing sharp teeth. A small taunting demon of guilt hid within the purse of Beryl Tree, peeping out to whisper of things that could have been done and weren't. I knew the demon and the gargoyle. We weren't friends, but I knew them.

The place was noisy. The bar was to my right and beyond it was the dining room and beyond the dining room was the bay and a view of Lido Key about a half mile or so away.

Carl Sebastian was at a table in the bar. He sat alone, a drink in his hand, his eyes on me as I approached. I sat.

"What do you have?" he said.

I felt like saying "a sense of humor" or "a desire for civilized interaction," but I didn't.

He was dressed in a perfect-fitting white jacket, a black shirt and a white tie and, from what I could see, a perfectly creased pair of white slacks. There was even a black handkerchief in his pocket.

I looked at him and smiled. I think it was a smile.

"You're in pain," he said. "Your chest—"

"Nothing to do with your situation," I said.

"I'm sorry," said Sebastian, starting to put a hand up to check the wave in his white hair and then changing his mind. "I've just been...don't know. I can't work. I can't...would you like a drink? I'm just having Bloody Mary mix with a slice of lemon. They don't have V8 tonight."

"I'll have the same," I said.

Carl Sebastian looked up over my shoulder,

made a slight gesture with his left hand and a waiter appeared. Sebastian ordered my drink and another for himself.

"She's probably still in the area," I said.

"Good," he said.

"She's not using her credit cards or checking account. Of course she could have used her cash to open another account under another name, but I don't see the point. Mr. Sebastian, I don't think your wife wants to be found. Not right now. She's not running, but she doesn't want to be found. I have some reasonable evidence that she plans to stay around for a while. I think she may come back on her own, call you or get to you through a friend. That's what they usually do."

He shook his head no.

I sat listening to the noise and looking to my right at the sun on the water.

"I don't want to think about who she might be with," he said. "What she might be doing. I can't sleep. I can't work. Find Melanie for me."

I shrugged and looked at the Bloody Mary mix with a twist of lemon the waiter had placed in front of me.

"All right," I said. "She rented a car. I may be able to track it down, find it, find her through it. There are other leads."

"The good Dr. Green," he said with as much sarcasm as he could muster.

"Maybe," I said. "You still think he might be with your wife?"

"Yes," he said emphatically, looking into my eyes.

"He says he's gay," I said.

"I know," said Sebastian. "He's lying."

"Pretending to be a homosexual?" I asked after taking a drink.

"Why not? He gets the homosexual trade. He gets women who feel comfortable with a homosexual who wouldn't be with a—"

"Straight guy, like you and me?" I said.

"You're mocking me, Fonesca," he said.

"Sorry."

"Shall I continue or do you want to smirk for a few seconds?"

"I don't smirk."

"Geoffrey Green gets women who feel comfortable with him and then seduces them. Maybe they think they're rescuing him from his choice or nature."

"And maybe he's gay," I said.

"Or maybe he is whatever the client wants him to be," said Sebastian. "I think he knows where Melanie is. I want her found. I'm sure I can straighten this out if she'll just talk to me face to face."

"I'll keep looking," I said.

He sat back and said, "Good."

I finished my drink, got up and said I had to leave. He looked at his watch and said he had to leave too. He dropped a twenty on the table and we made our way through cigar smoke and hoarse laughter and down the stairs and through the doors to the outside. Sebastian nodded to one of the young valets, who blinked and went looking for the right car.

"Find her for me, Fonesca," he said, putting a hand gently on my shoulder.

I nodded and started down the pier toward the parking lot. There were more gulls now but the pelicans were gone.

Sally Porovsky's apartment was in one of those two-story complexes in blocks of six or seven buildings. There was plenty of parking, the grass was green and the bushes and trees, including some stunted palms, were taken care of. This was not where the retired wealthy spent their golden years.

The apartment was easy to find. The buildings were clearly marked with large gold address numbers, which were easy to read by the complex's night lights. When I got to the door, I could hear voices inside, including one male voice I recognized: Harrison Ford. I pushed the button and waited. From inside, a boy shouted.

"Door. It must be Kevin Costner for you, Mom."

"Michael," said Sally, "how about a gesture of goodwill?"

A few seconds later, the door opened and I was facing a lanky teen in a blue T-shirt, million-times-washed jeans and bare feet. His hair was long and he had an earring in his left ear. He was still into acne, but it was minimal. He said nothing.

"I'm Lew Fonesca," I said, holding out my hand.

He shook and stood looking at me, holding the door.

"Can I come in?" I asked.

"Sure," he said, moving to a sofa against a wall and plopping into it. His feet went up on a low coffee table and his eyes turned to the television set, where Harrison Ford was scrambling along a rooftop.

I was standing in a small, neat living room with a bright comfortable sofa, an armchair, a dark wooden coffee table, a line of Georgia O'Keeffe flowers on the walls. The floor was gray carpet. I guessed the floors in all the apartments were management-gray carpet. The room and the dining room beyond it were clean and uncluttered.

I pushed the door closed behind me and said, "*Frantic.*"

"Yeah," Michael said.

"What's your favorite Harrison Ford movie?"

He looked up at me and said, "You care?"

"I think so. I'm killing awkward time till your mother comes to save me, but it'll be easier for both of us if we find something reasonably interesting to talk about. My favorite is *Witness.*"

Mike nodded and looked back at the television set. Harrison Ford almost fell.

"I like the first Indiana Jones too," I said.

"Yeah," said Mike.

"I've got tapes of both of them," I said.

"We don't have much room for tapes," said Mike. "But we do have the VCR."

"You can borrow my tapes," I said.

"That depends on if you go on another date with my mother."

"No, not really, but maybe. I live over by the DQ on Three-o-one."

"I go there all the time," he said, looking at me. "You eat there?"

"Every day," I said.

"No shit. Oh shit, I told Mom I wouldn't say 'shit' or..."

"I don't give a shit," I said.

He looked at my blank face and smiled.

Sally came hurrying out of a door across the room. She was putting in an earring.

"Sorry," she said. "Just got home. Home visit...I told you. You met Mike."

"Yes," I said.

"You said casual. I'm casual," she said.

She was wearing a loose-fitting dress with a belt, flats and the silver earrings. She'd done something to fluff her hair and she'd put on more makeup than she wore the day before. She looked alive. She looked great.

"I'm ready," she said.

Mike was transfixed by the television. He wiggled his toes.

"I'm ready," I said.

I was lying. I had the feeling she was too.

"One more thing," she said. She turned and called, "Susan."

A second door opened and a girl about nine came out. She was wearing cutoff jeans, a green blouse and sneakers. She was dark, pretty, with long dark wavy hair. She was definitely her mother's daughter.

"Susan, this is Mr. Fonesca," Sally said.

"Fonesca," she said. "Are there Italian Jews?"

"Yes," I said, "but I'm not one of them."

"I told you," Mike said without looking up.

"Nice to meet you, Susan, Mike," I said.

"Have you got the *X-Files* movie?" asked Mike.

"No," I said as Sally guided me toward the door.

Mike shrugged.

"Can I stay up till ten?" Susan asked sweetly.

"Nine. In bed, lights out. School tomorrow. You've heard this story every night for years."

"But tonight is different," she said, glancing at me.

"Nine. Mike?"

"Nine," he said. "What time will you be home?"

"Not late," said Sally.

"You look like that actor who plays the bad guy," said Susan to me. "You know the one."

"Stanley Tucci," said Mike without looking back at me. "He does funny stuff too."

"Is that his name?" Susan asked. "Two cheese?"

"Nine o'clock," said Sally, ushering me out the door and pushing it closed behind us.

"Well?" she asked.

"Well?"

"That was test one."

"I think I like them," I said. "You think I look like Stanley Tucci?"

"A little," Sally said, walking next to me as I guided her toward my Geo. "Where are we going?"

"I know a good pizza place," I said. "Then I've got some questions for you and I thought we might go looking for Adele Tree."

"Sounds like fun," said Sally.

"I'm sorry," I said. "I was trying to make a joke."

"No, you weren't," she said. "And I'd like to find Adele. You like anchovies on your pizza?"

"I love anchovies on anything," I said.

"You just passed test number two."

There were a few things wrong with Honey Crust Pizza. The place was small, crowded, with booths on both sides and tables with red-and-white tablecloths down the middle. The place was smoker friendly, but the smells from the open kitchen behind the counter at the rear overrode the tobacco. The waitresses were friendly, efficient and fast, and the pizza matched anything I had eaten back in Chicago. My mother was an Italian cook only because she was Italian. Her preference was for American staples: meat loaf, fried chicken, broiled fish and matzo-ball soup. There was no explanation for the matzo-ball soup, but my father, sister and I didn't need one. We liked it.

All this I told Sally, who was a professional listener. She paid attention, appeared interested and knew when to ask questions. She was

139

as good as I was, in a different way. Sally was animated, friendly, willing to talk herself. I am the quiet, sympathetic type. My basic affect was "I'm sorry for your trouble. I'm listening. I wish there was more I could do." Compared to my father, I was a blabbermouth. My father's usual evening conversation was "You all right. Kid's all right." My mother usually said "Yes." Sometimes, at dinner, she told about family slights, tragedies, inadvertent moments of comedy. My father ate, nodded and said nothing. He patted me on the head at least twice each night till I left the house and went out on my own. He always kissed my sister twice on the top of her head; once when he came home, the second time when she went to bed.

When we went to bed, he always said, "Good dreams. If you have a bad one, wake yourself up and try again." My mother claimed that was an old Italian saying. He always said it in English. Both my mother and father spoke Italian, though they had been born in the United States.

All this, too, I told Sally as we shared our large onion-and-double-anchovy pizza.

Sally had come to Sarasota a dozen years ago with her husband, whose name was Martin, Martin Herschel Porovsky. He liked to be called Jack because he admired John Kennedy. Sally had been born Sally Feldman. They had come to Sarasota because Jack, an engineer, was transferred by his company to the research lab in Sarasota to work on government military projects. Jack had died in an accident at work. Sally had never been given a straight answer about what had happened. She had been given a $125,000 death benefit and collected another $150,000 in life insurance. The money was in a mutual fund for the education of her children. Sally never touched it. She worked, lived carefully and spent as much time as she could with her mother in Dayton, Ohio. She hadn't dated in the five years since Jack died.

All this she said over coffee and a split order of cannoli.

"Why did you say yes?" I asked.

"To you, about tonight?"

I nodded. Like my father. Sally sighed and examined her coffee for an answer.

"You seemed safe. I meet a lot of people, good, bad, sad, troubled. I usually read them well. Maybe intuition. Maybe intuition is just experience. You looked sad, safe, troubled. No threat."

"Some people," I said, "think I look a little like Richard Gere. Those people are now safely locked away."

She smiled.

"Some people say I've got a sardonic sense of humor," I said. "I'm trotting it out in the hope of impressing you. I haven't been out with a woman, I mean like this, since my wife died."

"We're quite a pair," she said. "You said we were going to look for Adele. Unless my intuition has failed me this time, I don't think we're here having pizza and telling our life stories because you want to get information out of me."

141

"No," I said. "What I'm going to ask you I could have asked you in your office or over the phone. Your answers would have been the same."

"Ask," she said, brushing her hair back in a way that reminded me of my wife.

I went silent.

"What's wrong?" she asked.

"Time travel. I'm back. What's Adele's story? And Dwight?"

"Not much. She was delinquent at school. She was also selling herself at night on the North Trail. Court called in her father. She was living with him. Court ordered us to take on the case. Dwight Handford, who calls himself Prescott, is living proof of the many mistakes made by God or Darwin. Adele is a smart kid, a decent kid. She said she would go to school, stay off the Trail. She said she wanted to stay with her father. He said he wanted her."

"But...?"

"No hard evidence," she said. "Just hints and the fact that our Dwight spent time in prison for child molesting. I think Adele's afraid of him. I think Adele also wants to be with him and doesn't at the same time. I think, maybe, he knew she was hustling. She...it's not easy. I think Dwight has been molesting Adele sexually. I think he did it when she was a kid and started up again when she came looking for him in Sarasota. She wants to please her daddy."

"And the court said she could stay with her father," I said.

"That's it. No one knew there was a mother.

Courts send kids home if there's any way to do it. Doesn't matter what the parent or parents have done in the past, doesn't matter that a significant number of kids returned to abusive parents are abused again, some of them wind up dead."

"Now there's Beryl," I said.

"Now there's Beryl, but no matter what a court says, Adele is smart, street wise and able to run back to her father."

"It's worth a try," I said.

"It's worth a try," she agreed.

"So," she said. "I'll give you Dwight's address—the real one, not the one he gave the school—and we'll move the evening on to the North Trail, because if you find Adele you want me to be there."

"You've got it."

"You know how to show a girl a good time on the first date," she said.

"Richard Gere," I said.

"Stanley Tucci," she said.

"So I've been told."

The dividing line between Bradenton and Sarasota is just north of the airport, New College and the Asolo Center for the Performing Arts on North Tamiami Trail. Sarasota is a Culture town, capital "C" in Culture. There's an art museum, five Equity theaters, including one that only does musicals, a massive concert hall, a ballet company, and an opera company.

There wasn't much that could be considered big-C culture near the first phone booth outside the Warm Breeze Motel across from the Harcourt Inn. We checked the booth. The number was wrong. Sally went into the Warm Breeze to ask some questions.

While I waited outside, a prostitute took me for a Mister Right.

"Want some company?" she asked.

She was a washed-out brunette with sad eyes, rough skin and almost no breasts.

"No thanks, but I'd like to know if you recognize this girl."

I took out my wallet and handed Adele's photograph to the hooker, who didn't look much older than the girl she was look-ing at.

"Nice-looking kid," she said flatly and handed back the picture. "You a cop? I thought I knew all the cops in town. New?"

"I'm not a cop," I said. "I'm just trying to find a missing girl for her mother and ask her some questions."

"Thought you were a cop. Lots of cops last week or so."

"Why?"

"Why am I telling you this? You want conversation? Ten bucks."

I put Adele's photograph back in my wallet and removed a ten-dollar bill. She took it.

"A john got killed at the Yellow Sun, across the street there. Cops marched all the girls in, asked questions, found nothing."

Traffic whizzed by. A car slowed down. A

dirty-blond kid with a big round face stuck his head out of the window and in a redneck voice called,

"That the best you can do, man? You are really sorry."

And the car sped up.

The girl clenched her teeth, took a breath, and tried to jump back in the game.

"That worth another five?" she said.

I shook my head no.

"Hard times," the girl said, stuffing the ten in a pocket in her dress. "Her name's Suzanne, at least on the Trail. Worked from the Linger Longer."

She nodded over her shoulder. Across Tamiami Trail and two motels down was a tired neon sign with a flashing arrow pointing the way to the Linger Longer Motel.

"And?" I asked.

"Then she was gone," the girl said with a shrug.

"Who was working her?"

The girl shrugged again and looked across the busy street at nothing.

"That wasn't worth ten dollars," I said.

"All you're gettin'," she said. "Hard times, remember."

Sally came out of the Warm Breeze Motel. The girl saw her coming, turned around and tried to look as if she wasn't in a hurry.

"Anything in there?" I asked.

"Nothing," she said. "You get anything from Jean Ann?"

"You know her?" I said, watching the girl move away between motel neon lights and in between shadows.

"Yes. Not one of mine. Belongs to Medino Guttierez. I'll tell him she's out here again."

"Adele is calling herself Suzanne. She works out of the Linger Longer Motel. Hasn't been seen for a few days."

We drove across the street to the Linger Longer. There was a phone booth in front of it. The number was the one from which Adele had called her mother.

"Game plan," I said, looking over at Sally. "I go in alone. You stay here. If she spots you through a window, she may run. When I have her located, I'll come for you."

"And what do you do when you find her?" she asked.

"I talk," I said. "And you?"

"Not much more," she said. "I can have her brought in for being on the street. She's underage. I can keep it off her record. I've got friends in low places. She's better off in juvenile detention than out here and maybe—"

"Then that's the plan," I said, opening the door.

"Be careful, Lew," she said, touching my arm.

I nodded, gave what passed for a reassuring smile and got out.

The glass door on the Linger Longer Motel office said American Express, MasterCard, Visa, Discover were welcome and that German, Spanish, French and Canadian were spoken inside. It also said the clerk kept no cash. I pushed the door open. There was no lounge, no chair and not much room to linger. A coffeepot sat half full with white foam cups next to it. Behind the low counter, a kid sat reading a book. He put the book down and said, "Can I help you?"

"Why not Italian?" I asked.

"Pardon?"

"Sign on the door says German, French, Spanish. Why not Italian?"

"I don't know. Maybe they don't get Italian tourists."

"You speak German, French, Spanish?"

"A little."

He took off his big glasses and stood up with a polite smile.

I took out my wallet and the photograph of Adele and handed it to him. He put his glasses back on.

"Suzanne," he said. "Stayed here...oh, a couple of months back. Why? What'd she do?"

"Her mother's looking for her."

He cocked his head to one side and looked at the photograph again before handing it back to me.

"You're not a cop. If you're Children's Services or a private investigator, I'd like to see some ID."

"I'm not with Children's Services and I'm not a private investigator. I'm a process server."

I flipped open my wallet so he could see my card and photograph in living color. I couldn't believe the forlorn creature with half-closed eyes in the photograph was me. The kid behind the counter seemed to have no trouble believing it.

"You have papers on Suzanne?"

"No," I said. "Her mother's looking for her. I'm a friend."

The kid thought for a while, thumped his right hand softly on the counter, sighed deeply and said,

"I think she's in Port Charlotte, one of those clubs," he said. "She's a chanteuse."

"You get a lot of one-named chanteuses staying here."

"A surprisingly large number," he said. "Last year when I started here we had a surprisingly large number of one-named massage therapists."

"You like Suzanne," I said.

He considered the statement and said,

"Yeah, I like her. I'm a student over at New College. This job pays well and I get to read, do my homework and once in a while practice a little of my Spanish, German or French with tourists who don't know what kind of motel they've wandered into."

This time the pause was very long. He looked out the window at the passing traffic.

"Would five bucks help you think of something else that would help me find her?"

"No," he said, looking at me and pushing his glasses back up his nose. "She worked for Tilly. Room Five in the corner. He's in there now. If he asks you how you found him, tell him you tracked down a girl named Elspeth, tall bleached blonde, short hair, big lips, average breasts. Elspeth ducked on Tilly three weeks ago and headed back to San Antonio."

"Thanks," I said.

"I don't think I've done you a favor. My advice is get some help before you talk to Tilly. I hope you find Suzanne. She reminds me of a beautiful crippled bird my sister and I took in when I was a kid. The bird needed help but it kept biting us."

I went back out into the neon night and motioned to Sally to stay in the car. Room 5 was across the cement parking area toward the corner of the L-shaped motel. There were two cars parked: one a little blue Fiat, in front of Room 5.

"Who?" came a voice from inside the room when I knocked.

"Seymour," I said.

"Seymour? Seymour what?"

"Just Seymour," I said. "One name. Like a chanteuse."

An eye peered through the tiny, thick-glass peephole.

"You a cop?"

"Everyone asks me that," I said. "I'm not a cop. I just have a couple of questions to ask you and I'll drive away."

"Questions about what?"

"Suzanne. Her mother's looking for her."

"So am I," he said, opening the door.

"Tilly?" I asked.

"Come in, man," he said.

149

I went in and he closed the door. He was a lean, handsome black man about six foot and wearing a pair of clean jeans and a neatly ironed button-down long-sleeved white shirt. He couldn't have been more than twenty-five.

I looked around. The room was motel tacky. It didn't look like home.

"I don't live here," he said, reading my mind. "Why are you looking for Suzanne?"

"Her mother's in town. Wants to take her daughter home."

"Home? Mother. She's got no mother. Mother's dead."

"And you were kind enough to take her in."

"Hey, she's old enough to—"

"She's fourteen," I said. "Just barely. You want to talk to me or the Children's Services caseworker sitting in my car?"

"Just a second."

He pulled the drapes back enough to peek through and see Sally in the Metro parked across from him in the lot.

"Her mother's looking for her," I said.

"So am I."

I let that pass.

"You want a drink?" he asked. "Don't drink myself, but I keep a fridge for guest and visitors."

"No thanks," I said.

"Suit yourself," he said and went to the small brown refrigerator in the corner of the room. He pulled out a can of Mountain Dew and went to sit on a worn-out, rust-colored, two-seat sofa. I remained standing.

"Suzanne ran out on you," I said.

He laughed and took a sip of Mountain Dew.

"They don't run out on me," he said. "Once in a while I might ask a young lady to leave, but they don't want to go. I take a fair split and I never raise a hand."

"Elspeth," I said. "She ran away. You raised a hand to her, Tilly."

"She say that? I threw her out. She had a bad attitude, as her heading you to me proves. You know what I'm saying? Elspeth. Godawful name, but she wouldn't let me give her another."

"Suzanne," I said.

"Good kid. A little too sad in the eyes. A lot too smart, but a good worker and she didn't complain. That's all I'm giving without a fee."

"You worth a fee?" I asked.

He gave me a toast and a smile with his Mountain Dew.

I took out my wallet. I'd find a way to bill Carl Sebastian for the girl I had given the ten to on the street and the twenty I handed Tilly.

Tilly shook his head. Twenty wasn't enough. I gave him another ten. He took it, frowned. I shook my head. The thirty would have to do.

"I think she was turning her share over to a guy," he said.

"You think?"

"Okay, I know. Older guy. Good-looking if you're into that redneck type. Suzanne is."

"He came here?" I asked.

"Once," Tilly said, readjusting himself.

"He have a name?"

Tilly shrugged.

"Dwight something. I didn't catch another name, you know?"

"I think so," I said.

Tilly rolled up his right sleeve. A deep red gash was starting to form a scar.

"Dwight?" I asked.

"Yeah."

I pulled up my shirt and showed him the bruise on my stomach. It had grown bigger and was turning an interesting array of colors, mostly purple and yellow.

"Dwight?" he asked.

"Dwight," I said.

Tilly touched the can of Mountain Dew to his forehead and closed his eyes.

"I'll give old Dwight this," he said. "He's not a nigger-hating redneck. Just your all-out motherfuckin' son of a bitch."

Someone opened the door with a key. A heavily madeup young woman who might have been Hispanic with a touch of Asian stepped in. She was wearing or almost wearing a short, tight black dress. She smiled at me and looked at Tilly to confirm that I was a customer. Tilly still hadn't opened his eyes.

"Go get me a cup of coffee, Francine," he said. "Make it a big cup. And you have one too. Drink it before you come back. Put a lot of cream in mine. You know."

The smile disappeared from Francine's very red lips and she eased out of the room and closed the door.

"What the hell," Tilly said, opening his eyes and sitting up with his arms spread over the back of the sofa. "I'll tell you something if you give me your word that you won't tell where you got it."

"Why would you take my word?" I asked.

"I wouldn't, man," he said with exasperation. "I think it would be just fine if you found that girl and took her home to her mama. I think it would piss off Dwight and maybe a couple more people who I'd like to see pissed off. You follow?"

"Blindly," I said.

"Mr. John Pirannes," Tilly said with contempt. "Big operator out of the Beach Tides Resort on Longboat. Services tourists, mostly rich old white guys. Picked out Suzanne after she was here for a week or so. Came to me with Dwight backing him up, you know. Just like in the movies. Real tough like. Mr. John Pirannes makes me an offer to take over Suzanne. Piece-of-shit offer. I figure Dwight is looking for bigger bucks."

"And you...?"

"Took my hit from Dwight and accepted the offer," said Tilly.

"People-selling's a tough job," I said.

"You're telling me. No shit. Hey, I just

153

gave you free, key information. Don't stand there trying to give out free trips to Guilt City. I'm not taking the offer. There's always a catch."

He was right. Tilly emptied the can of Mountain Dew and placed it on the small white table in front of him. I had to give him credit. He didn't crush the can. He shot it toward the wastebasket next to the refrigerator.

"That it?" I asked.

"That's fucking it," he said, clicking on the television set behind me with a little black remote.

"Thanks."

"I'm doing you no favors. Getting that girl away from Mr. John Pirannes won't be a run to the 7-Eleven, if you know what I mean. I hope you know where to find a small army. Now if you'll just move out. You're blocking the screen."

"Last question," I said.

He hit the mute button and the voice of a vaguely familiar woman stopped in midsentence behind me.

"What do you think the best Italian restaurant in town is?"

"Say what?"

"The best—"

"I heard you. Are you nuts, man?"

"Italian."

"Bacci," he said. "Across from Barnes and Noble. Go on Wednesday and order the osso buco special. Now take your act somewhere

154

else and don't come back. We're not talking again."

I walked to the door and the woman's voice came back on. I glanced at the television screen just before I left. Mary Tyler Moore was trying to explain something to Ed Asner.

Francine was just inside the motel office when I passed. She was smoking and doing what she was told to do, having a cup of coffee. I pointed back to the room to show that it was all hers. The kid behind the counter looked my way and I nodded to show that everything had gone well with Tilly. He was safe. Adele wasn't.

I had left the key in the car. Sally had turned it on and was listening to *All Things Considered*, where a serious discussion was going on about the renewed interest in banjo music.

"And so?" she said.

"Ice cream?"

"Gelato," she said. "Classico. You know it?"

I did. Ten minutes later I was having a regular-size orange chocolate and she was having a regular half coconut, half chocolate almond.

"You ever hear of a man named John Pirannes?"

"I've heard. Even met him once. Name came up at the edges of a few of my cases and the middle of one. No one would say much but he's made the newspaper a few times. Pirannes," she said, trying to decide whether the spoon should go for the coconut or chocolate almond and deciding on the coconut, "likes to wear white, combs his white hair straight back, has nicely capped teeth and a decent vocabulary. He has slight lisp. Word is that he has all his money tied up in cash. Been here about five years. Very, very high-class call-girl operation. Reputation for angry public outbursts, usually with one of his girls. According to some police officers who know, he travels with an ever-changing backup man."

"You know a lot about Mr. Pirannes," I said.

I had finished my orange chocolate and was considering another, but I exercised restraint.

"Looked him up," she said. "Asked questions. Went to the library. His name kept coming up in my cases, other people's cases, always about young girls he had hurt. The police never got one of the girls to tell who hurt them, but some of those hurts were deep."

"I know him," I said.

"You do?"

"Couldn't be two men in Sarasota with that description. He works out early mornings at the Y. I see him there. Even said hello a few times. There's always someone with beef waiting for him and watching television in the lounge. Pirannes is a man of few words."

"But he reads a lot," she said. "Classics mostly."

"You know a librarian."

"I know the clerk at Barnes and Noble," she said. "A former client. I think Pirannes once had another name. I think he took up reading when he was in a place where there wasn't much to do. I think John Pirannes did something very bad and got caught."

"You know or you think?"

"A little of both," she said.

She touched my hand. I liked it.

"I've got to get home. Early meeting with a case manager. Lew, Pirannes has Adele, right?"

"Looks that way," I said.

"There's more?"

I took a half dozen beats before I answered.

"Her father dealt her to him."

Sally's head went down. She bit her lower lip and then lifted her head. Her eyes were moist. But there was anger too.

"The world would be a better place if people like Dwight Handford weren't in it," she said.

I didn't disagree.

"But not only are they in it selling their daughters, molesting their daughters and beating their wives, the courts give them... I've got to get home. Here."

She reached for a napkin, took a pen out of her purse, gave it a click and wrote something. She handed it to me.

"It's in Palmetto," she said. "I think that's where he lives. The Sarasota address he gave was to get Adele into Sarasota High."

"Thoughtful father," I said, folding the napkin and putting it carefully in my pocket.

I drove her home. We didn't say much on the way.

"You feeling...awkward?" she asked when we were about half a mile from her apartment complex.

"Yes," I said.

"Me too. We're not used to this."

"I never was," I said.

"Okay," she said, turning toward me. "We say good night at the door. We shake hands. We agree to see each other again. Okay with you?"

"Truth? I'm relieved."

She put her hand on my shoulder and smiled.

When we got to the front door of her apartment, we shook hands, a warm, friendly shake that lasted long enough to show that she was definitely friendly.

"Next time," she said. "Let's try Chinese or Thai and a movie. No business."

"Saturday?" I said.

"Why not?" she answered with a smile. "Six-thirty. A movie. Something funny. I need something funny."

She smiled. Tired smile, but real.

"I'll say one thing for you, Fonesca. You know how to show a girl a good time."

It was a little past eleven when I got back to the DQ parking lot. The DQ was closed. Traffic was slow on 301 and I got out of the car touching my tender but slightly better stomach. I thought about what Dwight Handford had done to his daughter and almost wished that he would come out of the shadows by the stairs. I went to the trunk, found the Geo's tire iron under the mat and closed the trunk. My tire iron upstairs was bigger but this was lighter.

I wondered what Ann Horowitz would say about tire irons as my weapon of choice. I had too much respect for her to think she would give me the old phallic response. It might be true, but we were beyond that.

Dwight did not appear out of the shadows. I went up to the dim-lit concrete balcony that led to my home, my office, the place where I wanted to feel reasonably safe and somewhat comfortably alone.

Something had happened to me in the last few days. I decided to call Ann Horowitz and hope she had time for an emergency visit. I had the twenty dollars.

Feelings were dancing in my mind and chest. Adele, Beryl, Sally and Dwight. And there was something about Melanie Sebastian. Something off. Something wrong. I was feeling it, but…My door was closed. Ames McKinney had fixed it. The lights were out. Tire iron dangling by my side, I turned the handle. The door was open. I stepped in, ready, and flicked on the light. Ames had put everything back in order.

Beryl Tree was sitting on the folding chair in front of my desk. Her hands were clasped together. Her head was back. She was looking up at the ceiling at nothing. Her face was red with blood.

I checked my second room. No one was there. I went to Beryl, touched a large vein in her neck. Beryl Tree was dead.

8

DETECTIVE ED VIVAISE'S GLASSES were perched on the end of his ample nose so he could look down at the few sheets of paper in front of him and then over the tops of his glasses at me.

"Lewie," he said, shaking his head. And then again, "Lewie."

He was a little under six feet tall, a little over fifty years old and a little over two hundred and twenty pounds. His hair was short, dark, and his face was that of a man filled with sympathy, the smooth pink face of a man whose genes were good and who probably didn't drink. He wore black slacks, a tieless white shirt. A black zipper jacket was draped on his straight-backed wooden chair.

Vivaise sat behind his desk in the Sarasota police station on Main Street. There were three other desks in the office, all institutional metal, all with papers and reports piled in metal mesh boxes or freestanding and about to topple. Vivaise and I were the only ones in the office. We had been sitting there for about an hour, or at least I had been sitting there an hour. He had gotten up and left the room four times, once to get himself and me coffee, and three times when the phone on his desk rang. All three times he had returned with papers.

In the hour, Ed Vivaise had said nothing to me but "Lewie, Lewie, Lewie," which translated into "Lewis Fonesca, what have you gotten yourself into."

"You don't mind if I call you Lewie, do you?"

"I prefer Lew or Lewis," I said.

Vivaise held up his hands in a gesture of peace and understanding.

"I understand," he said, leaning over. "I'll share a secret with you. I don't tell many people, but my real name is Etienne. French. Can you imagine me getting any respect if I used the name Etienne? I'd spend half my time telling people how to pronounce it."

"Thanks for sharing with me," I said.

He smiled, the pained smile of a man with severe stomach cramps.

"The victim's name was Beryl Tree," he said, looking at the top paper in front of him.

"Yes."

"No, I was telling you, not asking, but feel free," he said. "Age, according to the ID in her purse, was forty-two. She looked a hard-life forty-two to me."

He looked up.

"To me too," I said.

"So," he went on, putting the papers neatly in front of him and leaning back with his hands behind his head, "you tell me what you told Officer Bayles in your statement. New words, old words, whatever."

"Right," I said, leaning forward. "Beryl Tree came to me through a friend. I'm a process server."

"She needed a process server?"

Vivaise's eyes were closed now. He took his right hand from behind his head long enough to scratch his nose.

"No, she stopped at the Dairy Queen right near where I live, said she was looking for help finding her runaway daughter. She told the man at the DQ that she had come to the police, but she didn't think they were going to do anything much about it. There were too many run-aways from and to Sarasota. Check on reports for missing kids from Monday."

"It's all on computers," he said, eyes still closed. "It's been done. So far you haven't fallen from the tightrope. So she came to you?"

"It was convenient for her. I was right behind the DQ. I said I'd try to find her daughter."

"She gave you money."

"She gave me money. Not much, but I needed it. I don't need much."

"I'll back you on that," he said. "After seeing your place, you don't live high."

"I looked for her daughter," I went on. "So far I haven't found her, but I did find her father or, to be a little more accurate, he found me. Told me to stop looking, threatened Beryl and me. His name is—"

"I've got it, Dwight Handford. Did time. An unwelcome resident. We have his records."

"He's using the name Prescott," I said.

"Dwight Prescott?" he asked, writing the name on the pad in front of him.

"Yes. I took Mrs. Tree to stay with a friend. Handford found out she was there. She ran. I was out with a lady, came home, found Beryl's body, called nine-one-one."

"Makes sense," he said. "Sixty-two dollars and change in her purse. Wouldn't make much sense for you to bash her head in and call nine-one-one. Sense would have been to get rid of the body and go on with your business."

"Yes," I agreed.

His eyes were still closed. His hands were still clasped behind his head.

"But," he said, "there are lots of reasons for killing people and I've seen killers do some very dumb things. Common sense doesn't always prevail. You know what I mean?"

"Yes," I said. "But it makes sense that Handford killed her and I didn't. What reason would I have for killing her?"

"Who knows? She insulted your heritage, called you a queer, came on to you and you went nuts remembering some sexual trauma in the distant past."

I blew out some air, sat up with my back aching slightly and said.

"You've got imagination."

"Yeah. I'm a dreamer, aren't we all," he agreed. "Why do you have two tire irons in your office, one of which was found by your bed, the murder weapon according to lab, and the other on your desk?"

"Protection," I said.

"From?"

"Handford. Take a look."

I lifted my shirt. Vivaise opened his eyes and examined the large bruise.

"Looks like modern art," he said. "Colorful. My wife's an artist. Abstract. Portrait.

Landscapes. You name it. She'll do it. You can pull your shirt down."

"He killed her," I said.

"No prints on the tire iron," he said, closing his eyes again. "Not yours, not anyone's. Got any more suspects for me, Lewis?"

I thought. Had John Pirannes found out about Beryl and me looking for Adele? Was keeping a teenage prostitute a reason for murder? Maybe Adele found out from Tilly the Pimp. Maybe Tilly the Pimp had a change of heart and came looking for me, afraid I'd tell Pirannes Tilly had talked too much. Maybe he had walked in on Beryl and...Maybe a lot of things. Dwight knew where I lived and worked. Keep it simple. Dwight was the man.

"No," I said.

Vivaise opened his eyes, stood up and stretched.

"Your background checks. Got some nice words about you from the state attorney's office in Cook County. Said you'd gone a little flaky when your wife died, but that you were harmless. I'll go for Handford, see what happens. Is he smart?"

"He's smart," I said.

"Dangerous. Probably call a lawyer and refuse to talk if we pull him in."

"Probably," I agreed.

"Without evidence he'll walk," said Vivaise. "Smart ones usually walk, especially if they have money. Handford have money?"

"He's a tow-truck driver. I don't know what else."

"We'll see," Vivaise said. "You got a friend to stay with? We're still going over your place. I don't think we'll find anything, but sometimes you get lucky. You can go back in the morning."

"I'll get a room at the Best Western," I said.

"You want a ride?"

"I'll walk," I said.

"Nice night. A little cool. Beryl Tree, she was a nice lady?"

"Yes," I said. "She was a nice lady."

"Melanie Sebastian," he said.

"What about her?"

"You've got a file on her in your office. Mind telling me why?"

"I mind," I said.

"Suit yourself," he said.

"The Sebastian folder has nothing to do with Beryl Tree's murder."

"We'll leave that one open," said Vivaise.

"We made a copy of the file and your notes on Adele Tree. The file was on your desk. On that one, we don't care if you mind."

I hadn't left the file on Adele on my desk. I had left it under the seat of the Geo. I was in no position to complain and I didn't.

"You can go, Lewie. Things get anywhere, a trial, something, we may need you to come in and talk about Handford's threats, the artwork he gave you, the fact that he knew his wife was in town and was after her. You're our only witness. Take care of yourself."

"I will, Etienne," I said.

"You pronounced it right," he said, adjusting his belt. "Last question. You know where we can find the daughter?"

He looked at the papers on his desk and then at me over his glasses.

"Adele," he said.

"Haven't found her yet," I said. "She's supposed to be living with Handford but I hear she ran away from him."

"You hear?"

"You know, you hear."

"Take care of yourself, Lew."

"I will, Detective Vivaise."

"Ed will be fine."

"Ed," I said.

There was a vacancy at the Best Western. The night clerk, a thin woman with a slightly pinched face and a nice voice, asked pleasantly if I had any luggage. I knew why she was asking. Suicides sometimes checked into hotels without luggage. They knew they weren't going anywhere and didn't need a change of clothes. There was also the chance that I had a prostitute or someone's wife out of sight in a car and needed the room for a few hours. That was none of the management's business, but dead bodies and bloody walls were.

"Fire in my place, down the street, behind the DQ. Lost everything."

"I'm sorry."

"I'm insured," I said with my most plaintive Jobian smile.

I needed a shave. I needed a bath. I needed to think. The clerk gave me a complimentary disposable orange-and-white Bic razor and the key to my room. It was two doors down from the one Beryl Tree had sat in waiting to hear from me.

A shave, a hot bath, a shampoo of what remained of my hair and I was ready to think. It was nearly eleven. I turned on the television instead and watched the rerun of a soccer match on ESPN. Manchester United was playing someone. I didn't know who.

I lay in bed in my underwear with the lights out watching men running back and forth, crashing into each other, shouting, kicking and trying to score. I turned off the sound and fell asleep knowing that my inner clock would wake me in time to get back to my rooms, change clothes and drive the rented Geo to my appointment with Ann Horowitz.

My inner clock was off. I woke from a dream about a man dressed like the Joker in a deck of cards. The man was on a platform. There was a big crowd watching quietly. The Joker pulled out a small wooden box and held it up. He grinned and teased the audience with his hand, moving it as if he were about to open the box, and then pulling his hand back. He did this three or four times until three men wearing colorful shawls over their heads moved to the platform. The Joker looked at the men, bobbed his head and danced to make them smile or respond which they didn't do, and finally, resigned, the Joker opened the box and waved it, and small red pieces of paper came flying out. The audience went "Ah." The three men with shawls shook their heads in approval. The red paper came out in a storm that covered the floor up to our ankles. The audience was in a near religious fervor.

And then Beryl Tree was on the platform, Beryl Tree before her head had been shattered by a tire iron. The Joker handed her the box, which was still spewing red-paper snow. Beryl moved through the wildly applauding audience and handed the box to me. The audience went wild. Beryl said something to me. I couldn't hear her. The crowd was too noisy. I knew that she was telling me something important. And then a man somewhere said, "Is that everything?"

I woke up. The room was bright with sunlight. I hadn't pulled the drapes closed. On the television screen women were playing golf. The clock on the table near the bed said it was almost nine.

The man's voice said.

"Let's go."

I got up and went to the window. A man wearing a Cincinnati Reds baseball cap was loading his car trunk. A woman and a boy were getting in the car.

"That's everything," the man said and closed the trunk.

He saw me in the window, wasn't sure how

to react, and decided to smile. I smiled back and for some reason waited till he and his family had driven away before I got dressed, checked out and jogged to my office home.

The door was closed but not locked. There was no crime-scene tape. I went in. There was blood on the floor where Beryl's body had been. There was blood on the floor near my bed where the tire iron had been thrown. I changed clothes and hurried to the Geo.

I made my usual stop at Sarasota News and Books for two coffees to go with chocolate biscotti, left the car in a space in front of the bookstore and took my paper bag to Ann Horowitz's office a block away.

"Sorry I'm late," I said, handing her the peace offering of coffee and biscotti. I knew she was a sucker for sweets.

She placed the biscotti on a napkin on the table nearby, opened the coffee, smelled it and nodded her approval. She was wearing a bright yellow dress with a pattern of large red apples. Her earrings were matching red apples. The room was flooded with light.

"Thanks for seeing me," I said.

"Fortunately, the time was available."

"But still..."

"You are forgiven," she said. "Talk. I'll drink, eat and listen."

I talked. She dunked her biscotti, listened, nodded from time to time. When I stopped talking ten minutes or so later, she had finished her biscotti and was almost finished with her coffee.

"That's what happened, but how do you feel?" she said.

"About what?"

"About what?" she said with a hint of exasperation. "About the dead woman. About your date with Sally..."

"Porovsky," I said.

"Jewish?"

"Yes," I said.

"Because I'm Jewish?"

"You mean did I ask her out because you're Jewish? No, I don't think so."

Ann nodded.

"Wishful thinking on my part," she said. "You want me to tell you why you did it, asked her for a date? I don't know yet. You feel guilty about it, feel you are betraying your wife."

"Yes," I said.

"But you had a good time? You like this woman?"

"Yes. She's easy to be with."

"Sexual thoughts, feelings?"

I hesitated and then said, "Yes."

"Good," Ann said. "If you're not going to eat that biscotti..."

I broke it in half and handed one part to her.

"She reminds me of my wife in some ways. She doesn't in others."

"You plan to see her again?"

"Yes."

"How would you characterize what you did on this date?"

"I made it safe for both of us by spending most of the time searching for Adele Tree."

"She seemed to find this acceptable?"

"Yes. She said, 'You know how to show a girl a good time.'"

"Irony," said Ann, taking care of the last few biscotti crumbs.

"Yes. My grandmother made something like biscotti. I don't remember what she called it. It was good."

"And she came from Italy?"

"Yes, Rome. Spoke with an accent but her English was good."

"You find that observation relevant?" Ann asked.

"Yes, but I don't know why."

"We'll save that for another time. And now to murder and your dream. How do you feel about the dead woman, about what happened, about what the dream is telling you?"

"That's a lot," I said, finishing my now cold coffee.

"Jump in. Are you angry?"

"Yes, but I think I should be more angry. She seemed to be a decent person. I should have helped her more. She was murdered where I live. She...I'm still having trouble feeling. Even with this, I'm still having trouble feeling. My wife..."

I stopped and went silent.

"You want to tell me what you think the dream means?"

I shook my head no.

"Then I'll try. Is the Joker a messenger? Is

the Joker a jester? He is certainly handing the dead Mrs. Tree a box with a message for you, a message she gives you, an overflowing box of red pieces of paper. Anything?"

"Blood," I tried.

"Why not? She gives you the gift and wants you to accept it. She wants you to feel, to find the person who killed her. She wants you to find her daughter, to help her daughter. The three men in shawls are people you know who want to help, who want you to help find this murderer, to help find the girl, the child, Adele."

"And that's what my dream means?"

Ann sat back, shrugged and said,

"In the absence of an interpretation by you, that's what I want the dream to mean. I had a big breakfast. I shouldn't have had that last piece of biscotti, but..."

"No offense, but isn't there something unprofessional about telling me what you want my dream to mean?"

Ann touched the right earring.

"I'm old and can say what I wish to say. I want to cut through the baloney and get you jump-started. I want to prod you. That's what you came here for, isn't it?"

"Yes," I agreed.

"Then go get something to eat, find out who killed Mrs. Tree and find the girl."

"What about Melanie Sebastian?"

"Who needs finding more?" Ann asked.

"Adele," I said.

"That's your answer. Now, go forth, accept

the help of your three men in shawls and when you get a chance, call Sally Porovsky."

"I will," I said, getting up. "I think I know who one of my men in shawls is."

"Who?"

"You."

"Good," she said, reaching for the phone. "I have an opening the day after tomorrow at nine. You have twenty more dollars?"

"I'll be here," I said, moving for the door while she dialed.

"There's probably a frightened young man in my waiting room," she said. "Tell him I'll be with him in a few minutes."

The young man was there. He looked very frightened but he didn't look at me when I told him Ann would see him in a few minutes.

I went out the door and into the sun to have breakfast and look for Adele.

There's a Mennonite restaurant on Main, a small one, open mostly for breakfast and lunch to serve the downtown office workers, city government people and professionals—doctors, lawyers, therapists—in the area. The food was cheap, plentiful and, if you didn't mind the prayers in the menu, bright and cheerful.

When I finished, I left a good tip and headed for my office-home thinking about what Ann had said and about what I had said, thinking about a Joker with a box of red secrets.

I walked down to 301 and then the three blocks or so to the DQ parking lot. Dave was behind the open porthole serving customers, and the Geo was sitting where I had parked it. I checked it out. The file on Adele wasn't there. Either the police had it or left in my office when they had copied it or someone else had it.

I went up to my office. The drapes were closed and so was the door, but it wasn't locked. I went in. The contrast between sun and semidarkness took a few seconds to get used to. I started to reach for the cord to open the drapes and stopped. My eyes were getting used to the dim shadows.

In those dim shadows, I could see Beryl Tree sitting where I had left her body. She had one of my files open on her lap and she was looking up at me.

9

MY HAND WAS SHAKING but I reached for the drapes.

"No," she said. "Just turn on the light."

It wasn't Beryl Tree's voice. My hand was shaking a little less when I flicked the switch and the overhead tinkled on.

The resemblance to Beryl Tree disappeared. She was much younger, much better looking, and her dark green dress was much more stylish than anything Beryl Tree had worn in her life.

"You know who I am?" she asked.

"Yes," I said.

There was a floppy sun hat and a pair of sunglasses on my desk. The blood had been cleaned up. I moved behind my desk and sat looking at Melanie Sebastian. I knew two reasons why Carl Sebastian might want her back. She was as beautiful in person as she was in her photographs and the painting in his apartment. She also had a mellow voice that promised the possibility of music.

She closed the folder in her lap and handed it to me.

"You read in the dark?" I asked.

"There was enough light if I tilted it just a bit toward the window."

"And?"

"When I picked it up, I thought it was about me," she said. "Then I found the one about me. It wasn't very interesting so I went back to this one on Adele Tree."

"And this one is interesting?"

"And...there are really people like her father out there," she said. "You really think he—he sexually abused her?"

"Yes.

"The world can be a truly awful place," she said.

"Worse than that," I said. "It can be a low level of hell. Beryl Tree is dead, murdered right where you're sitting, probably by her husband. And Adele has been sold by her father to a high-class pimp named John Pirannes. You've heard of him?"

"No," she said. "You're joking."

"No."

"Why are you telling me all this?"

"You were reading the file. You seem interested."

"There are too many Beryl Trees. Too many Adeles. And far, far too many Dwight Handfords," she said. "I've seen them. I've...is Adele strong? Can she...?"

"She's strong. Why are you here?"

"My husband is looking for me. He hired you to find me. You talked to one of my friends, who told me. I don't want you to find me, not yet. When the time comes..."

"Not yet? You're going to let me find you?"

"When I'm ready," she said.

"Look, all I'm interested in is telling you your husband wants to talk to you, try to make things right," I said.

"I need a few days," she said. "I've spent a lifetime taking care of people. At least that's how it feels to me. I've taken care of my mother and father, children like Adele, my husband. I don't think many people can be saved and I certainly don't think I'm the person to save them. I don't know if you can understand or if I'm making myself clear."

"I understand," I said. "But you won't talk to your husband at this point?"

"I make that decision in a few days," she said. "I'm not ready. I just want some time for myself. I...Go find Adele Tree. When you do, then come looking for me. If you're good, you'll find me. I have a feeling you're good. I've left a trail."

"So," I said. "This is a rich lady's game with her husband and the dope he hired to find you."

"No," she said earnestly. "This is no game and I don't think you're stupid."

She meant it. I could tell that she meant it. I could feel it. I had questions.

"Just tell me—"

"No," she said, still sitting. "I can do a much better job of hiding than I'm doing now if I wish to. I can leave Florida. I'll stay if you promise to give me a few days."

"Is my promise worth anything to you?"

"Yes," she said. "Yes."

"Okay. I promise. You have Caroline Wilkerson's driver's license. Did she give it to you?"

"No, I took it when she was busy. Anything else?"

"Not now. What now?"

"Now I get up and step into the other room," she said, rising. She was tall. "When I'm in there, you open the drapes, stand there as if you're thinking and then you take the files on me and Adele and leave, locking the door behind you."

"It's broken," I said.

She was in the other room now. I was way beyond caring about how my cubbyhole and bed looked to this beautiful, rich runaway.

"Then just go. Stay away at least an hour."

"You think someone is following you," I said, moving to the window.

"No, Mr. Fonesca," she said. "Someone is following *you*."

Folders under my arm, I went back out into the sun and down the stairs, trying not to look around for whoever might be following me. The most logical explanation was that either the lovely Mrs. Sebastian had lost her mind or she was into some very heavy duty drugs. How could she know if I were being followed? And why would anyone want to follow me? Dwight? He knew where to find me, and if he had killed Beryl he probably wouldn't be within three or four miles of the DQ.

I didn't see anyone, didn't see any suspicious cars with tinted windows. I wanted to talk to Dave, but it had been clear that Melanie Sebastian wanted me to get some distance between me and my office.

I got in the car and drove to the Walgreen on Bahia Vista and 41. I made two calls. The first was to Sally. She wasn't in the office. I got her voice mail and said I'd get back to her soon. The police had copied my file on Adele. They might find Sally the way I had. I thought it would be better if the news of Beryl Tree's murder came from me. I was trying to protect Sally Porovsky, though it wasn't really my responsibility. I didn't think about it.

Then I called Carl Sebastian.

"Carl Sebastian," he said.

"Lewis Fonesca," I said.

"You found her?"

"No, but I'm getting close. Maybe another two days, three at the most."

"She's still in the area?"

"Yes."

"You're sure?"

"Positive," I said.

"Find her as fast as you can," he said. "Find her by tomorrow and I double your fee."

"It'll take at least two days," I said.

He sighed.

"Two days then."

"Possibly three."

He hung up.

I made another call.

"Texas Bar and Grill," came Ed Fairing's voice in the Texas drawl he had picked up from the movies.

"It's Fonesca," I said. "Ames there?"

"I'll get him."

"Can you spare him for an hour or two?"

"He's his own man," said Ed.

About a minute later Ames answered the phone.

"Yes."

"Ames, did you clean up my office this morning?"

"Yes. Watched the police leave, came in, went."

"You see a woman outside or inside my office? Beautiful woman?"

"No."

"Beryl Tree's dead."

Silence.

"Ames?"

"Here," he said.

"She was killed in my office."

"It was her blood then, her blood I cleaned up? How'd she die?"

"I don't think you want to know."

"I want to know, Lewis."

"Tire iron. I think I know where her daughter is. I think I'm going to go get her. You want to come?"

"I do," he said.

"Might want to bring a weapon," I said.

"I mean to," he said. "She with the person who killed Ms. Tree?"

"I don't know."

"I hope so," he said.

"I'll be there in ten minutes."

"I'll be out in front."

There were three people in shawls in my dream. Ann Horowitz was one. I had a feeling Ames McKinney was another.

Ames was waiting in front of the Texas. He was wearing a slicker over his denims and flannel shirt. It didn't look like rain and it wasn't cold, but I knew there was a very deep pocket inside the slicker, probably deep enough for a short or sawed-off shotgun.

Ames climbed in and closed the door.

"I plan to shoot him if it's the one who killed Ms. Tree," he said. "Thought I'd just tell you up front."

"I appreciate it," I said, "but I can't take you with me if that's the only choice you have."

I was on the way down Fruitville to 41.

"I'll hold off then," he said.

That was the end of our conversation. I

considered turning on the radio and decided against it. I made a right turn off of 41, drove past high-rises and over the bridge to Bird Key, and then kept going to St. Armand's Circle. The circle was alive with tourists. I swerved to avoid hitting a horse-drawn tourist carriage and then headed toward Longboat Key, over another bridge and down Gulf of Mexico Drive, the only road on the eleven-mile-long island.

Longboat is money. Resorts and high-rise beach condos on my left, very private home developments on my right. Wealthy French and Germans lived here in the winter. Movie stars had million-dollar retreats, and John Pirannes and others like him quietly sold damaged people, tainted land, and decaying schemes of wealth.

I pulled up to the guard gate at the Beach Tides Resort, rolled down my window and smiled.

"Mr. Pirannes is expecting us," I said.

The guard was old, but he wasn't stupid. He looked at Ames, who was staring ahead, and went into his glassed-in hut to call. He was back out in about thirty seconds.

"No answer," he said. "Sorry."

"I just have a—"

"Sorry," the guard said as if he were truly sorry.

I backed up, turned around and went back out on Gulf of Mexico Drive, where I did what I should have done in the first place. I drove to the small shopping mall a quarter of a mile down, pulled in and parked. Not much was open, but there were other cars. Ames and I walked back to the Beach Tides Resort, hoping a cop wouldn't stop us and ask questions. We kept close to the trees and found an opening in the shrubs we could get through. Security at the resort was fine as long as you tried to get through the front gate, but few of the resorts had fences or walls all the way around them.

My guess was that security was better at night, but I saw no signs of cameras in the trees. The Beach Tides Resort was badly in need of a security consultant.

We moved around a small pond where a white heron was dozing. A few dozen yards past a barbecue pit we hit the beach. I took off my shirt, slung it over my shoulder, and sauntered down the shore with Ames at my side.

"You're a big retired movie star," I said, waving at a trio of kids building a castle of white sand. "A cowboy like John Wayne."

"All the same to you," he said. "I'll think Buck Jones."

The three kids stopped building and looked at Ames. A jogger in bare feet, red swimsuit and a white T-shirt with Betty Boop reclining on his chest glanced at us as he passed and left footprints in the sand. I laughed as if Ames had just said something hilarious. Ames just looked forward. I was beginning to think that bringing Ames along was not such a good idea. In fact, my coming at all was probably not a good idea, but all I could think of was the fourteen-year-old girl whose picture was in my wallet, her dead mother, her father who had sold her, and John Pirannes who had bought her.

When we came up behind the Beach Tides on the beach, we walked around the pool, where a single old man treaded water, nodding at us as we passed.

We tried three buildings, checking names in the lobby, avoiding the security people who rode around on little golf carts. In the third building, we found a J. Pirannes and I pushed the button.

No answer.

I pushed again. This time a girl answered and said.

"Hello."

"John Pirannes, please," I said.

"He can't come to the phone," she said.

"Why?"

"I think he's dead," she said.

"Adele?"

"Yes."

"Adele, push the button and let me in," I said.

"Button?"

"On the phone, near the door, somewhere."

"Who are you, the police?"

"Good guess," I said. "The door."

I heard her put down the phone and waited, phone in hand, watching the driveway outside for the golf-cart patrol. Then, a buzz. I hung up the phone and went into the lobby. Pirannes's apartment was on the sixteenth floor. We were up and running down the corridor in about twenty seconds. Ames was almost keeping up with me in spite of the slicker, the shotgun and the more than thirty years I had on him. The door to Pirannes's apartment was locked. I knocked. I knocked again.

"Who is it?" Adele asked.

"You just talked to me on the phone. Open the door, Adele."

"I don't know," she said.

"I'm a friend of your mother," I said.

"My mother's dead," she said, sounding very much like the child she really was.

"I know," I said. "Who told you?"

"Mr. P. Someone called him. Then he told me. Why would someone want to kill my mother?"

She was crying now.

"I think it'd be a good idea if we talked about it inside."

"I can shoot the door open," Ames said evenly.

"A little noisy," I said.

"May be the best we can do," said Ames.

"Adele," I tried again, hoping the neighbors weren't listening. "Pirannes is dead?"

"Yes," she said. "I think so."

"We'll take care of it," I said.

"We?" she asked.

"Me and another friend of your mother. My name's Lew Fonesca. My friend, your mother's friend too, is Ames McKinney. Look, I know Sally Porovsky. We're friends."

The pause was long. Without looking around to see if anyone was watching, Ames pulled the shotgun from under his coat and leveled it at the door.

"I'll make a hole. You reach in and open the door if it doesn't pop," he said.

Before he could fire, the door opened.

Adele stepped back when she saw the gun aiming in her general direction. She covered her face and whimpered.

"It's all right," I said. "Ames isn't going to shoot you."

The girl in the middle of the all-white room—furniture, carpeting, walls—was a thin, frightened mess wearing a red mesh dress too old and too tight for her. She was barefoot. Her blond hair was all over the place and it looked as if she had been playing Dress-up and Makeup. Her lipstick was smeared. Her mascara was a dark splotch over her left eye and a running mess on her right.

Ames put his shotgun at his side.

"I'm so cold," she said.

The room was warm, but Adele was shivering. Ames stepped toward her and she backed up with a little whimper, her hands up to try to counter the attack she knew was coming.

Ames took off his slicker and draped it over the girl's shoulders.

"Help any?" he asked.

She took her hands away from her face and said, "Yes. I think so."

"Where's Pirannes?" I asked.

She pointed a red-painted finger toward a chair, a white chair facing the window.

"I turned him around," she said. "I really didn't look. I saw the blood and..."

Ames led the girl to a sofa and sat her down. I moved to the chair Adele had pointed to and touched the back. It spun around. I found myself looking down at a well-dressed man with dark hair and a graying mustache. He was looking up at me surprised. He had a hole in his head. The white chair was covered in blood.

I stood looking down at the corpse, knowing I should do something, that I should pick up the phone and call the police, ask for Detective Ed Vivaise and tell him the truth. Maybe he'd believe me. I wouldn't if I were the cop and he was the process server who had found his second murder victim in less than twenty-four hours.

"Ain't him," Ames said behind me.

"What?"

"Ain't Pirannes," he said. "When I went up on the murder charge, I met Pirannes. We had the same lawyer."

"Adele," I called.

She was shivering on the couch, Ames's slicker pulled tightly around her for comfort.

"Adele, you said Pirannes was dead."

"He is," she said, a shrill touch creeping into the fear. "Just look at him."

"I think you better look at him," I said.

"No," she said. "I can't."

"It's not Pirannes," I said.

"It is," she screamed.

"It ain't, girl," Ames said.

Adele got up and moved toward us. Ames went to help her.

"Spiltz," she said, looking at the corpse.

"Spiltz?" I asked.

"I thought it was...I mean I heard the gun, saw the blood. I turned the chair without looking at him and then I...I just sat there till you called. What is he doing here? Where's Mr. P.?"

"How long ago did you hear the shot?"

"I don't know."

"Where were you?"

"In the bedroom," she said, pointing behind her. "Doorbell rang. He told me to stay in bed. I...He went out. They talked a little. I wanted to take a bath or watch TV or something but I was afraid he'd come back and..."

"And?"

"Pirannes and whoever it was argued."

"Two men," she said.

"You recognize any of the voices?"

"For sure?"

"For sure."

"None but Mr. P. for sure. Maybe him," she said, waving at the dead man without looking at him. "He was here yesterday night."

"And the other man?"

She shook her head no.

"Was it your father?" I asked.

"Don't know," she said. "I wanted him to come. He wouldn't have come without seeing me."

187

She was crying now.

"I wanted him to come, say he made a mistake, take me back. I'll say it. I hoped it was my father. I hoped he killed Mr. P., but...Can I smoke?"

It was a bad time to give a lecture on the evils of tobacco.

"Sure," I said.

She went to a table near the front door, lifted the cover on a white wooden box and took out a cigarette. She placed it between her lips and started to look around for a lighter or match.

"There's one here. Got to be," she said, running frantically from table to table, back through the door she had indicated was the bedroom. She came out again, sighed, took the cigarette from her lips and dropped it on the sofa.

"I don't feel so good," she said.

"What did he do to you?"

"Mr. P. gave me some stuff. Made me feel good. I thought I knew what he wanted but I wasn't even close. I was hoping he was dead, wishing it. You know what I mean?"

"You know this guy's first name?"

"Tony, I think," she said. "Tony Spiltz. I've got a good memory. I don't feel so good."

"Can you clean yourself up?" I asked.

"I don't know," she said.

"Do your best and do it fast," I said.

"I don't want to be alone," she said.

"I'll go with you," Ames said, putting a hand on her shoulder.

He led her back and through the door to the bedroom. I stood looking down at Tony Spiltz and wondered what had happened. Where did Pirannes go? Why did he go? Was he with Dwight Handford? Had someone called the police?

Spiltz had no answers. I looked for the gun that had killed him. I did it carefully and wondered what, if anything, Ames or I had touched. No gun.

When Adele emerged ten minutes later, she looked like a fourteen-year-old girl. No, she looked even younger without makeup, with her hair combed out and in a pair of tight jeans and a loose-fitting black sweater that probably belonged to John Pirannes.

"Let's go," I said.

"I'll need the slicker, child," Ames said.

"I'm not so cold now," she said, handing him the slicker.

He didn't put it on. He wrapped it around the shotgun and put it over his arm. We left, Adele between us, and I closed the door with with my shirt. It probably wasn't necessary, but some young cop or security guard might be very smart.

We didn't meet anyone till the elevator stopped at the thirteenth floor. An old couple wearing robes and carrying towels got on with a small boy in a bathing suit carrying an inflated yellow plastic duck.

The old couple looked at us. The woman looked with concern at Adele.

"You all right?" she asked.

"Fine, ma'am," Adele answered.

The woman looked at me and Ames. Adele moved close to Ames, who put his arm around her. This seemed to satisfy the woman.

"Did you notice what floor we got on from?" said the thin old man, with a knowing grin. "Thirteen. Most buildings don't have a thirteen. Actually, they do, but it's fourteen, if you understand."

"I do," I said.

"We live on thirteen," he said. "We even pay less for our place because people don't want to live on thirteen. But if they're on fourteen, they're on thirteen."

"Sol," the old woman warned.

The little boy made a popping sound with his lips and moved the plastic duck around as if it were an airplane. We came to the lobby and the elevator doors opened. The old couple and the boy went left. We went through the front door.

To our right, where the guard gate was, beyond a stand of bushes and short palm trees, a light was flashing. My guess was that it was a police car. I didn't need a guess about where they might be going, though I wondered who had called them.

We moved right around the building and headed for the beach.

The old man was still in the pool alone. The beach was crowded. We hurried but didn't run. Only the joggers were running, and we didn't look like joggers. We found our way back past barbecue pit and pond. The heron was gone.

We pushed through the first line of bushes and stayed back behind the front stand of flowers and trees as we moved toward the mail. We made it in a few long minutes and got in the Geo.

"Where are we going?" Adele asked from the backseat, where Ames sat at her side, an arm around her shoulder.

"I'm thinking about it," I said.

I couldn't take her to Flo. Handford knew about Flo, had called Beryl there. She couldn't go to the Texas, and she sure as hell couldn't come to my place.

"He should have taken me back," Adele said behind me as I drove well within the speed limit past the entrance to Mote Marine Laboratory to the left.

"He maybe should have just fuckin' left me with Tilly," she said. "Tilly isn't all that bad. He's not like Mr. P. I never met anybody like Mr. P."

When we got back to the mainland, I pulled into the parking lot at the Denny's a few doors north on the Trail. I had a phone call to make and I wanted to get a good look at the '98 blue Buick that had followed me from the parking lot on the beach.

10

ADELE SAT ACROSS from Ames in the booth at Denny's. Ames had left his "hog leg" in the car. Adele ordered a cheeseburger special, chili and a strawberry shake. She wasn't trembling, but there was a vacant look about her while she waited for her food.

Denny's was crowded. The waitress was in a hurry. I ordered a bowl of chowder, and Ames wanted nothing but coffee.

When we had first seated Adele in the booth, Ames and I had stood away for a moment. I had told him we were being followed. He said he knew.

We got lucky in our choice of booths. Through the window you could see the parking lot and the Buick. Its engine was off, but no one emerged. Ames nodded toward the window to let me know he would keep an eye on the car, whose windows were darkly tinted.

I made my phone call and went back to the booth to tell Adele what we had to do. My chowder was waiting, complete with a small basket of crackers. Adele was alternating between chili and burger, washing them down with the shake. She didn't seem to be getting any great joy from the feast.

"What kind of car does your father drive?" I asked, crumbling crackers into the white chowder.

"Dwight has a pickup with a tow winch," she said. "No car."

"Dwight?" I asked.

"Always call him Dwight," she said, her mouth full. "Since I was...before he went away when I was a kid, and now."

I didn't pursue this conversational line, but went on with,

"What kind of car does Pirannes drive?"

She stopped chewing and looked through the window into the parking lot. She was a bright kid.

"Big, black," she said. "I think it's a Lincoln or something."

"Tilly, what does he drive?"

She put down her sandwich. There was a touch of ketchup on her upper lip.

"What's this about?" she asked.

"Being careful," I said. "If any of them show up, I want to know about it as early as I can."

"You know Tilly?" she asked.

"I met him last night."

She nodded, took another bite and looked at Ames, who pointed to his upper lip and then at Adele. She got the message and used her napkin.

"Tilly drives a sort of sky-blue Jap car with one of those black canvas-like tops. Looks like a convertible but it ain't...isn't. It's not all that new. He got it used. Looks good. He keeps it clean. Tilly is not a big-money dealer on the North Trail, if you know what I mean."

"He and your father get along?" I asked, working on my chowder.

"I guess," she said. "You know something? I don't feel much like talking or thinking."

I nodded in understanding and said,

"Then you can listen. I just called Sally Porovsky."

Adele took on the look of a trapped cat. Her hands were on the table. She was ready to get up and run, but since she was smart, she knew better under the circumstances.

"I told her I found you," I said. "She knows about your father, about Pirannes. I didn't tell her about the dead man, Spiltz. I don't want to put her on the spot. If you want to tell her, fine."

"My mother's really dead?" she said, trying to think something through.

"Yes," I said.

"Then I don't have to go away. I can live with my father."

"Adele," I said. "Your father is a violent, abusive child molester. He abused you. He beat me up. He sold you to a pimp and he probably killed your mother."

"You don't mean 'abused,'" she said. "You mean he screwed me."

"Did he?"

The wary cat looked at me and Ames.

"No way," she said, shaking her head. "He's good to me."

"He sold you," I repeated as the waitress reappeared and said, "Anything else?"

"Pie," said Ames. "Apple if it's fresh. Nothing if it's not."

Adele and I were eye to eye. The waitress didn't know what was going on and didn't much care. She moved away from the booth.

"I didn't say he did," Adele said, playing who-blinks-first.

"Tilly says he did," I said.

She shook her head.

"You figure Tilly's going to tell that to a cop or a judge or a social worker? You think anyone would believe him?"

There was no reason to go on with this. I would leave that to Sally. Back in Chicago, I was on a case in which a dying black drug dealer, a kid a few years older than Adele, had been stabbed six times in the stomach. He was in a hospital emergency room when I saw him. He was dying and he knew it. The cop I was with asked the kid who had knifed him. He said it was his best friend, his street partner, but he wouldn't give a statement against him.

"Him and me," he said. "We was always tight. He was good to me, like, you know, a brother. He was real good to me till he killed me."

The waitress came back with Ames's apple pie.

"Fresh enough?" she asked.

"It'll do," he said, reaching for the fork.

"I'm real happy to hear that," said the waitress, putting our check on the table and moving away.

Adele started to eat again, her eyes down. She was either thinking hard or working hard at not thinking.

Ames nudged me. I looked at him and he nodded toward the window.

The door of the Buick was opening.

A man I recognized stepped out. It was my guardian angel, the short, tough-looking

195

bulky little man with less hair than I had, the one who had saved me from a hospital-size beating, or worse.

He didn't look in our direction and Ames and I looked away before he caught me.

"What're you two doing?" Adele asked, looking out the window.

"Ever see that man before?" I asked, still working on my chowder. "Man closing the door on that blue Buick?"

"No," said Adele. "Wait. Is he coming in here to get me or something?"

"No," I said. "I'm just being careful."

"Fucking paranoid," she said.

"I'd appreciate your watching your language when you're in my presence," Ames said.

"Who the...?" Adele began and then found Ames looking at her, fork holding a piece of pie.

Adele shrugged and pushed her plate away. Ames finished his pie. The bulky short man came into Denny's and headed for the men's room without glancing our way. He almost waddled.

I considered following him into the men's room, asking him what was going on, what did he want, who did he know, but I dropped the idea. He wouldn't tell me and I owed him one. There was also no long-term point in getting out and running while he was occupied. He knew where to find me. There was, however, a short-term reason for losing him: Adele.

"Let's go," I said. "Now, fast."

I dropped a twenty on the table, a too-generous tip.

Ames put down his fork and Adele slid slowly out of her side of the booth.

"The guy in the Buick," she said.

I didn't answer. We moved toward the door.

"He's after me," she said, looking toward the men's room.

Ames touched her arm, guided her quickly toward the door. Adele was shaking again. When we got in the car, Ames sat in the back with Adele while I drove.

"I didn't believe you," she said.

"About what?"

"About my mother being dead. You were just trying to get me to say something bad about Dwight."

"No, little lady," said Ames. "Your mom's dead."

In the rearview mirror I could see Adele looking up at him and seeing the truth. Her mouth was open. The first cry was more of a scream, and then the tears came. Ames put his arms around her. She leaned against his chest, her fists clenched. Her right hand went up and for a second it looked as if her thumb was searching for her mouth. It stopped short and her fist rubbed against her cheek.

She didn't stop crying until we pulled up in front of Sally's office building.

Sally was waiting downstairs in front of the glass doors. Her arms were folded across her chest. She was wearing a very businesslike black skirt and a matching black jacket over a white blouse.

"I'm not telling her," Adele said as I pulled up in front of Sally. "About the dead guy."

"Up to you," I said, getting out of the car.

Adele got out too, but Ames stayed where he was. Before she moved toward Sally, Adele looked at Ames. He looked back at her. There was something going on, some understanding, maybe some respect on her part.

"Adele," Sally said, stepping forward, her arms now at her side.

"Sally," Adele said cautiously.

"I can use a small hug," Sally said, looking at me. "Or a big one."

Adele moved to Sally and put her arms around her.

"I've got to go," I said.

Sally nodded and met my eyes.

"I'll call you later."

"Do that," she said, one arm now around Adele, who was crying again.

As she led the girl through the glass door and into the building, I got back in the car.

"She'll run," said Ames. "If they don't lock her up, she'll run to him."

"I know," I said, driving forward.

"What if he wasn't there to run to?" asked Ames.

"That's what I was thinking," I said. "He killed Beryl. He has a record."

"I was thinkin' somethin' faster, surer," he said as we drove north on Tuttle.

"You can think it," I said, "but don't do anything more than think it. You know where I'm going now?"

"Yes," he said.

"If you come with me, we do it my way," I said.

"Till your way doesn't work anymore."

I looked at him. He didn't look at me. He seemed to be admiring the trees and houses and, particularly, a concrete mailbox shaped like a manatee.

Sally had told me Dwight Handford worked out of a Texaco station on University Parkway, east of I-75. It was easy to find. It was a self-service place with a double-bay garage and two tow trucks. A good-looking blonde in shorts was pumping gas at one station. The others were empty.

We parked in front of the station, got out of the Geo and stepped inside. There was no one at the cash register, but there were two men working on cars beyond an open door that led to the garage. The hood of one car, a Mazda, was up. A heavyset man with a mop of white hair was leaning deep into the open mouth of the Mazda. He was wearing overalls. The heavyset man was talking to a kid in similar overalls. The older man's voice echoed within the Mazda.

"Here, see this, right here. Leak."

"I see," said the kid, leaning forward.

The kid was skinny. Grease spotted his overalls.

"We'll have to take the whole damn thing out," said the heavyset man, easing back out from under the hood. "I told him it might happen. 'Shit happens,' I told him. You know what I mean, Arch?"

"I know what you mean," the kid said. "Shit happens."

The big man patted the kid on the back once and said,

"You'll learn something with this one."

The big man started to clean his hands with a cloth. He looked away from the Mazda at us.

"What can I do for you?" he asked.

"Dwight Handford," I said.

"Don't know the man."

"Dwight Prescott."

The big man gritted his teeth, looked away and said,

"He's not here."

"When will he be here?" I asked.

"Never," he said. "If he shows up, I go for my gun and the phone. Son of a bitch should be locked up again."

"You fired him?"

"Two days ago," said the big man. "Who are you?"

"Friends of his wife," I said.

The big man looked at Ames and then back at me.

"He's married?"

"He was till yesterday," I said. "She's dead."

"He kill her?"

Arch was fascinated by the conversation. He stood listening, mouth slightly open.

"Between you, me, Arch and my friend here, I'd say it was a good bet."

"Violent bastard," said the big man.

"Why did you fire him?"

"I told him to do something, go out on a call. He said he had somewhere he had to be. I was tied up with a hurry-up. Arch was off. I told Dwight to go. He started lipping off, came into my space. I had a wrench in my hand and more than a belly full of that son of a bitch."

"You knew he had done time?" I asked.

"I did more hard time than he did, but that was some time back and for armed robbery. I've raised a family since. A friend asked me to give Prescott a chance. I did. He blew it."

"You know where he is now?" I asked.

"No," he said. "Don't want to know. I've got a home address for him."

"In Sarasota?"

"Yeah," he said.

"I'll take it, but I think it's not where he really lives," I said. "Did he ever say anything about his daughter?"

"Daughter?" asked the big man, looking at Arch.

"Adele," said Arch.

"Yes," I said.

"Adele is his daughter?" asked the big man.

"I figured," said Arch.

"You didn't tell me," said the big man.

"He had her with him two or three times. I figured she was his girlfriend, a little young, but...the way he—"

"She's fourteen," I said. "Just barely."

The big man looked at the stained cloth in his hand.

"My oldest is fifteen," he said. "I got a late start. If old Dwight comes around, I just might go for the wrench."

I handed him my card and said, "If he comes back and survives, I'd appreciate your giving me a call."

"You a private detective?" he asked.

"Process server," I said.

"You've got papers on Handford?"

I smiled and held out my hand.

"Fonesca," I said.

"Lopez," he answered, taking my hand.

Ames and I left. Dwight Handford Prescott, I thought, was developing a long pregame lineup of people who wanted him to disappear.

I considered going back to my office, but I wasn't sure what or who might be waiting for me there.

Instead I went to the Texas Bar and Grill. It was late afternoon. There were only a few people having beers, maybe a bowl of chili here and there. The television over the bar faced toward the tables. There was a baseball game going on. It wasn't baseball season. It looked like the rerun of a game between St. Louis and Chicago. People didn't get tired of seeing

Mark McGwire and Sammy Sosa hitting home runs. It beat the news hands down.

Ames disappeared behind the bar and headed for his room.

Ed Fairing brought me a beer. I took it and moved to the telephone at the end of the bar. I called the DQ. Dave answered.

"It's me," I said.

"Lewis," he said. "Business has been brisk. So have the inquiries about you and the visitors to your door. Some of the most recent visitors were the police. It's a good day to be out on the water. There are times when I...forget it. And my suggestion is that you don't come back here for a while. You know a guy with an Italian face, no offense, who looks like photographs of Tony Galento and drives a late-model Buick, blue?"

"I know who you mean."

"He pulled in about half hour ago, bought a root-beer float then parked across the street in the acupuncture-and-dance-studio parking lot," said Dave. "He finished the float and threw the container out the window. Then he sat there about twenty minutes and took off. I'm going to have to go there and pick up his mess. Can't leave a Dairy Queen container littering a parking lot. And you wonder why I prefer the sea to land."

"He ask about me?"

"No," Dave said.

"If he comes back and asks, tell him...nothing."

"That's what I'll tell him. Hold on. A lady with two kids is waiting for dinner."

He was gone about two minutes.

Mark McGwire hit a home run. High-fives all around the field as he rounded third and headed for home with a big grin.

"Back," said Dave. "I'm thinking of selling out. Or maybe I'll hire Dawn full-time and semi-retire. I'm beginning to think I don't like many grown-up people. You are an exception. Don't ask me why. Can I ask a question?"

"Sure," I said, taking a slow drink of beer.

"Who was the litterer across the street?"

"My guardian angel," I said.

"Angels come in a variety of sizes, shapes and colors these days," he said. "Some can fit on the head of a pin. Others can tuck the universe in their ears, though why they would want to do it I don't know. Old Testament is filled with angels, warrior angels."

"I've got to find a guy," I said.

"We talking about a bad guy?"

"Very bad. Name's John Pirannes. Ever hear of him?"

"I have," said Dave.

"Know where he might be found or know anybody who knows where he might be found?"

"I understand he has a place at the Beach Tides on Longboat."

"I have it on good authority that he has vacated the premises, at least for now."

A thin black guy in a threadbare sports jacket sat down next to me. He nodded in greeting. His name, the only one I knew, was Snickers. Snickers had a sweet tooth and connections.

Snickers was reasonably adept at breaking and entering.

"He has a boat docked at the Sunnyside Condos across Gulf of Mexico Drive and almost at the north tip of the Key," said Dave. "I've seen him there. Big boat, can't miss it. Sleeps who knows how many. Called the *Fair Maiden*."

"Keep it to yourself," I said.

"Lewis, it's no big secret except from the cops," he said. "Oh, I read that John Marshall article. I think I'll pick up a biography of Marshall. I've got to go now. Customers."

"Thanks, Dave."

"Captain Pirannes is a good man to avoid," he said. "Take care."

He hung up and so did I.

"Snickers," I said. "How's it going?"

"Fine. Hell, not so fine. You want to buy me a beer or three?"

"Sure."

Snickers was bobbing up and down to some inner music. He looked up at the television screen.

"Sosa's the man," he said.

I motioned to Ed to set up a beer for Snickers, who, considering the candy he consumed, must have been blessed with perfect genes. His teeth were even and white.

"He's the man," I said.

"Hey, that's right. You're from Chicago. So, what's been going with you?"

"Well," I said, getting halfway through my

beer, "a tow-truck driver beat me up, a client was murdered in my office, I rescued a kid who had been sold to a pimp by her father, and I discovered a dead guy with a bullet in his head in an apartment on Longboat."

Ed placed the beer in front of Snickers, who looked at me to see why I thought this was funny. But I was paying, so he smiled and shook his head.

"You know a pimp named Tilly?" I asked.

Snickers put down his beer and nodded knowingly.

After talking to Snickers and watching McGwire pop another home run, I dropped a five on the bar and left. Hell, it was going on Carl Sebastian's bill.

I considered flipping a coin or playing a game to determine which of the two not-very-bright moves I was going to make. I didn't consider taking Ames with me. Ames looked a little like Jefferson on Rushmore, but there was a determination behind that face of stone that shouldn't be there in a man who had access to guns and had killed another man.

No, I was on my own. It was either that or forget the whole thing and go to the police. Detective Etienne Vivaise, otherwise known as Ed, seemed not the greater of two evils but the one unlikely to get me anywhere except in trouble.

If the next five plates I saw were from Florida, I would head for Longboat and the

Fair Maiden. If I spotted an out-of-state, I'd go to the address I had for Dwight Handford.

Ann Horowitz asked me every other session or so if I was having feelings of self-destruction. I always told her I wasn't and she answered, "Not consciously."

At the moment, I wanted to face Pirannes and Handford for what they had done to Adele and probably to Beryl. I wanted to know why creatures like this walked the earth. I wanted to argue with God and say, "I don't know why you do what you do, but you'll get no praise from me till you accept the guilt you should feel for what you've done."

I was finally feeling angry about something. I was feeling grimly determined about a whole lot of somethings.

I counted license plates and found out where I was going—at least where I was going right now.

11

SUNNYSIDE CONDOMINIUMS WAS ON Gulf of Mexico Drive on the bay side of the key about five minutes north of the Beach Tides Resort, where Ames and I had rescued Adele and left a corpse.

There was no gate and there were no guards. The Sunnyside apartments were protected only by a tall, tight hedge of flowering bushes. The parking lot was crushed shell and just a few steps to the right past the bushes. There were about a dozen cars parked on the lot. There was room for two dozen more.

From Gulf of Mexico Drive, it was impossible to tell how big the Sunnyside was. Once I was inside and walking along the narrow concrete path that curled around the two-story buildings and past a trio of tennis courts, I realized that there were at least a dozen buildings.

I had no trouble finding the docked boats. I just veered toward the bay. I had no trouble finding the *Fair Maiden*. I just looked for the largest boat. I know nothing of boats. They were a passion of Dave's. He turned boats into vessels of philosophical speculation as he mixed Blizzards and served burgers and fries. He told tales of the open sea that he felt brought him near a sense of a supreme power.

When I was on a boat, I thought only of how soon the voyage, even an hour into Lake Michigan or on the bay, would be over. I longed for the land. I couldn't live on a key. The possibility of being trapped on an island when a hurricane went wild filled me with dread. That didn't, however, stop me from admiring the isolation that a boat promised.

I thought of this as I moved out on the narrow wooden dock toward the *Fair Maiden*. It was a deep thought. The thought on the surface was images, images of the frightened runaway, images of Beryl Tree. There was right and wrong, and sometimes they were clear.

I stopped at the end of the dock and looked at the clean broad deck in front of me. There was a tower with a steering wheel on my left. The tower was surrounded by glass or see-through plastic and a blue metal roof. There was also a closed door at the base of the tower on the deck. I guessed the length of the power boat at about fifty feet. My second guess was that it could probably take John Pirannes very far away very quickly.

There was a table on the deck with two places set for lunch. A bottle of wine chilled in a silver cooler on the white-clothed table. Another bottle of Perrier water sat ready next to two thin-stemmed glasses.

I stood, waited. Someone was below the deck. I could hear voices.

I closed my eyes. A breeze.

There is in some men a natural ability to kill. My grandfather, my father's father, had told tales of the gangs in Rome, of the intimidation before the first war and the killing of Nazi sympathizers during and after the second war. He had already left the old country, but most of his family had stayed. They wrote. There were tales of cousins, uncles, distant bandits with the name Fonesca or DeFabrio or Tronzini who carried guns and knives in their belts and needed no reason beyond honor to use them.

I was not born with the ability to kill. I had never developed it. Even standing in front of the *Fair Maiden* I didn't want a gun. I realized when I heard the voice that I wasn't sure what I wanted, but that I would know when I found it.

"Can I help you?" came the voice.

I opened my eyes. A man stood on the deck, legs apart. He had stepped out of an ad in one of the *Vanity Fair* magazines in my allergist's office. He was wearing white slacks, white deck shoes and a black shirt with a little white anchor over his heart. His hair was white and blowing with the breeze. His legs were apart, his hands folded in front of him. I knew who he was.

"Permission to come aboard," I said, remembering *The Caine Mutiny* and trying to inject a hint of sarcasm into my request.

Pirannes looked at me as if I were some kind of lunatic.

"Manny," Pirannes called calmly toward the door through which he had no doubt come.

A man in a white sweat suit came on deck. He was a big man, sun-brown and unsmiling. He was dark haired, well shaven and definitely Hispanic. Manny stood in front of the door, hands behind his back. I wondered if he had something in those hidden hands.

"I know you," said Pirannes, running his tongue over his lower lip, trying to remember.

"The Y," I said. "I work out there most mornings. You show up with Manny. We've said hello a few times."

Pirannes smiled, a problem solved. He looked at Manny, who looked at me and said nothing.

"I remember," said Pirannes.

His voice was mellow, his grammar nearly perfect. If he had a lisp, I didn't hear it.

"Can I come on board?" I asked again.

"Why?"

"To talk," I said.

"Talk about what? Who are you?"

He was smiling amiably.

"Adele Tree," I said.

The smile was gone.

"Dwight Handford," I went on.

Manny took a step toward me.

"Tony Spiltz."

Manny took another step toward me.

"Tilly the Pimp."

Manny leaped onto the dock. There was nothing behind his back but thick, dark callused hands. He patted me down, even into my crotch and with a finger in my shoes. Then he turned and shook his head no to let Pirannes know I wasn't armed.

"What's your name?"

"Lew Fonesca," I said.

"What's your business?"

"I was hired by Beryl Tree to find her daughter."

"She's dead," said Pirannes.

"I'm still working for her," I said.

"You know who I am. You know about Tony Spiltz and you come here like this? Are you a lunatic, Fonesca? Are you suicidal?"

"Maybe both," I said. "If Manny will move out of the way, I'll come on board the *Guida Merchant*."

"Okay. We'll play games for a few minutes. Come on. You have lunch?"

"No," I said as Manny stepped to the side, let me pass and step down on the deck in front of Pirannes.

"You want something? I'm having shrimp in the shell, a fresh French baguette."

"Water," I said.

Pirannes motioned to table and I sat while Manny, on the dock, looked down at me and folded his hands in front of him. Then Pirannes pulled a small, flat cellular phone from his pocket, hit some buttons and looked at me as he said,

"We're going to have a late lunch. Come in an hour. No, make that an hour and a half. I'll have Manny put a deck chair on the dock in case we have to take the *Maiden* out for a while. Wear your floppy hat. Bring your sunglasses. Sunscreen, and bring a book...Shrimp, tarragon chicken salad, sorbet...raspberry or lemon."

He pushed a button and put the phone back in his pocket. Then he sat across from me and poured us both a glass of mineral water.

"Now," he said. "What do you want?"

"I've got Adele," I said.

He didn't blink. He whipped out the phone again and hit a single button. He said nothing, and then hung up and looked at me.

"Who answered my phone?" he asked, picking up his water.

"Probably the police," I said.

"What's going on, Lewis?"

"John, I don't want to play games," I said.

He leaned toward me and whispered, "Lewis, you don't look like the kind of man who can threaten me."

"I'm a little crazy," I said. "Remember the question you asked me? My therapist thinks I'm suicidal. A suicidal lunatic on a mission can be a dangerous thing no matter what he looks like."

"True," he said, holding his glass of water up so the sun hit it.

We watched the light hit the bubbles for a few seconds and I said,

"You leave Adele alone. And you keep her name out of what went on in your apartment."

"What went on," he repeated. "What are you talking about, Fonesca? What are the fucking police doing in my apartment? No, wait. She tried to kill herself."

"No," I said.

"Then...?"

"Spiltz," I said.

"Spiltz what?"

"He's dead. Big surprise, huh?"

Pirannes sat back.

"No," he said. "Tony Spiltz had enemies but—"

"And you don't know he was killed in your apartment?"

"No," said Pirannes. "Give me a second here."

He sat thinking, looked at Manny, whose

head moved ever so slightly, indicating, I think, that he hadn't shot Spiltz.

"Okay, Fonesca, here's the way it is," Pirannes said. "I know you're not carrying a wire and I know who lives in every condo facing this dock. No one's listening to us. I'm still taking a little chance, but you are definitely beginning to irk me."

"I'm sorry about that, John."

He shrugged.

"It happens in my business. I gave Dwight Handford, who is, by the way, a piece of diuretic mongrel shit, good money to get the girl. And don't bother telling me you can't buy and sell people. I do it. Lots of others do it. Now think about it. What's her life like if she stays with Dwight or Tilly?"

"What's it like with you?"

He laughed.

"Her life with me can be goddamn good. Listen, I give her a great apartment she shares with a couple of other girls, maid service, great food. Clothes. Walk to the beach. No one hits her. I don't let her have drugs or drink anything stronger than a little wine. I keep her in shape till she gets too old."

"Then you send her back to Tilly or Dwight," I said.

"You don't get it, Fonesca. It's not that simple. Life's not that simple. Where have you been living, aboard the *Enterprise*? When Adele retires, which I hope is a long time away, she'll have more money than you'll ever have and I'll get her a straight job, hostess

214

at a restaurant, something like that, far away from here. I have connections. If she wants to go to school while she's with me, that can be worked out. My clients are top-drawer people, high level. No one is going to hurt her. Whatever crap she's already been through with Dwight and Tilly, this will be heaven. I've got a doctor who checks out the girls, takes care of them. I guarantee my girls are disease free, guarantee."

"You're a saint, John," I said.

"You are a stupid wiseass," he said, shaking his head. "So you keep her. Then what? She goes to a foster home? She'll run away. She goes back to Dwight, which is a distinct possibility because if I can't get to her, I bankroll good old Dwight and get him the best lawyer in the state. The judge will not only give her back to her loving dad, but he'll probably get a Father of the Year award. And then he'll give her back to me, with the same visiting privileges he has now. You want another scenario? Fine, you can adopt her. You don't like me. You don't like Dwight. You adopt her, keep her from running away. You prepared to be pop to Adele, Lewis?"

"You killed Tony Spiltz," I said.

"How?"

"Shot him in the head. Last night Tony and Dwight came to the apartment while you were in bed with Adele. You came out, argued. You shot Spiltz. Then you and Dwight ran off, leaving Adele with Tony's body."

"That's a stupid story," said Pirannes.

"Look, I'm hungry and I'm starting to get a migraine. I have migraines. My mother had them. My two sisters have them. You're giving me a migraine. I've got a lunch appointment and I have to call my lawyer about Tony getting killed in my place. The truth is, Lewis, I wasn't home last night. I left Adele with Tony to watch her, maybe, you know, teach her a few things. Tony was a gentle guy with a lot of experience."

"Adele says otherwise about what happened," I said.

"Adele's trying to protect her father, you simple-minded asshole. Handford probably came to my place last night looking for money, wanting to spend time with his kid, who knows. Tony said no. Dwight brought a gun or took Tony's and...you know the rest. I'm getting hungry. Maybe that's why I'm getting a migraine."

He took out one of those plastic one-week pill containers, popped open one of the compartments, removed a large white pill and swallowed it with a Perrier chaser.

"You leave Adele alone," I repeated.

"You are getting boring, Fonesca. And you don't listen. Adele is a smart sixteen-year-old who knows the world better than you do."

"She's barely fourteen and she doesn't know much of anything," I said.

"Fourteen?" he said.

"Change things?" I asked.

"For the better, Lewis. For the better. I've got clients who'll be very happy to get the news.

216

They trust me, know I wouldn't lie about something like that. You've brought me good news, Lewis. Walk away and I'll forgive you your trespasses. As far as I'm concerned, when the cops find me, I've got an all-night alibi and I've never heard of Adele. As far as I know, Tony was in the apartment all alone last night. He must have let one of his friends in. They had a fight, and...You like that story?"

"Stay away from Adele," I said again.

Pirannes got up, rubbed his forehead gently with the fingertips of his right hand and said, "You like to swim?"

"No."

"I do. There's a drawer of swimming suits below. Pick one out that fits you and then come up. I'll take the *Fair Maiden* out a few hundred yards. We'll have something to eat and you'll have a nice swim. You do swim, don't you?"

"A little."

"Good, because it would be very unfortunate if we were a few hundred yards out there," he said, pointing beyond the rising waves, "and you couldn't make it back to the boat or the shore. Manny, help Mr. Fonesca find a swimming suit. You'll like it, Lewis. Water temperature is eighty-one degrees."

Manny was on the deck now, reaching for the rope that had us moored to a pile on the dock. There was probably an anchor too. I'm not fast. I'm not slow, but I didn't think I could get past Manny. Diving into the water wouldn't do me much good either. I had lied to Pirannes. I really couldn't swim at all.

I reached for the bottle of champagne. My plan was to whack Pirannes and take my chances, which were not very good, with Manny. I looked at Pirannes, who had figured out my plan and nodded his head to show me I was making a mistake.

I had already made my mistake. Pirannes's plan was simple. He didn't even have to be involved. He could put my clothes on the shore with a towel and let the police assume I had swum out too far and drowned. Ames wouldn't believe it. Dave wouldn't believe it. Flo wouldn't believe it and I didn't think Sally would believe it, but that didn't do me much good. I had not underestimated John Pirannes. I had not estimated him at all. I was looking at a man who killed people who annoyed him.

"This doesn't give me pleasure," said Pirannes as Manny unwrapped the loose rope around a piece of metal shaped like a Y that was screwed into the deck.

I must admit it didn't look as if Pirannes was particularly happy. He checked his watch as Manny moved to the rear of the boat toward the anchor. If I were going to run, this was the time. Pirannes stepped in front of me. Maybe I could take him. Maybe I couldn't. He could certainly keep me busy till Manny made it across the few yards across the deck.

I think I was the first one to see the man coming. He was walking down the dock toward us, hands at his side. There was a little waddle and a little swagger to his step.

Pirannes spotted him and said, "Manny."

Manny looked up from where he was turning a winch to pull up the anchor. He saw my guardian angel.

"Don't do something very stupid," whispered Pirannes. "He's probably going to one of the other boats. If he's here to talk to me, you stay seated and stay quiet. The best you can do is get you and our visitor killed."

He kept coming, straight, eyes ahead, steady pace.

Manny moved across the deck to face the dock. When it was clear to all of us that the stocky bald man was not going to another boat, Pirannes shouted, "Can I help you?"

The angel said nothing, just kept coming. Manny jumped on the deck over the two-foot gap created when he had pulled in the rope. He stood facing the approaching man. Manny was four or five inches taller than my angel. Manny had muscle. Angel looked as if he had eaten far too much lasagna. It was no contest. When the smaller man kept coming, Manny's arms came up, one palm open, the other in a fist.

The smaller man didn't even pause. He came faster, leaned over and plowed his head into Manny's stomach. Manny groaned but didn't go down. Angel stepped to the side and shoved Manny off the dock and into the water. Then he jumped for the deck of the boat, almost missed and moved toward Pirannes, who didn't back down.

"What do you want?" Pirannes asked.

The man didn't answer. He grasped Pirannes in a bear hug, lifted him off the deck, walked to the bay side of the boat and threw the society pimp into the water.

Then he turned to me and said,

"Let's go."

Manny was wading heavily toward the shore. Pirannes was swearing at us. I followed the man up the dock and back to the parking lot.

When we stopped at my Geo, he was breathing heavily. His Buick was parked right next to me.

"How did you find me?"

"I know the places you go," he said, almost bored. "You don't come back to your office. I check around, saw your car parked near that bar. I followed."

"Thanks," I said.

"Do your job," he said.

"Which job?"

"Find her," he said.

"I found her."

"No," he said. "Not the kid. Mrs. Sebastian. Find her. Do your job."

"Who are you?" I asked as he turned his back and opened his car door.

"Just do your job," he repeated.

He got in the car, leaned over, opened his window and said,

"Get in your car and get the hell out of here."

I got in my car and got the hell out of there.

• • •

I drove off the key and wondered how much I could count on the little man with the big body. He had probably saved my life for the second time. Was he working for Sebastian? Himself? Someone else? And why was he following me?

I decided to put off looking for Dwight for a while. I wasn't sure I could keep counting on my angel. I'd need backup when I found Dwight and I'd also need a plan—which, I had to admit, was more than I really had when I went looking for John Pirannes.

Had Dwight killed Tony Spiltz? He came to Pirannes's apartment to be with Adele. Maybe Tony said no. They fought. Dwight had a gun or took Spiltz's. It was over. He told Adele the story she fed me and Ames. She would do anything for Daddy.

I went back toward my office, waving at Dave, who was framed in the DQ window. He waved back and shouted, "Your friend is pulling into the lot across the street."

"I know," I shouted back and headed up the stairs and into my office-home. There was no one waiting, dead or alive. No one had taken the place apart.

I picked up the phone and dialed Harvey the computer whiz.

"What've you got, Harv?"

"Our lady is getting careless," he said. "She's using her credit cards."

"Where?"

221

"Mostly in Bradenton, once in a gift shop on Anna Maria. Lady has a ton of cash. Is she trying to get caught?"

"I think so," I said. "Keep looking till she lets you find her."

"I prefer tracking to being led," Harvey said, his zeal definitely gone.

"Stay with it, Harvey."

That done, I decided to hurry the search. I still had a killer to find and a kid to protect from the thing she called her father. I picked up the phone again and called the office of Geoffrey Green. His secretary said he was in but that he was with a patient. I said I would call back.

I went down to the Geo and drove to Palm Avenue. The blue Buick was right behind me, not trying to hide anymore. I found a parking space near a gallery. I didn't see where Angel parked.

The receptionist looked up at me with a smile and a hint of recognition.

"Yes, sir?" she said.

There were no patients waiting.

"I've got to see Dr. Green," I said.

"If this is an emergency, I can take your name and number and—"

"Now," I said.

"He has a patient in his office for ten more minutes," she said. "If you'll tell me what this is about, I'll let him know before his next patient arrives and maybe—"

"No maybe," I said calmly. "I'll sit here ten minutes and then he'll see me. Tell him it's

Lewis Fonesca. Tell him I'm here about Melanie Sebastian. Tell him there's a full moon tonight and I'm feeling its power. Tell him I love him. Tell him whatever you have to tell him, but don't forget to tell him that I'm coming in to talk to him in..." I looked at my watch and said, "Nine minutes."

"I'll tell him," she said. "Please have a seat."

I sat. What I really wanted to do was go back to my little room with a stack of videotapes. I wanted to watch Bette Davis, Joan Crawford, Cary Grant, Kirk Douglas, John Wayne and Errol Flynn while I ate a pizza. I wanted the search for Melanie Sebastian to be over. I wanted Dwight Handford to disappear. I wanted Adele to be a kid again and live somewhere safe. I wanted to have soft-shelled crabs with Sally Porovsky and talk about her childhood.

I sat. I waited.

12

"SOMEONE IS PLAYING GAMES with me," I said as Dr. Geoffrey Green closed the door to his office behind me.

He went behind his desk and stood while I moved in front of his desk and did the same. It was late in the afternoon. I was sure I needed a shave. I wondered why he didn't. I guessed that he shaved between patients.

Always well groomed and imperially slim.

"I have ten minutes, Mr. Fonesca," he said. "If you want to make an appointment—"

"No, I'm in a hurry. I'll take the carry-out analysis," I said.

His suit was soberly dark. His tartan tie perfectly Windsored. His manner calm.

"I'm not sitting and I'm not asking you to sit because this will have to be very brief," he said. "Someone is playing games with you? If I were going to give you the standard carry-out answer, the two egg roll, wonton soup and chow mein answer, I'd say you were possibly paranoid. But I'll give you the benefit of the doubt. Who is playing games with you? What games? And why are you telling me?"

"All right," I said, spreading my palms on his desk, invading the wall between him and his patients, "Carl Sebastian hires me to find his wife. He says she ran out with all his money. No reason. No excuse. He pushes me to you. You don't tell me much of anything. You're her therapist—notice I didn't say 'shrink.' You hint. You send me off to the next square. I roll a six. Melanie Sebastian leads me around by the computer. She's smart. Maybe you're helping her to be smart. She tells me she'll let herself be found in a few days. Why the wait? Meanwhile, a very tough, overweight muscle mass follows me around, saves my life and tells me to get back to the job of finding Melanie Sebastian. Game. I'm being pushed around the board. I'm the pawn, the silver wheelbarrow, but who are the players

224

here, Green? You and Melanie Sebastian? Concerned Carl?"

"Are you frequently like this?" Green asked calmly.

"I'm never like this," I said. "I didn't sleep well last night. I've got another job, which is more important than finding Melanie Sebastian. A woman I liked was battered to death with a tire iron in my office. I've got a long story, but you said I only had ten minutes. So..."

"Sit," he said, considering something important, possibly my sanity.

I sat.

He adjusted his tie, scratched his left eyebrow and said,

"I know where she is. If you tell Carl Sebastian, I'll deny it. I'm sorry he brought you into this. This is really between Melanie and Carl. She is my patient and my friend. I can't say more."

"But you know more?"

He nodded.

"Who is this guy who keeps saving my life and insisting that I find Mrs. Sebastian?"

"I don't know," said Green.

"I was tired. I was frightened. A man named John Pirannes—ever hear of him?—had just tried to kill me. I should have asked the ball of muscle why he didn't go find Melanie Sebastian."

"Yes," said Green. "We've got five more minutes."

"Yes?"

"I've heard of John Pirannes. I don't know

him. And yes, you should have asked this man why he didn't try to find Melanie. My guess is that he doesn't know how to find people, intelligent people who don't want to be found."

"He had no trouble finding me," I said. "Don't comment. I'll take the flattery. I know how to find smart people, especially smart people like Melanie Sebastian who want to be found, but on their schedule. Am I making sense?"

"Yes," he said.

"Are you and Melanie Sebastian lovers?"

"I'm gay, Mr. Fonesca. I told you."

"Why do they call it gay? Most of the homosexuals I've known are smiling on the outside and depressed on the inside," I said.

"Like you?"

"There is a distinct similarity," I said, sinking back into the chair. I considered asking him to prescribe a tranquilizer for me. I'd been on antidepressants for almost a year after my wife died. I wasn't depressed now. I was manic. I must have looked confused. He reached over for the pad on his desk, picked up a pen, wrote something, tore off the sheet and handed it to me. It wasn't a prescription for tranquilizers. It was two suggestions. I looked at them.

"More games," I said.

"I'm afraid so," he agreed. "We're out of time."

He got up and so did I.

"Two people have died in the last two days, both murdered," I said. "I shouldn't be playing games for rich people, for you, Carl Sebastian, his wife. I've got a girl in real trouble, not just a spoiled rich runaway wife."

"And you think it's your responsibility to find a murderer?" he asked. "Mr. Fonesca, it's the responsibility of the police to find murders. Time's up."

"So," I said, following him to the side door. "I'm not paranoid."

"In general? I don't know. In this instance, no, I don't think so."

He opened the door. I folded the note he had given me and placed it in my shirt pocket.

"You're going to call her now—Melanie—aren't you?" I asked.

"Yes," he said.

I stepped out and he closed the door behind me.

The blue Buick was parked half a block ahead of me on Palm. I considered walking over to it, asking the guy who had saved my life to have a cup of coffee and help me out with some answers. From my minimal contact with him, I didn't think he'd be a great conversationalist and I doubted if he would give me any answers.

I drove down Palm slowly and headed for the law office of Tycinker, Oliver and Schwartz. Harvey was in his computer room. He didn't look happy to see me. I handed him the note Geoffrey Green had given me and told him to look at item one.

"I can get an answer to that one in an hour,

maybe less," he said, looking a bit happier. "But I'm working on something for Matt Schwartz now. I can have an answer in two, three hours. You want overall? You want details?"

"Overall for now," I said. "Details when you have the time."

"I can't print out," he said. "I don't want hard evidence."

"I trust your memory," I said.

Harvey grunted slightly and reached for a mug of tea with the little string and tab hanging over the edge.

"It ain't what it used to be," he said.

I wasn't sure what "it" was.

"Someone's playing games with me, Harvey—with us."

"I like games," he said, pushing a button on the gray keyboard in front of him. "What I don't like is your Melanie Sebastian waving a virtual-reality carrot in front of me."

The computer clicked musically and came to life.

"I'll buy you dinner, you name the place, when this is over," I said.

"My tastes are modest, Lewis," he said. "That was not always the case."

"Good. I'll call you later. You'll be here?"

"I'm always here," he said.

"Mind if I use your phone?"

The second of the two scrawled items on Geoffrey Green's pad was just two words: Caroline Wilkerson.

I had her number and all the other ones, plus fragments of notes I had made that I had trouble reading, in the little notebook I kept in my back pocket. Her voice came on: answering machine. I left a message, told her I still wanted to talk to her again and would call her back.

Then I called Sally at her office. It was getting late but I knew the kind of hours she kept. I had to wait about three minutes because she was on another line.

Harvey ignored me. He sipped tea, watched the screen, hit buttons and talked to his computer.

When Sally came on, I asked,

"How's Adele?"

"I checked with my supervisor. We filed charges so we could hold her at Juvenile." Sally sounded tired. "I think she'd run away otherwise. I explained it to Adele. She wasn't happy in some ways. In others, she was. Juvenile is safe, but it's only for a few days. We'll drop charges. We'll keep her in detention, try to find a foster home, hope she doesn't run again. Hope a judge doesn't send her back to her father. She told me what happened."

"She told you."

"Spiltz," she said. "I'm writing a report now. I have no choice, Lewis. I could lose my job, maybe even be up on charges, obstructing justice."

"You told your supervisor?"

"I told my supervisor."

"Can I buy you dinner?"

"I don't know when I'll be done," she said.

"I'm not in a hurry."

"I told the kids I'd have dinner with them," she said. "I'm picking up fried chicken. You want to come over?"

"You think Michael and Susan would go for that?"

"They think you're interesting," she said with the first touch of amusement.

"Give me a time," I said. "I'll show up with the chicken."

"Eight," she said. "That should be safe. You don't happen to know someone who wants to become a foster parent? Someone who might want and be able to control Adele. We're talking about a saint here. You know any saints?"

"Not exactly," I said.

Harvey chortled. I have heard few real chortles in my life, but this was definitely one of them. He chortled at a list of telephone numbers on the screen in front of him.

"On the other hand," I said, "I may know someone who might be willing to take on the challenge."

"Give me a name," Sally said. "I'll turn it over to the department that handles placement."

"I'd better talk to her first," I said. "See you at eight."

I hung up. I was procrastinating. I was avoiding. Now that I was starting to feel alive, I was also starting to look forward to things, like a bucket of fried chicken with Sally and her kids. I had realized while John Pirannes was telling me to put on a pair of swimming trunks that I was not as suicidal as I had been only a few days ago.

Ann Horowitz would definitely be pleased. I was feeling fear, pain, possibility and anxiety. There was much to be said for the alternative, depression.

I didn't want to go talk to Dwight Handford now, at least not for the same reasons I had wanted to before. But I did have to talk to him.

"Couple of more calls," I said, figuring out a way to avoid Dwight.

"Many as you like," Harvey said as telephone numbers scrolled rapidly down the screen. "Bingo. Bingo. Bing. There it is."

"What?" I asked, pushing buttons on the telephone pad.

"Not your job," Harvey said. "I don't think you'd be interested, but I can tell you when I crack something like this, when it hits the screen, it's better than any drink or the best coke I ever had."

"Great," I said.

Harvey had traded one set of addictions for a healthier one.

"What can I do for you?" Flo asked.

Unlike Harvey, she had not found a substitute for the loss of her husband. She bathed in the smoothness of expensive whiskey. I could hear it in her voice.

"It's me, Lew," I said.

"You find the kid?"

"She's okay," I said.

"I screwed up, Lewis," she said. "I let Beryl go, let her get killed. I'd like to find her bastard husband and blow a hole through his head, but that won't bring her back."

231

"I'm sorry, Flo," I said. "I shouldn't have brought you into this."

"I live with more, maybe even with worse."

"Can I come over tonight, late, maybe eleven?"

"Come ahead. Something on your mind?"

"Something's on my mind," I said. "I'm going to offend you now."

"Offend."

"Have something to eat, take a shower and—"

"Be sober," she continued. "Okay, but that's an agreement, not a promise. I've learned not to make promises."

"See you at eleven if I'm not in jail," I said.

"Expecting to be?"

"I'll let you know if I am."

I hung up. Harvey was singing softly now to the numbers on his screen. I didn't know what he was singing.

I made one more call. It was almost six. Detective Etienne Vivaise was still on duty. He was busy. I asked the woman who answered the call to tell him Lewis Fonesca was on the phone and wanted to talk to him about Tony Spiltz.

"One moment," she said.

Vivaise was on the phone within seconds.

"Fonesca," he said. "You want to come in and confess to a pair of murders? You doing a murder a day? Forget it. My mind's on something else. You know something about the Spiltz murder? It's got something to do with...hold it. Beryl Tree?"

"I think they were both killed by the same person," I said.

"Do I come to you or you come to me?"

"I'll be there in ten minutes," I said. "I'm not far."

"Ten minutes," he said and hung up.

I touched Harvey's shoulder, said I'd call him latter.

"An hour, two tops," he said.

I headed for police headquarters on Ringling. The blue Buick followed. I wondered what he made of my route. My guess, based on my brief encounter with him, was that he was not high on imagination. That was probably his greatest asset.

The cop at the desk asked me if I knew the way. I told him I did. He waved me on. In the room outside of Vivaise's office, a scaffolding and a paint-stained plank suspended between the rungs of two ladders stood against one wall. Desks, file cabinets, chairs were covered with paint-splattered white canvas drop cloths. One wall had been painted the exact color it had been before. Before the painters had quit for the day, they had gotten halfway finished with the second wall in front of the scaffold.

The only uncovered piece of furniture in the room was a bench against a wall. Two men, both black, were seated on the bench, hand-cuffed together. One man was in his late thirties, groomed, suited, with a neat tie and trim mustache: Eddie Murphy without an

233

attitude. His eyes were closed. The young man he was handcuffed to was short, wearing jeans and blue polo shirt. He didn't look like anyone I could think of. He saw me, turned his head.

Inside his office, behind his desk, sat Vivaise in a position from which he could see the two men on the bench through his open door. Vivaise motioned me in, pointed to the chair across from his desk and rubbed his forehead.

"Headache," he said. "I live with them. Allergies, migraine, whatever's possible, I have it."

"You look it," I said, sitting. "I met someone else today who suffers from migraines, John Pirannes."

Vivaise stopped rubbing.

"Let's talk Spiltz first," he said. "You want a coffee?"

"No, thanks," I said.

"Sometimes caffeine is good for a headache. Cola, coffee, pills. Hey," he shouted over my shoulder, "where are you going?"

From behind me a voice said,

"We got to piss."

"Both of you," Vivaise said wearily.

"Both."

"It can wait. Sit down. Your lawyer's on the way. When he shows up, I'll let him walk you to the toilet."

Vivaise turned his attention back to me.

"So, who killed Spiltz? And how do you know?"

"Dwight Handford," I said. "Killed his wife. Killed Spiltz."

"You have some evidence, a witness, a story?"

The door to the outer office behind us opened and Vivaise shouted, "You're right on time, Charlie. Your clients are having bladder-retention problems. You want to walk them down the hall? I called the county attorney's office. They're sending someone."

"Who?" the voice behind me asked.

"I think it's Angie Fairchild," Vivaise said.

"Good," said Charlie. "I'll walk my clients down the hall and confer."

The door behind me opened again and then closed. Beyond it I could hear the handcuffed men talking. And then there was silence.

"Story," said Vivaise.

"You saw my file on Beryl and her daughter."

"Got it right here," he said.

"A street pimp on the North Trail named Tilly told me Dwight Handford sold Adele to Pirannes. Tilly was in no position to argue. I went to Pirannes to check out his tale. I found Adele there. No Pirannes. She said some men came during the night. She was in the bedroom. She heard a shot. She came out. Spiltz was dead. The men were gone. Adele was in shock, shaking. I got her something to eat, turned her over to her therapist and caseworker. She's in Juvenile now."

"Go on," Vivaise said.

"It was stupid. I panicked. I should have called you when I found the body, but all I could think of was taking care of the girl," I said. "I realized my mistake an hour or so ago. I called you. I'm here."

"Who was the other guy with you at Pirannes's place?"

"Other guy?"

"Old guy with long hair wearing a yellow coat," said Vivaise. "I've got the report right here, pulled it when you called. Hard copy. Guard at the gate said a sad little balding guy, which I assume was you, and a tall old guy with long hair wearing a coat in eighty-degree weather tried to get in to see Pirannes this morning. When a couple of residents reported seeing these suspicious characters, the guard called the police. We went to Pirannes's apartment, found Spiltz's body. Between you and me with no tape rolling, the departure of Tony Spiltz from the earth was not a great loss to humanity. Thirty-eight arrests here and in New Jersey and New York. Spent time in Attica twice, once for racketeering, once for conspiracy to commit murder. If someone asks, I'll contribute ten bucks for his funeral. Who was the old guy?"

"The guard made a mistake," I said.

"The guard made a mistake?" Vivaise asked. "That's what you're going to say when you make a statement on the record, the guard made a mistake?"

"I don't know," I said. "I'll ask my lawyer. If there was an old man in a slicker with me, which there wasn't, he might have an arrest record. He isn't part of this, if he existed, which at this point he doesn't."

"I'm having trouble following you," Vivaise said. "It's been a long day. I need coffee. Our coffee isn't all that bad if the pot was emptied recently and someone made a fresh batch. Sure you don't want any?"

"I'll take some," I said.

Vivaise rose heavily and left me sitting and thinking while he went out. I came up with nothing new while he was gone, but he wasn't gone very long.

"Luck," he said, handing me a large white foam cup. The cup was hot. The liquid black. "Fresh pot. I sent Charlie and his clients downstairs to wait. I wanted to give you my full attention."

He went behind his desk, sat and sipped his coffee. I put my cup down and looked at him.

"You were talking about mistakes you made," he said. "You were talking about John Pirannes."

"I went to see John Pirannes," I said.

"Where?"

"He has a boat, the *Fair Maiden*, docked at the Sunnyside Condos on Longboat."

Vivaise was taking notes now.

"Why did you go to see him?"

"You said you had a daughter about Adele's age. Maybe you'll understand. I was angry."

"You had a plan?"

"No," I admitted. "I wanted to warn him, tell him to stay away from Adele. Maybe he'd tell me that Dwight Handford killed Tony Spiltz."

"Brilliant," said Vivaise, having some more

coffee. "Of course, he agreed to stay away from Adele and confessed to either killing Spiltz himself or being present when Dwight Handford did it."

"No," I said, hiding in my cup of coffee.

Vivaise was right. The coffee wasn't bad.

"You found out fast that Pirannes is smarter than you are," he said.

"Yes."

"And that he has a very short fuse."

"Yes."

"Confession time here, Lewis," he said in a stage whisper. "Pirannes is smarter than I am. He is slick. He had great lawyers. We've got nothing on him. We'll look for him, find him or maybe he'll come to us. He'll have a great story to cover where he was when Spiltz was killed and an even better one to cover why Spiltz was in his apartment. We know what Pirannes does, who he does it with. But nothing to crucify him with. And so far you've given me nothing."

"He tried to kill me or, at least, he planned to kill me," I said.

Vivaise shook his head in a way that said, What did you expect, you moron?

"He told me to put on a bathing suit, made it clear that he was going to dump me in the bay. I can't swim."

"You annoyed him. We have it on good authority that he doesn't like to be annoyed, that others have annoyed him and have gone swimming in the gulf or the bay and never made it to shore. He told you straight out that he was going to kill you?"

"No."

"Doesn't matter," Vivaise said. "All we'd have is your word. What else do you have?"

"Pirannes told me he had an alibi for Spiltz's murder, that he hadn't been back to his apartment last night, that he could prove it."

"He could prove he hadn't been there whether he had been there or not," Vivaise said. "What else?"

"He was on his boat with a big man named Manny."

Vivaise wrote and said, "Manny Guzman. And?"

"He was waiting for a woman. She was coming for lunch."

"Very helpful, Lewis. How did you get away from Pirannes?"

"Luck," I said.

Vivaise thought for a while. We both drank coffee. I was feeling a little better.

"How's your headache?"

"Better," he said. "Okay. We've been looking for Pirannes all day. You find a body in someone's apartment. You look for him. Pirannes is probably still on the boat. Maybe he even went back to the apartment. It's sealed, but he has a key and he can claim he doesn't know what this is all about. Maybe the girl's lying. Maybe she saw her father or Pirannes, or Manny kill Spiltz, for who knows what reason, and she's afraid to talk?"

"I don't know," I said. "I don't think so."

"Hell, I'll talk to her. In the morning. I'm going home, kiss my wife, probably have an argument with my kids."

"And me?"

"Leaving the scene of a crime. Withholding evidence," he said, standing up and finishing his coffee. Then he looked at me for a long time and added, "You were trying to protect the kid. Go home. Stay out of trouble. No charges on this one. If I find out you're lying, you'll get those charges and some I'll invent."

"I'm not lying," I said.

I hadn't finished my coffee.

"I don't think you are, but I've seen liars who believed their lies and convinced me. Go home."

I didn't go home.

"Kentucky Fried," Susan Porovsky said when she opened the door and saw the two bags on my arms.

"Is that good?" I asked.

"It is if there's corn and mashed potatoes with gravy. Is it extra crispy?"

"Half and half," I said as she pulled one of the bags toward her to peek into it.

"Can I come in?"

She took the bag she had been peeking in and led me into the apartment.

"Your mom home?"

"Coleslaw?" she asked, leading me through the living room to the dining room table.

"Coleslaw," I said.

"I hate coleslaw."

We started to unpack the bags. Susan seemed to be searching for something.

"What's this?" she asked, holding up a bag.

"Broasted chicken, for your mother. She doesn't eat fried chicken."

"I know," she said. "But she takes the crispy off and eats it when we get it fried."

We had it reasonably laid out and ready now, right down to the paper plates, paper napkins and paper cups. A bottle of Coke and another of Diet 7UP stood next to each other.

"Your mother's not home?"

"No," she said. "She called. Said if you got here first to wait ten minutes and then eat without her."

"Your brother?"

"Michael lives in the bathroom."

"He's in the bathroom."

"Confirmed," she said, nodding her head. "When he isn't in the bathroom, he watches TV, reads, goes out with friends to R-rated movies he shouldn't see and he plays basketball. I play basketball. I play the recorder too. Want to hear?"

I sat at the table and said,

"After dinner maybe."

"You don't think I can really play, do you?"

"I think you can really play. I just don't know how well. I play a harmonica. It sounds all right to me. Other people think I stink."

"You have a harmonica with you?"

"No, I haven't played since...for a while."

241

She sat across from me.

"That's because you're not happy."

"You are very wise for a child who has not even lived one lifetime," I said.

"What?"

"That's from *Dracula*."

"I don't remember that part. I can't think of anything else to entertain you. Mom said I should entertain you."

"You're doing a great job."

Michael emerged from the bathroom and said, "Kentucky Fried, great."

"Hi," I said.

"Hi," he answered, reaching into a bucket for a chicken leg.

"Wait for mom," Susan said.

"I'm starving," he said. "I'll just eat one and then I'll wait."

"Do Borgs eat?" I asked.

He sat and thought about it, drumming the chicken leg against a finger.

"What are Borgs?" Susan asked.

"Borgs are like zombies in *Star Trek*," Michael explained.

"I don't like *Star Trek*," she said to me. "My father was big. Mom thinks Michael looks like him and is going to be big. He's already pretty big."

"I think Borgs don't eat because they're mostly machines," he concluded. "It's a good question."

"I don't like mashed potatoes when they get cold," Susan said.

"We can microwave them," Michael said,

looking at me. "Mind if I ask you a question? I'm not trying to offend you or anything."

"Ask," I said.

"Are you making moves on my mother?"

"Michael," Susan shouted.

"It's okay," I said. "No, I'm not. I won't lie to you. If I keep seeing her, I probably will, but now we're friends. I lost my wife about four years ago. Car accident. I haven't...you understand?"

He said he did and took a bite of the chicken leg as the door in the living room opened and Sally stepped in, a black canvas bag in one hand and a briefcase in the other.

"Sorry," she said.

She came to the table, kissed Susan on the cheek and Michael on top of his head, and then she looked at the table.

"Looks great. I'm hungry."

"He got you broasted," Susan said.

Sally sat and said,

"Then what are we waiting for."

We ate. We talked. Mostly about nothing much. Kids feeling me out. Me playing. Sally listening, watching. I was having a good time. I didn't forget what was outside and what was deep inside me, but I enjoyed myself.

"Easy cleanup," Sally said when we were clearly finished.

Susan got a white plastic garbage bag while I consolidated what was left of the chicken into one bucket to go into the refrigerator.

There wasn't much privacy in the apartment,

but there was a small balcony with three chairs and a telescope. Sally and I went out while Michael and Susan watched television.

I told her everything.

"Sometimes…there are people I'd seriously consider shooting if I could. Dwight Handford is one, right at the top of the list. There's a real possibility that Adele will actually be sent back to him and I might not be able to do anything about it. I know what he's done to her and will keep doing. The courts know what he did to his niece. I've never hit one of my kids. I've never hit anyone. I've never held a gun. The Dwight Handfords of this world make me think about going to one of the many gun shops in this town."

"And Pirannes?" I asked.

"I've got a little list," she said.

"Of society's offenders who may well be underground," I said.

"Gilbert and Sullivan," she said. "I did *The Mikado* in high school. Played one of the three little girls."

"And I may have a foster home for Adele," I said, "providing my candidate passes whatever tests you give."

"I don't give them, but others do."

"Her name is Florence Zink. She's rich. She's tough. She drinks. She swears, but she's a good woman. Like to meet her?"

"When?"

"Tonight."

"I can't leave the kids. Tomorrow. Give me a number. I'll have someone call her."

"And," I said getting up, "I'll go talk to her. Who looks at the stars?"

"We all do," she said, touching the gray telescope fixed on an eye-level tripod. "I do it when the kids go to bed. Reminds me of how little we are."

"You want to be reminded?"

"Makes me feel better to think that what happens on earth isn't all that important. Makes me feel that I should concentrate on what I've got and enjoy it. And then I take my eye away from the lens and go back to the Adeles and Dwight Handfords. I've got paperwork."

Michael and Susan were watching a sitcom I didn't recognize. Sally walked me to the door.

"How did the Baby Ruth candy bar get its name?" I asked.

"Easy," said Susan. "The fat baseball player who hit all the home runs and drank beer before Mark McGwire."

Michael slumped, arms folded, and didn't bother to answer.

"No," I said. "Grover Cleveland got married after he became President of the United States. His wife had a baby named Ruth. It was a big thing. There were Baby Ruth dolls and a Baby Ruth candy bar."

"I'll tell Maggie and Shayna tomorrow," Susan said. "You know a lot of stuff."

"Yeah," I said. "Stuff."

Sally left the front door barely ajar behind us when we stepped out.

"You're a good man, Lewis," she said,

245

kissing me with sincerity but no passion as she held my hands in hers.

"Thanks," I said. "I'll talk to you tomorrow about Adele."

I started toward the stairs.

"Michael's going to an overnight basketball weekend and Susan's staying at her friend Maggie's on Saturday," she said.

"Saturday," I repeated.

13

THE HARD PART wasn't convincing Flo to consider being a foster parent. The hard part was dealing with a Flo Zink I had never seen before, a Flo Zink, complete with big-buckled denim skirt and bespangled blouse, who seemed to be on the verge of tears.

"They won't let me, Lew," she said.

"I've got a friend in the right place," I said.

Flo had poured me a beer without asking. I drank it. I had no idea what the glass with clear liquid and squares of ice in front of her contained. We were sitting in her living room listening to Johnny Cash.

"I don't know if I can cut this stuff out," she said, holding up her glass.

"Cutting back might be a start. Flo, I'm not handing you a present. I'm giving you one great big problem kid."

"I liked Beryl," she said.

"I did too."

"Well, if I can get her, bring her on. I'm old but I'm good at taming tough ones. Want a snack?"

"I've got to go."

Flo walked me to the door. The drink wasn't in her hand.

"I'd love to get a bead on the forehead of Beryl's husband—what's his name?"

"Dwight Handford," I said.

"If he'd come when Beryl left, as Hank Williams is my witness, I'd have killed him and Beryl would be alive."

"Lot of people feel that way about Dwight," I said. "Good night, Flo."

It was late now, after eleven. I wondered if the blue Buick was out there in the dark waiting. I didn't see it, but I hoped he was out there and hadn't gone home for the night or gone wherever it was he slept. I would sleep better knowing he was watching my back.

I didn't want to think. I wanted to wash, shave, put on some shorts, put a chair under my door, watch the tape of *The Mad Miss Manton* I'd bought at a garage sale for three dollars. I wanted to ease the nagging throb just below me ribs where Dwight had hit me.

There were no ghosts nor any of the living waiting in my office. I didn't feel haunted by Beryl Tree. She would know I was on her side and that there was no point in my going out on the road in search of Dwight Handford tonight. I needed rest. I needed someone with a weapon to go with me. I needed to think of a really good threat or a really good lie to frighten Handford off. None came to mind.

I was lying back on my three pillows when the phone rang. I hit the pause button and went into the office.

"Fonesca," I said.

"Where is she?"

I recognized the voice.

"Dwight, I've got some advice. The police are looking for you. John Pirannes is looking for you and tomorrow I'm going to be looking for you. I've got something to tell you."

"Say it now," he said.

"No. Worry about it overnight. You're a smart man. Running would be better than satisfying your curiosity."

"Where is Adele?" he demanded.

"Have a good night," I said, hung up and disconnected the phone.

I was back in bed and pushing the pause button again. Barbara Stanwyck started moving in black-and-white as the window in my office exploded.

I went to the floor, rolled over and crawled to the window. I counted five and looked out from the darkness of my room. A pickup truck with a tow winch was backing out of the DQ parking lot.

No one but me lived in the office building. The DQ was closed. Traffic was light on 301. I waited in the window for ten minutes. No sirens. No police. No one had heard the shots or, if they had, no one had reported them.

I was reasonably sure he wouldn't be back

tonight. He knew I would probably call the police and he wanted to be far away with some kind of alibi. But there was also the chance that he would think it over, figure that he had nothing much to lose with two murders behind him in the past two days and come back not just to scare me off, but to stand outside my window and blow holes in me.

Dwight Handford was a piece of work.

I grabbed my things, got dressed fast and went into the night. There was a rumble somewhere in the west but it wasn't raining. I went to the Geo, got in and went back to the Best Western, making sure I wasn't being followed by a pickup truck. I didn't see one. I didn't see anything behind me. My blue angel had missed another chance to save me.

I checked in, went to my room, showered, shampooed and climbed into bed after I checked the thermostat and found that the room temperature was seventy. I was hot, hot the way I had been until a few months ago whenever I drove a car. I turned the room temperature down to sixty.

Then I lay in bed, in the dark listening to the cold air rushing in and doing nothing to cool me.

I had a dream about rain and endless bowls of soup with tiny people splashing around in the soup and crying for help as they drowned. There were soup spoons in each bowl. They could have climbed out on the handles of the spoons or at least clung to them to keep from drowning, but they thrashed around and cried for help in tiny voices, hundreds of tiny voices, hundreds of bowls of soup, white chowder, red tomato, clear broth, green cream of broccoli.

When I woke up, I was hungry and I was certain of something. The dream had told me this, though it had nothing that clearly suggested what I was thinking. I got out of bed and stood for a minute. The room was cold, but I wasn't.

I made a call to the Texas Bar and Grill. Ed Fairing wouldn't be there this early. The only one who might answer was Ames. He did after twenty rings.

"I'll pick you up in twenty minutes," I said. "Bring your hog leg."

"Fine," he said.

I hung up, shaved, dressed and went to the car.

The sky was black with the threat of heavy hot Florida rain. I picked Ames up in front of the Texas. He was wearing his slicker. This time it was more than possible he would need it. I was sure the shotgun was under the yellow coat. I was positive when he climbed in the car and put it across his knees. Then I told him where we were going and why. He nodded. I drove.

And that's where I began this story. The dead man in the house in Palmetto was Dwight Handford. There was enough left of him to make the identification certain. I didn't know how many times he had been shot and I didn't care, probably six or seven. It had happened up close and very personal, a handgun.

Now, with the rain still coming down dark and dangerous, I drove back, this time down the Trail, down 41. I knew who the people in the soup were now. Their tiny faces had been clear but I had blocked them out. They were the faces of people I knew, one of whom had driven out to Palmetto and shot Dwight Handford dead.

Dwight's house hadn't been all that hard to find. What I had done others could have done in the same way or a different one. My blue angel could have done it, could have been waiting somewhere when Dwight shot out my window the night before, could have followed him home. My angel had been thrashing in pea soup. Then there was Pirannes, who had been cursing in a chilled peach fruit soup. And, though I didn't remember seeing them, there must have been Sally and certainly the rigid old man at my side, Ames McKinney, and Flo. There were probably two or three others I hadn't thought of yet and others I'd never heard of.

On the one hand, I didn't really want to find the truth, but, on the other, I had to know. I couldn't walk away. I might not turn the killer in, but I had to know.

"Ames, did you come out here last night on your scooter and kill Handford?"

"No," he said, looking straight ahead.

"But you're glad he's dead?"

251

"I am."

"So am I," I said.

I dropped Ames back at the Texas and told him we hadn't been to Palmetto, hadn't found the body.

He nodded, took out his key and went into the door of the grill. I went back to my office. There was no reason to stay away any longer. John Pirannes might still be a bit upset with me, but there was nothing much I could do to him. He was a prime candidate for Dwight's murder, he or Manny or someone he paid a few dollars to.

In spite of the overhang that ran along the concrete outside my door, the wind had been strong enough to tear down the drapes inside the broken window. The floor was slick and wet with blown-in rain. Blood, rain. When this was all over, I'd seriously consider finding another place to live, if I had enough money and energy for it. But then again, these two rooms were beginning to feel like home.

It was only nine. People were getting to work. Some had been there a while. I was hungry. The DQ wasn't open and I was soaked through and didn't feel like changing and going back out into the rain.

I did take off my wet clothes, throw them in the general direction of a far corner and put on dry ones.

Then I called the office of Tycinker, Oliver and Schwartz. Harvey was in.

"Harvey, I'm glad you're there."

"I've been here since seven. I'm trying to

track the bastard who put a real killer virus on-line. It's called Buga-Buga-Boo."

"I thought you couldn't track the source of an Internet virus," I said. "You told me that."

"Well, I may be the first. I'm close. When I track him, I'm going to shut him down."

"Great," I said. "How about the search you were doing for me?"

"Finished it last night," he said.

I could hear the clack of computer keys as his fingers reached into cyberspace to hunt the virus planter.

"And?"

He gave me the information. I wrote down what I needed of it. It wasn't much, but Harvey loved to describe the chase. I didn't disappoint him by cutting him off.

"Thanks, Harvey," I said.

"I'm shredding the hard copy of what I just told you," he said.

"Fine."

"And tell your friends, don't download Buga-Buga-Boo."

"I'll tell them," I said.

We hung up. I needed time to think, not conscious thinking, but deep down, almost the dream state. I had a feeling that I'd probably fail because I wanted and didn't want to know who had killed Handford. Maybe I could convince myself that it was Pirannes since it probably was.

I had another case, another client. I looked at the number of Caroline Wilkerson and punched the buttons. Six rings, the machine.

"It's Lewis Fonesca," I said. "I've got to talk to you about Melanie. If you—"

She picked up.

"Yes?" she said, panting.

"Sorry to wake you," I said.

"I've been up for hours," she said. "And, at the moment, I am on my StairMaster. What's this about?"

"Geoffrey Green thinks you have something to tell me that will help me find Melanie."

"Geoffrey Green is a quack," she said. "A charming quack, as quacks should be. I have nothing to tell you. I wish I did. Carl and Melanie belong together. Without her...don't know what will happen to him."

"I have something to tell you," I said.

"What?"

"In person. I guarantee you'll be interested."

She gave me her address and told me to come over in half an hour. She had a doctor's appointment, a facial and shopping to do. I told her I'd be right there.

I hung up. I already knew her address and phone number, but it didn't hurt for her to be cooperative. I found an old crumpled London Fog coat, back in my small closet. My wife had given it to me. Not a birthday or holiday gift. Just something she thought I needed.

I went out, down the stairs with the rain waterfalling off the roof and from the sky. Rolls of thunder, flashes of lightning. It would have been nice just to sit and watch and listen.

The Geo was at the rear of the lot, as close

to the stairs as I could get. I had left the doors unlocked so I didn't get too wet when I climbed in. There was just enough time for a quick breakfast. I had the feeling that the advances I had been given by Beryl Tree and Carl Sebastian were almost gone. I didn't want to check.

I found a space right in front of Gwen's Diner a minute away from the DQ. I ran in. There weren't many customers. The go-to-work rush was long over. Old Tim from Steubenville was at the counter, in the same seat he had been in the last time I was here. There was no Corky Spence, the trucker who had thought I had served him with papers. I sat next to Tim, who looked up from the magazine and coffee in front of him.

"Process server," he said, pointing a finger and smiling.

Gwen Two said, "Eggs, bacon, hash browns, coffee?"

"Right," I said.

She brought coffee immediately.

"Reading something interesting here," Tim said. "About the Sargasso Sea. Hundreds of miles of floating sea plants in the middle of the Atlantic."

He pointed east toward the Atlantic.

"Filled with little animals, weird fish, big worms, turtles."

"That a fact?"

"A fact," Tim said. "People used to be afraid centuries back, thought they'd get tangled in the plant life, but it's thin stuff. Off

255

of Bermuda out there. Animals, plants. They die. Drop down thousands of feet. Animals down there eat it. Food chain."

"Just like on land," I said.

"Cynical comment," he said. "Place I'd like to go is Galapagos Islands. You know Darwin was always seasick on a boat?"

"No," I said.

Gwen Two put the hot plate of food in front of me. The eggs were over very easy. Orange marmalade for my rye toast. I had become a semi-regular. Listening to Tim, having Gwen Two know what I wanted, helped take some of the horror out of the morning. I ate, paid attention to Tim and checked the clock.

Caroline Wilkerson had a less than modest house just over the north bridge leading to Siesta Key. Siesta is smaller, more ambling and less upscale, less high-rise and less resort-lined than Longboat Key. Siesta still has the sense of lush greenery and the memory of village. That's not to say Siesta has less wealth that the longer, thinner finger of its rival to the north. Siesta's money, generally, is more tastefully secluded.

The home of Caroline Wilkerson was big and new. Eight steps led up to a large double door with frosted-glass square windows etched with fleurs-de-lis. On each side of the doors were two white pillars, which probably did nothing to hold up the floor and enclosed balcony above. The house itself went for a balance between almost-orange brick Florida and Mount Vernon. It was about the right size and shape to decorate the back of a new U.S. Mint coin. Yes, a commemorative pink, Florida half dollar, the Wilkerson house on one side, a flamingo on the other.

It was still raining and thunder rolled, but far away inland.

I parked in the brick driveway behind a red Jaguar, hurried up the steps and pushed a well-hidden white button. A hum, somewhat like the musical sound made when Harvey turned on his computer, sounded inside the house.

Caroline Wilkerson opened the door. She was in pale blue tights, a towel around her neck, her white hair a bit frizzled, her face pink, handsome and without the trace of a line or wrinkle. She hadn't gone to any trouble anticipating my visit.

"Come in," she said.

In I went, following her across pink terrazzo floors to a patio beyond a living room, dining room, kitchen and a big, cozy-looking library. The patio was under a room above it that provided a roof. There was none of the screened-porch look to this house. It was open. The bugs that plagued the houses inland did not come in from the gulf on the keys. In front of the broad terrazzo patio was a swimming pool with a Jacuzzi and a small waterfall from it to the pool. Beyond the pool was a broad inlet. I stood watching a long-necked white bird glide through the rain, looking down for a feast of fish brought to the surface by the rain.

I was feeling poetic. I was feeling as if I had just eaten a large breakfast. I was feeling like not thinking about what I knew I had to do.

The table was white wicker with a glass top. The chairs were matching wicker.

"Will this take long?" she asked. "I'm running late."

"Nice house," I said.

"Thank you," she answered, making it clear that the opinion of a short, balding Italian process server would not make her day. "Please have a seat. Coffee, tea, juice?"

"No, thanks," I said, sitting.

She toweled off and sat.

"Well?" she said.

"Why did Dr. Green tell me to come see you again about Melanie Sebastian?"

"I don't know," she said. "I'd ask him when I see him, but we're not really on social speaking terms."

"Why?"

"I don't think he's given Melanie particularly good advice," she said. "Excuse me."

She got up nervously, went into the house and left me sitting and looking at the rain now coming down more reasonably but still hard. The rain had not cooled the morning. When she came back, Caroline Wilkerson was without towel and carrying a glass of clear, white liquid.

"Water," she said, seeing me look. "I don't drink."

"None of my business," I said.

"You're quite right," she said, sitting and looking at me.

"Mrs. Wilkerson," I said. "I'm trying to find your friend. I think she's in some kind of trouble. The way she's acting just doesn't make sense. Does she have a history of emotional problems?"

"Did you discuss this with Carl?"

"Not yet. I'm just following up Green's suggestion."

"Why not ask him, then? He's the psychiatrist."

"He wouldn't tell me. Patient confidentiality. That may be why he sent me to you."

"Oh God," she said, looking into the sky. "I hate this." Pause. "Melanie was depressed, profoundly depressed, probably still is. She even talked to me several times about suicide. She was supposedly working through it with Geoff Green."

"What was she depressed about?"

Caroline Wilkerson ran a finger over her moist upper lip, looked at the moisture and said,

"I don't know. Maybe something from her past. She didn't talk about her past much. Just before she ran away she had visited a relative up north, an aunt or something, her last living relative I think. Melanie's older brother had died in Vietnam. Her father died when Melanie was a baby. Her mother, I don't know, Melanie didn't talk much about her but from a few things she dropped from time to time I got the impression that her mother had some serious mental problems."

"You think Melanie may be…"

"Disturbed," she said.

"Suicidal?"

Her head went down.

"Yes. I talked to a doctor friend. From what little I could give him, he thought the problem might be chemical imbalance, inherited. I think it very possible that Melanie might do something to herself if you don't find her soon."

"And Carl Sebastian loves his wife?" I asked.

She gave me a look that suggested she was examining a demented lower species.

"Adores her," she said. "You should have seen them together. Melanie is Carl's life. He's a remarkably strong and resilient man for his age, but I think if Melanie…if you don't find her, he won't survive long or, if he does, he'll be a broken man. My husband always said Carl was a genius, that Carl had an instinct for the right deal, the right moment. Carl helped make my husband wealthy. Find Melanie, Mr. Fonesca."

"You have no idea where she might be?" I asked.

"None," she said. "I have no idea why Geoffrey Green sent you to me."

"You know a little man who looks like a bear, not much hair, tough face, drives a blue Buick?"

"No."

"When did you lose your driver's license?"

She turned her head away and then back to me.

"How did you know I lost it?"

"My job."

"What difference does it make?"

"Melanie used it. Got her picture pasted over yours, laminated it. She's you when she wants to be."

Caroline Wilkerson tapped the red fingernails of her left hand on the glass top of the table.

"What does Melanie Sebastian like to read?" I asked.

"Like to read? I don't know. What has this got to do with...?"

"She have a favorite food?"

"I really never noticed," she said with some irritation.

"Maybe if I know these things I can check them out, see if she's bought a new book, gone to a restaurant where they serve her kind of food."

"I see," she said.

"Her favorite movie or movies?"

"I'm not sure."

"Is she a Democrat, Republican, Libertarian? None of the above?"

Caroline Wilkerson shook her head.

"I wish I could help, but we never talked about such things."

"What did you talk about?"

"Clothes, people, you know, gossip, what happened at a party. It sounds superficial, but we had more substantial things we did on our own."

"Like what?"

"What do I do?"

"Yes."

"I do volunteer work at the Women's Center. I serve on the boards of...This is really none of your business."

She was definitely not pleased with me.

The rain was stopping. I wished it wouldn't.

"What did Melanie do? Substantial, I mean."

"Children, she worked with children. Raised money, gave money to local groups that support abused mothers, children. She couldn't have children of her own."

"Why?"

"Some illness," Caroline Wilkerson said, running a narrow manicured finger around the rim of her water glass. "I don't know what it was. She didn't talk about it. I have to go."

I got up and said, "That's about all I have for now. You've been very helpful."

"I hope so."

Now she got up and looked at me without the contempt I'd felt since she first opened the door.

"Find Melanie," she said. "Find her quickly."

"I will," I said.

She put out her hand. I shook it gently and she walked me back through the house and out the front door.

Melanie Sebastian and Caroline Wilkerson might have been best friends, but Caroline knew very little about her buddy. Maybe Melanie wasn't the kind who shared. Maybe Caroline made it clear she wasn't interested in getting too close and knowing too much.

There are people who live on the surface. They don't want to get below their own veneer and they certainly don't want to get below the surface of others. There is something behind the face we show the world that threatens the life of people like Caroline Wilkerson. Caroline Wilkerson would remain plastic surgery, diet, exercise and makeup handsome to the last second and then she would repaint the veneer with peach self-deception.

The truth was that I didn't know what I was telling myself. It was a fantasy that felt true but might be a lie. It probably came from my having a surface that hid almost nothing, at least nothing I was aware of.

I drove off. When I left the Key over the north bridge, the reality of Dwight Handford hit me again. I had put it away, but it wouldn't stay down. I had to make the rounds. I had to ask questions that risked my losing the few friends I had.

Well, Lew Fonesca did hide his gargoyles and demons and he told no one about his grandfather's mandolin. Why hadn't I told Ann Horowitz about them? Reminders of guilt and pain soothed by a childhood memory of an instrument now plucking out "The World Is Waiting for the Sunrise," my grandfather's arthritic fingers moving madly. There are some secrets we want to hold on to, cling to—the last piece or two of flotsam that keeps us afloat in our private sea of doubt. Did the Handfords of the world have secrets, doubts? Did he take some piece of jagged driftwood memory to his grave? I hoped not. We, at least I, need monsters. Without monsters there are no heroes. Something has to be black and white.

Ames had told me he hadn't killed Handford. Ames wouldn't lie. He would know that I'd never turn him in. I knew I'd never turn in one of my other friends if they had killed Dwight. I just had to know.

First stop, Flo Zink.

The sun had come out when I was about halfway to Flo's. I knew it was now hot and humid, sweat-drenching hot and humid, just outside the air-conditioning of the Geo. A little old man in a big new car swerved out of his lane and almost forced me off of Tamiami Trail. I looked over at him. He was hunched over and looking dreamily ahead. He had no idea what he had done. I accepted this hazard of Florida life and drove on.

Flo was home, waiting. She opened the door, the voice of a man behind her sang about the Texas wind and Flo announced,

"One drink so far today," she said with pride. "I'm shooting for four a day. How do I look?"

She was wearing a beige knit skirt and matching top with a brown sweater. Her hair was brushed and her earrings small and silver.

"Fine," I said. "What's the occasion?"

"I thought we were going to see some people about that foster parent business?" she said.

"I haven't worked out the details yet."

"There's a phone. Work it out."

Flo didn't sound or act like a woman who had shot a man a few hours ago, but maybe she was in a mood for celebrating after having done a righteous deed.

"Flo, Dwight Handford is dead."

"Maybe there is a God," she said solemnly. "Makes things a lot easier. Who killed him? Forget it. I don't care."

"I had the idea that you might have done it," I said.

She put her hands on her hips, cocked her head to one side and said, "Lewis, I'm flattered. But I didn't kill him. How did he die?"

"Lots of bullets from a handgun."

"Sounds like what I'd do if I did it but I didn't. Can you make whatever calls you have to make now?"

"Who's that?" I asked, looking at the tape player.

"Roy Acuff," she said. "Not much of a voice, not much emotion, but he sounds like the real thing and the words get to me. The phone, Lewis."

I called Sally on her cell phone.

"Hello," she said.

"It's Lew," I said. "When can you set something up for that foster placement for Adele? I'm here with a very expectant lady."

"My office, one P.M. I'll have someone there who can take care of it."

"I have to talk to you, Sally," I said.

"Can't talk now," she said. "I'm in a client's home. See you at one."

She hung up.

265

I hadn't told her about Dwight Handford's body up in Palmetto. I knew why. I wanted to catch her off guard, see how she took the news. She had sounded normal on the phone, but that didn't mean much.

"One o'clock," I told Flo. "You sure you know what you're letting yourself in for?"

"Lewis," she said, touching my cheek. "You sure you know what I've been through in my life? Someday I'll tell you some stories. Right now I'd like a drink, which means it's up to you to take my mind off of it."

"Let's go to Mote Marine," I said.

"Never been there," she said. "Fish."

"It'll take your mind off of human life," I said. "I like it there."

We went to the Mote Marine Aquarium on City Island between St. Armand's Circle and the bridge to Longboat Key. We smiled at a shark, grinned at a giant grouper, examined eels and searched for alliteration in the clear seawater tanks.

"You're right," Flo said. "It's...a different world."

The blue angel was there, in his car not far from where I parked. I wanted to invite him in. I had the feeling he would like the fish, several of which resembled him. Some probably resembled me. I also wanted to talk to Angel about the death of Dwight Handford.

"Lunch?" Flo asked when we had finished the cycle and seen every fish and sea creature.

"Had a late breakfast," I said, "but I'm up for salad."

"Columbia?" she asked. "They have a mean house salad."

"Sure," I said, and we walked back to my car. I let her in and asked her to wait for just a second.

"Mind if I turn on the radio?"

"No," I said, and moved toward the blue Buick.

I knocked at the driver's side window and he rolled it down and looked up at me. No music played in his car, but there was a pile of magazines on the passenger seat. The top one was the latest *Cosmopolitan*. He said nothing.

"Dwight Handford is dead," I said.

"Who?"

"The guy who tried to beat me up. The guy you saved me from. The guy who shot a hole in my window last night."

He nodded, accepting the information.

"You followed him last night after he blew my window out."

He shrugged.

"You kill him?"

"No. What'd I tell you yesterday? Do your job."

"I'm doing it," I said. "What's your job?"

He rolled his window closed. I couldn't see through the tint. I gave up and went back to Flo, who had found a country-and-western station on the radio.

"Who's that?" she asked, nodding toward the Buick.

"An angel," I said.

267

She seemed satisfied.

"Who's that?" I asked, nodding at the radio.

"Eddy Arnold," she said. "Got all his CDs. They ran a special on television a while back."

The Columbia, a Cuban restaurant on St. Armand's Circle, wasn't far. The original Columbia was opened in 1908 in Ybor City in the heart of Tampa. I'd been there once to serve papers on a computer salesman. Old, big, authentic, lots of colorful tile, lots of big solid wood tables. Zorro country. The night I served the papers there was a quartet of flamenco dancers. My wife would have liked it. She would have liked the sense of stepping into the past.

The Columbia in Sarasota was modern with lots of light and the house special 1908 Salad, which I ordered. Flo was hungry. She ordered the seafood paella. It took twenty minutes to prepare, but we were in no hurry. I looked through the window at the passing traffic and across the street at the large circle surrounded by sidewalks around trees and bush-lined paths with benches where tourists could eat their ice creams from Ben & Jerry's or Kilwins.

A man was standing on the concrete path on the circle across from the Columbia. He was looking through the window at me. Cars passed in front of him. Through one break in the traffic, he motioned to me.

"Flo, I've got to do something. I'll be back in a few minutes."

"The guy on the circle?" she asked.

"Yes," I said, getting up. "He's a client, Carl Sebastian."

"Just happened to be there and saw you?" she asked, reaching for her second warm, crisp roll.

"I doubt it. I'll make it fast."

"Take your time," she said. "I like it here. You think a glass of wine would be..."

"A good idea," I said.

The air outside the Columbia was warm and after-rain muggy. There were puddles and patterns of water in the street and on the sidewalk. I crossed between cars and faced Sebastian on the path.

"I knew some of the people," he said. "The ones who have stars."

The concrete sidewalk around the circle was embedded with stars honoring famous circus performers, much like the stars on Hollywood Boulevard. These bronze stars included information on the performers.

"Knew Emmett Kelly slightly. Lou Jacobs. The Wallendas," Sebastian said, shaking his head. "Looking at those stars always brings back memories. I love the circus."

"I'm fond of it myself," I said. "You followed me out here to talk about circuses."

"You said you'd find Melanie," he said.

"I said I'd find her in two or three days. This is day one."

"It's day two," said Sebastian.

"Look, Mr. Sebastian—"

"Tomorrow then?"

"The next day at the latest," I said, knowing

that Melanie Sebastian might change her mind about letting me find her and that Harvey might not be able to follow her on the Internet highway to where she was hiding.

"I'll give you a bonus if it's tomorrow," he said.

"You said you'd double my fee. When we talked last time you said you'd double it."

"Double, then. Just find her. I can't sleep. I can't work. I can't think."

He put his head down and rubbed his neck. Then he looked up and said, "Sorry. You said you understood what it was like to lose your wife. You remember? You said that?"

"I remember," I said.

"Then find her. Find Melanie."

There were tears in his eyes. He turned away and walked up the path that ran through the middle of the circle.

I went back to the Columbia. Flo was working on her paella. My 1908 Salad sat waiting.

"This is great," she said. "What did he want?"

"Everything," I said. "Everything."

14

JOHN DETCHON SAT BEHIND the reception desk at the Children's Services office. He looked up from a pile of papers he was sorting and smiled.

"The sad detective is back," he said.

"I'm not a detective, John."

"Indulge me in my fantasy," he said. "I'm trapped behind this desk eight hours a day. I need to bring home tales of corruption and intrigue to my roommates."

"I'm a detective, John. I carry a derringer in a tiny holster near my crotch. I've been shot five times and killed four people. I may not look tough but I turn into a raging revenge-seeking monster when provoked."

John grinned.

"Beautiful," he said. "Beautiful. I don't believe a word of it, but it's beautiful. I didn't think you had an imagination."

"I'm learning," I said.

"Can we cut the crap and get on with our business," Flo said.

"And you," John said, "must be Mr. Fonesca's mother."

Flo went tight.

"Listen, sissy," she said. "I'm broad-minded, but I don't take shit on a silver spoon from anyone, especially sissy boys."

"Sissy? God, the last person who called me that was my grandfather when I was six."

"I've got better words," she said.

"Flo, don't blow this," I said.

She shrugged, nodded to show that she was under control and said,

"Sorry."

"Apology accepted," said John. "I like your sweater."

"Thanks," said Flo.

"Miss Flo," said John. "The word of choice is 'gay.'"

"I know," said Flo.

"Sally is expecting you," he said. "Go right up. You know the way."

We got on the elevator. The doors closed.

"He's okay," she said, looking at the door. "I'm just fucking nervous."

"Flo, if you have to, say 'freaking.'"

"Can't," she said. "It's a PG-rated coward's word. Let's get on with this."

Sally stood as we approached. There was a woman with her. The woman was in her fifties, a little off in her color combinations and in need a a good hairbrush. She looked frazzled. Sally smiled at me. I liked the smile. She didn't look like a woman who had shot a man this morning, but she might be smiling about it. I didn't know her well enough yet.

"This is Florence Zink," I said.

The two women stepped forward to shake Flo's hand.

"And this," said Sally, "is Edna Stockbridge. She'll talk to Mrs. Zink in my supervisor's office. She's at a conference."

"This way," said Edna Stockbridge, motioning to Flo.

Flo followed, after looking at me. There was warning in my look. I hoped she read that warning.

When they were gone I sat in the chair next to Sally.

"She'll be fine," Sally said. "And we need foster homes so badly that she'd have to be an ax murderer to be rejected. She's rich. She wants to deal with Adele. What more can we ask for? All she has to do is convince Edna that she can handle Adele."

"She can handle Adele," I said. "Dwight Handford."

I watched her face for a sign. I didn't see one as she said,

"I talked to our lawyer this morning. She thinks there's a fifty-fifty chance at best of keeping Adele from him. The power of a mistaken belief that children should be with their parents whenever possible combined with the likelihood of a really expensive lawyer representing Handford make fifty-fifty look optimistic."

"Handford's dead," I said.

"What?"

"Dead."

"Really? When? Where?"

"His house. The real one in Palmetto. You want to know how he died?"

"Not really," she said, taking a deep breath. "I'm trying to deal with the fact that I suddenly feel relieved and I don't feel guilty."

"Why should you feel guilty?" I asked.

She looked at me. It was a very serious look.

"Because a man is dead and and I'm troubled because I don't care. Why else would I feel guilty?"

"He was murdered," I said flatly.

"I'm not surprised, though death in an alcoholic stupor or a bar fight wouldn't surprise me either. I've got to think about what this means to Adele, how to tell her. I'll have to call our lawyer. Sometimes death is good news."

"You wanted him dead," I said. "You said you could kill him."

She was silent. Her mouth opened slightly.

"Lewis, you think I killed him?"

"It's possible," I said.

"I didn't."

"You're offended. I'm sorry."

"No, I'm not offended. I guess it's a reasonable question. Do I need an alibi? When did he die?"

"My guess is early this morning, very early."

"I was home with the kids."

"When did they get up?"

"About eight," she said.

"You could have gone out, killed Handford and gotten back before they got up."

"I could have, but I didn't. Lewis, are you trying to back away from me, from—for want of a better word at the moment—our friendship?"

"No. I'm asking you questions the police might ask you, maybe today, maybe tomorrow. There's a smart detective named Vivaise who—"

I stopped in midsentence. I had another suspect. Ed Vivaise had a daughter. He had said something about the benefit to the world of Dwight Handford's death.

"Too many suspects," I said, leaning back. "The only way I'm ahead of the police is that

I can eliminate me from the list. Are we still going out Saturday?"

"We're still going out," she said, touching my arm. "You pick a place to eat. I pick the movie."

"Thanks," I said. "I'm sorry."

"For what? Being honest with me? Now the hard part of my day," she said. "The downside of Dwight Handford's death. I'm the one who'll have to tell Adele her father's dead and I have no idea how she'll react. I think I'll do it now. I don't want to carry it around all day."

"Let me know how she takes it," I said.

"I will. Saturday. That was interesting," she said. "Being a suspect. Am I clear now?"

"Yes," I said, but I lied.

Flo had to stay with Edna, get papers filled out. Edna would drive her home. She came out of the supervisor's office and told me this. She was nervous and glowing. They were hurrying the process.

I told Sally what Harvey had told me about the Buga-Buga-Boo virus. She made a note to E-mail everyone in her computer address-book to warn them. I left.

I was sure Handford had murdered Beryl, but I wasn't too sure about who had killed Tony Spiltz and Dwight Handford. The loss mankind would suffer due to their deaths was nonexistent.

My vote went to John Pirannes. Had a fight

with Spiltz, who was doing his part to train Adele. Pirannes wanted Handford out of the way because he was probably a witness to the Spiltz murder and because he was a loose blunderbuss, ready to explode, dangerous. Pirannes probably knew Dwight had killed Beryl. My vote definitely went to John Pirannes.

That should have closed the file for me, but it didn't.

I had to know for sure. I knew why I had to know.

My wife had been killed by a drunken hit-and-run driver. The driver hadn't been found. There was no closure. I needed closure, certainty, in my life. I'd talk about it with Ann Horowitz as soon as I could.

The blue Buick followed me back to the DQ parking lot. I went to see Dave, who leaned out the window.

"How's business?" I asked.

"Slow," he said. "Rain always makes it slow. I don't mind. You went to see Pirannes?"

"Yes," I said.

"You survived. Congratulations. The *Fair Maiden* pulled out this morning, headed who knows where," said Dave.

"Doesn't surprise me."

"You want a burger, Blizzard?"

"Had a big salad for lunch. Diet Coke."

Dave nodded over my left shoulder. I turned and found myself facing two policemen. Their car was in the lot a few feet away.

"Lewis Fonesca?" one cop said.

Both cops were young. There was a thin one

with a smooth face and a heavyset one with an amber mustache.

"Yes," I said.

"Would you come with us, please? Detective Vivaise would like to talk to you."

"Do I have a choice?"

"No, sir," said the thin cop.

I knew better than to ask if I could drive my rented Geo. I climbed into the backseat of the police car. Until recently, the Sarasota police car insignia on the door was a picture of the statue of Michelangelo's *David*. A copy of the statue stood in the courtyard gardens of the Ringling Museums. A copy of a copy had graced the doors and hallways and official vehicles of the city. Many of these tributes to distant art still remained. I don't know much about art but, I liked the Ringling, the polished dark wood floors, the old-worldliness of the galleries of ornately framed paintings Ringling had collected in his European travels. I had been told by someone who should know that the paintings on display were the worst of the great masters—Rembrandt, Titian, that whole gang.

"You ever go to the Ringling Museum?" I asked the young thin cop at my side as we drove.

"When I was a kid, once," he said.

"You?" I asked the driver.

"No," he said. "My wife has."

"She like it?"

"Said she did."

I considered asking Vivaise about the Ringling Museum, but when I stepped into his office he was seated and patting his desk with his left hand.

"Dwight Handford is dead," he said.

I sat across from him.

"Not sorry to hear that," I said.

"I'm not either, but it's my problem."

"Where did he die?" I asked.

"You know damn well he died in his house in Palmetto."

"Why would I know?"

"Don't wear me out," he said.

He had stopped drumming.

"A neighbor saw two men going into Handford's house this morning. Tall man with a yellow raincoat and a short bald man. They came in a little white car and left in it a few minutes after they went in. Sound familiar?"

"Anything else?"

"Manatee medical examiner is looking at the body. At this point all he's sure of is that Handford is dead and that he died sometime last night or early this morning, very early, before you and your friend were there."

"And?"

"You're going to play games with me, aren't you, Fonesca? Handford was murdered. Shot. Between you, me and the painters out there if they're listening at the door, I say the world's a little better place today. Fonesca, did you kill him?"

"You mean did I drive out to Palmetto in the middle of the night, kill him and then drive back in the morning, discover the body and not report it?"

"Did you kill him?" Vivaise repeated.

"No, did you?"

"Not funny," he said.

"Not meant to be. You have the weapons, the reason. The same reason I'd have. You're happy he's dead."

"My guess is a lot of people are happy he's dead," Vivaise said.

"Why is it your case if it happened in Palmetto?"

"Because I think Handford murdered his wife and probably murdered Tony Spiltz, who died within the jurisdiction of the Sarasota Police Department, died in my county. And the Palmetto police are happy to give it to me as long as I keep them informed."

"Pirannes's boat pulled out this morning," I said.

"I know. We're looking for him."

"What now?"

"You feel like confessing?"

"To what?" I said.

He threw up his hands.

"To anything. A plot to kill the President. Crossing Proctor against the lights. I'll take what I can get. Have you been to confession recently?"

"I'm not a Catholic," I said. "Episcopalian, very lapsed."

"Do you know who killed Handford or Spiltz?" he asked.

"I'm working on it. Let's pin it on Pirannes. If he didn't do the murders, I'm sure he did others we know not of. He gave me reason to believe."

"That the way the police think in Chicago?" he asked.

"That's the way," I said. "But I'm not a cop."

"You're not even a private investigator," he said, beginning to steam. "You're are a goddamn little process server with a big nose that gets into places where it shouldn't be."

"I agree," I said.

"Get out, Fonesca," he said, both hands on the table. "I know where to find you."

"What happened to those two guys last night? The black guys in handcuffs?"

"You are a piece of work, Fonesca," he said with a grin almost as sad as mine.

"I can't help it," I said.

"They got off," he said. "They're car thieves, but we didn't have enough to keep them without a confession. They didn't confess. They went home. That's the way it usually is."

"Another question?" I asked.

"Why not?" Vivaise said.

"Have you ever been to the Ringling Museum?"

"You are nuts, Fonesca."

"Maybe, but I'm taking a sort of survey."

"I've been to the museum. My wife and I have taken the kids. We're museum members. I like it there. It's peaceful, old. It's a refuge, a garden of sanity, a sanctuary from the mad chaotic world outside, the world where people like you drive the streets and ask crazy questions. You satisfied with my answer?"

"Yes," I said.

"Get out, Lewis," he said calmly. "I sort of like you, but that can change quickly."

I got out. The two young cops who had brought me here were waiting outside Vivaise's door watching the painters, talking to them, laughing. They offered to take me home. I told them I'd walk.

I went down Main Street past the YMCA. I hadn't been there for five days. I longed for that bicycle ride and workout. I wanted my routine back. I wanted my loneliness back. I looked at the people beyond the glass on the exercise machines. I thought, waited for an epiphany. None came. I walked back to 301 and headed south toward home.

When I passed the Crisp Dollar Bill across from the DQ, it hit me. It hit me hard. It was the only thing that made sense. I didn't like the sense it made.

The blue Buick was parked in the DQ lot. The blue angel was sitting at one of the tables eating what looked like the deluxe burger. He had probably seen the cops pick me up and had decided it wasn't a good idea to follow a police car. He was waiting for me.

I didn't want him with me where I was going, so I went into the Crisp Dollar Bill. It took my eyes a few long seconds to adjust to the darkness. There was no music. I had lived across from the bar for more than two years and had never been in it before. It wasn't as big as I thought it would be, just a line of wooden tables to the right and a long bar with stools on the left. There were no booths. One man sat alone at a table. He was a silent solitary drinker, his eyes fixed in the past. He was wearing a colorful Hawaiian shirt and I guessed his age at fifty.

There were two people at the bar, talking quietly. One was a woman who looked as if she were a retiree from the North Trail. The man wore a rumpled suit and had his back to me.

I went to the bar and ordered a Budweiser from the lean, long-haired bartender, who might have been any age between forty and sixty. He gave me a friendly smile and wink and said, "Coming up."

No music. I liked that. I never understood why, when you got in someone's car or went to their home to talk, they turned on music.

The television over the bar was off and the place was dark. I liked it here. I wondered if it was like this at night. I didn't think so. Late afternoon was the time to come to the Crisp Dollar Bill. I'd remember that.

"Phone?" I asked when the bartender came back with my beer.

"Back there by the john," he said. "Need change?"

I checked. I had a handful of quarters and other change in my pocket.

"No," I said.

"Give me a nod if you want your bill or another Bud," he said.

"There's no music," I said.

"Music-free bar," he said. "Watch a football game once in a while. Sundays, Monday night. Quiet most nights."

He moved down the bar toward the man and the woman. The bartender knew I needed space. He was one hell of a good bartender.

I made my call and went back to finish my beer.

Ten minutes later, my glass empty, I paid my bill and left a good tip.

I went out the door and looked over at the DQ. The blue angel had finished his burger. He was probably back in his Buick watching the parking lot and my door. I walked back to Main Street and stood in front of the Main Street Book Store across from the Hollywood Twenty movie theaters.

Ames pulled up on his motor scooter a few minutes later. He was wearing his blue zipper jacket and a helmet. I moved to the scooter and he handed me a helmet. It was a duplicate of his, green.

I had told him on the phone where we were going. I hadn't told him why. It was too noisy on the scooter to carry on a conversation. I waited till he had parked in the lot on Longboat Key, about fifteen minutes later. Ames locked the scooter and ran a chain through a hole at the rear of both helmets. He locked the chain to the scooter with a padlock he kept in his pocket and we began to walk as I explained.

"We go in the same way?" he asked.

"Worked before," I said. "This time we do a better job."

There were two long-necked white birds in the pond beyond the bushes that surrounded the Beach Tides Resort. One of them looked at us as we moved.

We didn't go to the beach this time. We didn't have to search for the building. We knew where it was. We watched for security guards in their golf carts, didn't see any and moved to the rear of the building where John Pirannes had an apartment.

There was no one in sight. We could hear the voices of people at the pool and beach, but their possible view of us and ours of them was blocked by a hill, a bed of red flowers and tropical trees.

"Here," I said. "Right?"

We were standing in a plot of tall grass. Ames looked up at the building.

"Yes," he said.

"A lot to look through," I said.

"Seems so," said Ames.

We bent and started to go through the grass with our hands. In twenty minutes of looking, I managed to find a golf ball, a soggy eyeglass case and an ant hill. I got two bites on my hand. My stomach was feeling better, but far from healed. Bending was not easy.

"Nothing," I said, looking at Ames.

"Still light," he said, looking at the sky.

Fifteen minutes later Ames found it, about fifteen yards from the building, next to a short palm tree, in plain sight. He pointed to it and I took the plastic zippered bag from my pocket.

I lifted the gun by the barrel and carefully dropped it into the bag.

Half an hour later we were back downtown. I was constantly thanking Ames, but I
did it again.

"Anytime," he said as I got off the scooter
and handed him the green helmet. "I owe
you."

"You've paid me back," I said.

"I like you," he said.

"I like you too, Ames," I said.

He looked at me, gray eyes serious.

"We're friends," he said. "I haven't had
more than three real friends in my life."

"Friends," I said.

He drove away. A crowd of people waiting
in line at the movie theater for the early-bird
show looked at him as he shot into traffic.

I walked to the DQ, got a Diet Coke to go
from Dawn and went to my office, moving past
the blue Buick.

My window was boarded up. I went in,
locked the door, turned on the light, put the
bag with the gun on my desk and sat down. I
was pretty sure what it could tell me. I didn't
need a lab report.

I made a call and set up an appointment.

Then I put the bag with the gun under my
dresser and lay on my bed. The sound of
traffic on 301 put me to sleep. I didn't dream.
At least I don't remember dreaming.

I woke up to the sound of people arguing.

Moist and groggy, I rolled over, got on my
knees and reached under the dresser to con-

vince myself I hadn't dreamed the day. The gun was there, inside the bag. I moved to the window near my television set, pushed the drapes aside and saw a couple in their twenties standing in the parking lot of the DQ. They were arguing.

The woman, bedraggled, probably pretty beneath defeat, was carrying a child about a year old in her arm. The child had a pacifier in its mouth. The child was looking at what I assumed was its father, who was pointing a finger at the woman as he shouted. The young man's neck was stretched in anger, tendons taut. He was wearing a baseball uniform sans cap.

I moved away from the window and checked my watch. I had to hurry.

Five minutes later I was in my car. The gun was tucked under my seat. Angel was close behind. We didn't have far to go. I wasn't sure where the room I was going to might be, so I just parked on the street, locked it and went in. I left the gun behind. I knew there was a metal detector in the building.

Sally was waiting in the lobby.

"What is this, Lew?"

"I'm not sure," I said. "I'm pretty sure. I don't think you should know. Not yet. Maybe never."

"Susan thinks you might be a little crazy," she said. "My daughter likes you but—"

"Ten-year-old girls have a sense of things like that," I said. "She may be right. Don't trust people who say 'Trust me,' but, Sally, I'm asking you to trust me."

She sighed, checked her wristwatch and said, "All right. Let's go."

We went through the metal detector and signed in at the desk. We had an appointment. Sally was known at the Juvenile Security Center. If I could have gotten in without her, I would have.

"You told Adele that Dwight is dead?"

"I came to see you right after you left my office," said Sally. "She didn't know how to react. She just stood there for a while. Then she cried for a bit while I held her. When the crying stopped, she gave a deep sigh like she was letting go of something. I think she's relieved and isn't ready to admit it to herself. She may never be."

"And Flo? You told her about Flo?"

"I told her. She agreed. I don't think she can take it all in yet."

I followed Sally to an elevator. We went up three floors and were met by a woman in uniform who was waiting for us. She led us down the hall to a room with a sofa and some chairs. There was a single window. It was covered by metal meshing.

We stood while the woman went away and returned in about three minutes with Adele.

The girl looked smaller than I had remembered. In fact, she didn't look like the same girl at all. Her face was pink and fresh. Her hair was combed out, hanging back and touching her shoulders. She wore a sleeveless summer dress, green with little white flowers. She looked at least a year younger than fourteen. It was her eyes that looked forty.

She looked at me and then at Sally, who stepped to her and gave her a hug.

Adele ticked a smile, a very small, cautious one.

"Remember me?" I asked.

"Sure," she said. "Denny's. What you want?"

"To talk to you," I said.

"'Bout what?"

"Sally, can I talk to Adele alone for five minutes?"

I could feel the word "Why?" forming inside of Sally.

"Something you don't think I would want to hear?"

I nodded.

Sally looked at Adele. Adele was looking at me warily.

"Adele," Sally began, "if you..."

"It's okay," Adele said. "Nothing he can say can make things worse than they are and I might as well have it all in one day."

"Five minutes," said Sally. "I'll be right outside the door."

Sally left, closing the door behind us. I walked to the steel-meshed window and looked down. There was a drive-in spot for trash pickup. Two large green Dumpsters sat waiting. One was bulging with garbage. Fat green plastic bags looked as if they were creeping out.

"Let's sit," I said.

"I like standing."

She moved to the wall, put her back against

it and folded her arms. I moved about five feet from her and put my back against the same wall.

"I know who killed Tony Spiltz," I said.

"Mr. P.," she said.

"You," I answered.

She shook her head and said,

"You are somethin'. My mom and dad get murdered. I get thrown in here and you come...You are sick. I've seen 'em sick. But you are really sick."

"I can prove it," I said.

"You can't, because I didn't."

"I've got the gun," I said. "Found it below Pirannes's balcony, near a palm tree. Took Ames and me about half an hour, but we found it."

She shook her head no.

"Smith and Wesson thirty-eight. Silver barrel."

"I don't know nothing about guns," she said, looking at the ceiling.

"You didn't have to. You just pulled the trigger. I've got the gun in my car. It has your fingerprints on it. When I leave here, Sally will stay so you can remain in this room. You walk to the window, look down. I'll be parked right in front of the Dumpsters. I'll hold up the gun."

"I didn't shoot him," she said weakly.

"Your story was terrible," I said. "You're a smart girl. You could have done better. You could have done all kinds of things. You could have wiped your prints off the gun."

"You think I wanted to get caught?" she said,

turning to me with a look, a typical teen look, that said, Are you nuts?

"I think so. I can make up a story to fit, but it would be faster if you just told me what happened. I'm not out to get you, Adele. I'm out to help you."

"No," she said, back to the wall again, arms folded, eyes looking up at the ceiling.

"Okay. Pirannes wasn't in the apartment with you. Spiltz was. Just you and Spiltz. He was there to keep an eye on you. You weren't exactly a volunteer. Spiltz went after you. You got his gun, shot him, panicked and didn't know what to do. You threw the gun over the balcony, managed to get Spiltz's body into the chair and then you cleaned up the blood where you shot him."

"No," she said.

Tears were coming. She fought them back.

"I've got the gun. It has your prints. The police, if they know the story, can find the spot you killed him. There'll be blood traces."

"I shot him in bed," she said, her eyes closed. "I wrapped him in the sheets and blankets and dragged him into the living room so there'd be no blood and so it'd be easier to move him. There's a washer and dryer down four, five doors down. I washed the sheets and blankets, dried 'em and put 'em back in the cabinet. Then I put new sheets and a new blanket on."

"He had to have a holster," I said. "Ames and I didn't find one."

"I figured a holster would be too easy to find.

Reason I took it off him was I...I thought if he was wearing one when he was found dead, the cops might wonder where the gun was that went in it. I figured if he didn't have a gun or holster, the cops would figure whoever shot him came and went with his own gun. I rolled the holster up neat and put it in one of Mr. Pirannes's drawers."

"That was smart," I said. "No gun. No connection. Police would think the holster was Pirannes's. Holsters aren't registered and they're not illegal. It might even suggest that a gun might have been in it and it might have been the gun Pirannes used on Spiltz. You really think it out that far?"

"No," she said, eyes still closed. "I just..."

"It's full of little holes, but it's pretty good."

"I was gonna go back when it was safe, find the gun, bury it fast, but I'm here and you got there first. What's gonna happen to me?"

"I'm working that out," I said.

"He was gonna rape me," she said so softly I could hardly hear. "No one ever did it to me without saying I was willing. Nobody, not my dad, not Tilly, not any man. You won't understand the difference. A man wouldn't. Most women wouldn't."

"Maybe I'm the exception," I said.

She looked at me.

"Our five minutes are just about up," I went on as I checked my watch. "The gun disappears. You stick to your story. The only one who knows it's not true is Pirannes. The police won't believe him if they catch him. The problem is that Pirannes has probably figured out that you killed Spiltz."

"He'll come for me," she said. "He'll kill me."

"No. I'll get Sally to keep you in here a couple of more days. I'll find Pirannes and convince him you didn't kill Spiltz."

"How you gonna do that?"

"You're not the only one who can tell stories," I said.

"And me?" she asked, turning to me again and pointing to herself. The question came out in a thin, plaintive whine like the air escaping from a balloon.

"You? You get out, go live with Flo Zink and live happily ever after," I said.

"I'll give it a try," she said. "I'll try. I really will."

"You'll make it," I said with a certainty I didn't feel.

"You don't have to show me the gun," she said. "I believe you."

The door opened and Sally came in. She looked at Adele, who was looking down at the floor, her arms folded. Then she looked at me.

"You all right, Adele?" Sally asked.

"I'll be fine. Sally, can I stay here a few days, just a few days? I've got some thinking to do, things to work out about my dad, stuff. I gotta get used to going to live with that lady."

"I think that can be arranged," Sally said.

"I've got to go," I said.

Sally looked at me with questions in her eyes, questions I might never answer. Then she turned and moved to comfort Adele.

15

THE AFTERNOON WAS GONE. I headed down Fruitville, driving into the setting sun. I flipped down my visor till I hit Tamiami Trail and turned right. The sun was big, low and bright over my left shoulder.

I thought about what I was going to do with Tony Spiltz's gun. I thought about how many laws I was breaking, started counting them and gave up at six. I'd worry about that, if I had to, when and if there was peace for me here in Paradise.

People in business usually arrive early to prepare for the day or the night. They make sure the furniture or stock is in place, the cash register is still working, the pictures on the wall and the merchandise are straight. Lots of things.

Pimps are no different. Tilly was no different. I pulled into the parking lot of the Linger Longer Motel, parked, locked the doors and moved quickly to Tilly's home away from home.

I knocked. No answer. I knocked louder. No answer. I went to the office. The kid with the big glasses who spoke a dozen languages looked at me.

"Tilly?" I asked.

"If he's not in his room, I don't know," he said. "I just got here."

I needed Tilly.

"Take a guess."

"He usually eats at the Mel-o-dee before he begins his night. Always goes alone. He says he needs some alone time to think before things start. Girls usually start when it's dark."

"Thanks," I said.

The kid didn't answer.

The Mel-o-dee was a little farther north and on the west side of the Trail. I'd eaten there a few times. Down-home food, small but good salad bar. The place was full. It was dinnertime. People in the neighborhood, low-budget tourists, men and women just getting off of work who lived alone or didn't want to go home yet ate at the Mel-o-dee.

A quartet of elderly people, three women and one man, was waiting to be seated. I nudged past them, looking for Tilly. He was in a booth on the left next to the window. His back was turned to me but he was easy to spot. He was the only black customer in the room. There was another room in back, but I knew I had found him.

I walked past singles, doubles, trios and quartets of people eating and talking. A pair of families, both with babies in high chairs, one with two kids in high school, were seated at booths to the right of Tilly.

I sat across from him in the booth. He had a bite-sized piece of meat loaf on his fork and a newspaper next to his plate. He was wearing glasses. He was dressed in a white turtleneck shirt with a black jacket. He looked like a car salesman or a clerk at Circuit City.

"What the hell do you want?" he asked with exasperation, taking off his glasses and putting them in his pocket.

"You know Handford's dead?" I asked, watching his eyes.

"No," he said. "But as my grandmother would say, 'Hallelu and Praise the Lord.'"

"Convince me you didn't kill him," I said.

He put down his fork and looked at me with even greater exasperation.

"Go away, man. I didn't kill Handford. I wouldn't go near him. I don't kill people. Where'd the profit be in killing Handford? I'm a businessman."

"Peace of mind," I said. "With Handford gone you'd have a little peace of mind."

"If I killed every motherfucker whose death would give me peace of mind, I'd rack up a better record than John Wayne Gacy. Now go away."

"You convinced me," I said.

"That makes me very happy," he said. "Now, I want to finish my dinner and read my paper. I've got to get to work."

"Adele is at the Juvenile lockup," I said.

"She's none of my business anymore."

"If she ever tries to come back to you, I want you to call me."

"You scare the shit out of me," he said with a smile. "I wouldn't take her back. Pirannes would have me disappear in a minute if he found out. Are you finished now? Can I eat now? My food is getting room temperature."

"Where's Pirannes?"

"Okay. I tell you, you go."

"I'll go."

"Word is he's on his big boat hiding out somewhere, probably Texas, maybe Mexico, waiting for his lawyer to clean up some stuff he's into. I don't know what."

"That's the word," I said. "But where is he really?"

"You're smarter than you look."

"It helps in my business. Pirannes?"

"Tell me and I go," I said.

"Just when I'm beginning to enjoy your company. He finds out I told you and I'm a dead man."

"That's what you said the last time we talked about Pirannes. He won't know."

"Word is he sent the boat out to make it look like he was waiting things out across the gulf. Cancun. He's got business here. He leaves for three, four days and it all falls apart here. You know what I'm saying?"

"I know," I said.

A waitress approached and asked if I was eating. I said no. She moved away.

"I'm not supposed to know it," Tilly said, leaning forward, "Nobody's supposed to, but a lot of people do. Pirannes likes to hang out at a place he owns a piece of out on Proctor, gated, town houses, big houses. Place is called New Palm Manors. Pirannes uses the name Steele. Now you know. Now you go. Looking for that man is a bad idea. I told you once. He boils over real easy."

"I know," I said. "He tried to kill me."

"And you're going to look for him again?"

"Yes."

Tilly shrugged and put his glasses back on. "Have a nice forever," he said.

He looked down at the newspaper. Our conversation was over.

I drove south down the Trail past an endless line of malls small and large, gas stations, office supply stores and restaurants. Sarasota has lots of restaurants. People on vacation eat out. Retired people with money eat out. This is an eat-out town. There were no really good Chinese restaurants. I missed that. Chicago had more than a hundred first-class Chinese restaurants. My favorite Chinese restaurants in Chicago were in China Town. My wife and I had gone there at least once a month for dim sum.

I drove warily, slowly, watching other drivers, waiting for one of them to cross the line coming at me and hit me head-on, or one of the ancient drivers to sideswipe me into another car.

I turned on the radio. G. Gordon Liddy was answering a caller's question about morality and loyalty. G. Gordon said he had gone to jail in the Watergate case because he refused to lie under oath. He praised Susan McDougal and said something about the importance of loyalty. You give your loyalty to someone and you don't betray it even if the person you've given it to abandons you. At least it was something like that.

I had given my loyalty to Beryl Tree. I

hadn't given it to Carl Sebastian, but I was still working for him. I owed him what I had promised to give. I'd promised to find Melanie. But right now I was trying to bring Beryl's case to an end.

I drove down Proctor, past walled-in and gated developments on both sides, across the bridge over I-75. The New Palms Manor was on the right. I drove up to the gate and waited. A woman in a gray uniform came out of the gatehouse. She wasn't wearing a hat or jacket. She was slim, dark and serious. I considered asking her if she was Italian.

"Yes, sir?"

"I'm here to see Mr. Steele. We have an appointment. My name is Dwight Handford. Is there a clubhouse, community house, here?"

"Straight ahead to the right."

"Busy in there tonight?"

"Wouldn't know for sure, but it's Friday night and there's almost always people playing cards, talking, having drinks or parties."

"Good, will you tell Mr. Steele that I'll be waiting for him in the clubhouse."

She nodded and went back into the gatehouse. I watched her pick up the phone, hit some buttons and start talking. She looked over at me once and then talked some more. She hung up and came out.

"Mr. Steele will meet you in the clubhouse in a few minutes," she said.

She went back in the gatehouse, did something, and the gate went up.

The clubhouse was easy to find and there

were about thirty cars in front of it. I parked the Geo as far from the entrance as I could get.

Immediately through the doors I found myself in a large room full of couches, tables and chairs. Most of the chairs and couches were full. A few clumps of people were standing. There was a small bar to the right, behind which stood a small bartender in a white shirt and a red vest. The people of the manor were dressed casually, in simple dresses, skirts and blouses, slacks and short-sleeved shirts. The people of the manor were generally not young.

I found a vacant couch to the right of the door and sat.

Pirannes came in alone five minutes later. He was wearing slacks, a shirt, a tie and a light-weight tan jacket. He was overdressed and he didn't look happy. He found me and sat down at my side without looking at me.

"You're dead," he said.

"How did you know I wasn't Dwight Hand-ford?"

"Handford's dead," he said. "I knew about it by noon. Besides, Angela described you."

"Angela, at the gate. Is she Italian?"

"Her name's Angela Conforti. And my name is Richard Steele and your name is mud. How did you find me? Who told you?"

"Your secret is safe with me, but I've got to tell you, about a third of the criminal population of this community knows about Mr. Steele's manor retreat."

"What the hell do you want, Fonesca?"

I looked at him.

"Did you kill Dwight Handford? Not that I care much. Just for my peace of mind. I can't prove anything and it's just between you and me. You can deny it later."

"You're wearing a wire, carrying a tape recorder," he said.

"Get friendly. Check me out."

"Let's go in one of the private rooms," he said.

"I might not walk out," I said.

"I'm not going to kill you here. I'm not an idiot."

I followed him through a lounge on the left, where people were playing cards at two tables. Beyond the lounge were two doors. We went through the one on the right. Pirannes turned on the lights, faced me and patted me down. He wasn't gentle.

The room was small, had tastefully wall-papered walls, sconces with teardrop lightbulbs, furniture with the look of something old and French.

"I didn't kill Handford," he said. "And I didn't kill Tony Spiltz. The kid lied about me being there. I'll tell you something, Fonesca."

He was starting to get worked up. That was not a good sign.

"I'll tell you what I think," he went on, pointing a finger at me. "I think Handford set me up. I think he came back to get the kid when I wasn't there. I think he killed Tony. I think maybe she helped him. He told her the story about me being with her. I'll tell you that if someone hadn't killed Handford, I would have done it myself, personally. But I didn't."

"Leave Adele alone," I said.

He laughed and shook his head. He even started to choke a little. I was being very funny.

"I wouldn't..." he managed to get out and then paused to regain his voice and some of his anger. "I wouldn't take her back. I wouldn't go near her. She might kill a customer. She might kill me. But I tell you what I do want, what would keep her safe."

"What?"

"The money I paid for her," he said.

He ran his hand back over his hair and pulled himself completely together.

"How much?"

"She went cheap," he said. "Eight thousand. Handford didn't know what he could have gotten. I'll take the eight thousand. I'll be very nice. I won't ask for any of the money I could have made on her."

"You're a man of principle," I said.

"Sarcasm will get you killed," he said.

"I thought I was already a dead man."

"No. I like you. I'd offer you a job, but I don't think you'd take it and I don't think I could trust you. I get the eight thousand by tomorrow noon and you live and I leave the girl alone."

"What have we got going here that tells me I should trust you?"

"Simple," he said. "I've got no reason to lie. If I wanted you dead, I'd have my man waiting outside the door follow you to your little white car. He'd kill you quietly, pack you in the trunk—"

"I don't think I'd fit. It's a Metro."

"Shove you on the floor in the back," he said. "Drive you out of here smiling at Angela, and leave you somewhere quiet and peaceful."

"How would he get back?"

"You always think like that?" Pirannes asked with a smile.

"Almost always. I can't stop."

"Another car would be following him, pick him up, bring my man somewhere else. Any more questions? I advise you not to get me mad."

"Where do I deliver the eight thousand?"

"Main post office. Noon on the button. Woman in a white dress. Blonde. Young. Pretty. Cash in an envelope. If there's anything traceable, marked, you die. You want to die for eight thousand dollars?"

"No," I said.

"You have eight thousand dollars?"

"No, but I can get it."

"I don't need eight thousand dollars, you understand. But I have to have it."

"The principle."

"The principle. You walk out of here now. You never come back. You never look for me again. You forget you ever met me."

"Met who?"

He smiled and put his right hand on the side of my neck and patted not too gently.

"Right question," he said. "You've got three minutes to be back on Proctor Road."

I left. I didn't see anyone outside the doors of the clubhouse, but that didn't mean they weren't there. I was on Proctor Road heading home in less than two minutes.

It was night. It wasn't late. I drove to Flo's. The lights were on. Her 1994 Jeep was probably in the garage.

She opened the door a few seconds after I rang. She had a drink in her hand.

"Lewis," she said. "You here to check up on me?"

"No, Flo."

"Smell this, taste it," she said, holding the glass in front of my face.

I took the glass, smelled it, tasted it.

"Ginger ale," I said.

"Seven-goddamn-Up," she answered. "Come in."

Flo was wearing a blue buttoned shirt and a denim skirt. A familiar voice was singing through the house. He was singing something about the rose of San Antoine.

"Roy Rogers," she said. "Underrated singer. Sons of the Pioneers backing him up. You've got news? You want a drink?"

"No drink, thanks."

We sat in the kitchen. I had caught Flo in the middle of dinner. There was a plate on the table, knife and fork. Chicken, green beans.

"Mind if I eat while we talk?"

"No," I said.

"Hungry?"

"No."

She ate.

"Edna Stockbridge called me, said Adele had to stay put for a few days, said she had to clear

303

the papers we worked on and get a judge to approve me. Said there wouldn't be a problem. Hell, Lewis, I'm going to be a mother after all these years."

"She won't—"

"Be easy," she finished for me. "Tell me something new."

"Eight thousand dollars," I said. "I need eight thousand dollars cash."

She ate some chicken and said,

"When?"

"Tomorrow morning at the latest," I said.

"Big bills, little bills, what?"

"Doesn't matter," I said.

"I'll get it after I finish eating unless you're in a hurry."

"You want to know why I need it?"

"If you want to tell me," she said.

"It's about Adele," I said. "We're—you're insuring her from her past."

"Eight thousand isn't much to insure that."

She finished, threw her bones in the red kitchen garbage can, rinsed her plate, knife, fork and glass and put them in the dishwasher. Then she went to a drawer, opened it, took out a small screwdriver and motioned for me to follow her. We went across the living room to the opposite side of the house and down a hallway I'd never been in before. She led me into a little room with carpeting, two recliners and a television set. The lights were already on. Roy Rogers was loud and clear in here too. He was singing about a pony now.

Flo went to the television set mounted on a dark wood table with rollers. She rolled the television out of the way and opened a little built-in cabinet. There were books in the cabinet. She handed them to me and told me to put them down. I put them on one of the recliners. Then she reached back and edged the back wall of the cabinet out with the screwdriver.

We weren't through. There was a black safe with a dial and white numbers.

"I use my birthday backwards," she said, turning the dial as she said, "Thirty-four, twenty-nine, nine."

The safe swung open. It was piled thick and tight with bills. She pulled out a stack on the left, counted off hundreds and handed them to me. She pocketed a pile of bills and put everything back the way it had been. When I handed her the last book and she had put it in place, Roy Rogers sang, "Yippie ti aye oh."

"Thanks, Flo," I said.

She waved off my thanks as she rolled the TV back into place.

"Need an envelope for that?"

"Yes."

She went to a table between the recliners, opened a drawer, pulled out an envelope and handed it to me.

"My husband, Gus, and me used to practically live in this room," she said. "Now I do. Watch TV, read, write letters, drink, listen to music. That was his chair. This is mine. I like this room. I like it being small."

"I like it too," I said.

I meant it.

"I'm going to wait till Adele's here before I redecorate the guest room down the hall, turn it into hers. She can do what she wants with it long as she keeps it clean."

"Don't spoil her, Flo."

"I'll work her. Don't worry."

"And don't let her know about the safe," I said.

"Lewis, you've known me two, three years. Am I a fool?"

"Definitely not."

"Then don't act is if I might be one. I know what the girl's been through. She's not coming to me out of a finishing school. She's a tough orphan. I'm a tough widow. Good combination."

"Good combination," I agreed.

"You bet your ass it is," she said, guiding me down the corridor to the door, holding on to my arm, screwdriver peeking out of her pocket, smile on her face.

When I left, Roy Rogers was singing "Happy Trails."

With eight thousand dollars in my pocket and a murder weapon under the seat, I headed home. The blue Buick was right behind me. Well, not right behind me but not far enough back that I couldn't see him.

I hadn't eaten with Tilly and I hadn't eaten with Flo. Pirannes hadn't offered me anything. The problem was that I wasn't hungry. The DQ was doing burn-up business now. The parking lot was almost full. I retrieved the gun, dropped it in my pocket where it did not fit snugly and wouldn't have even if it hadn't been in a ziploc bag, and went to my office-home.

The window was fixed and the broken air conditioner gone. Ames. Always Ames. I locked the door, put the chair in front of it, pulled the plug on my phone and went to bed with the gun and the envelope full of hundreds under the bed. There wasn't a decent place to hide anything here and I didn't want to part with gun or money.

So I put them where even a retarded blind chimp could find them. Then I watched my tape of *Mildred Pierce* for the three or four hundredth time.

When I woke up in the morning after dreaming of Ann Blyth coming to shoot me, I reached under the bed and found gun and money. I needed a shave. It was a little after seven in the morning. I was hungry. I staggered into the office and plugged in the phone. It was ringing.

"Hello," I said.

"Lewis, your phone is broken or you were out all night."

"I unplugged it."

"It's me, Harvey."

"I know," I said, mouth and tongue dry.

"Bingo," he said.

"Straight line or four corners?"

"Melanie Sebastian," he said. "Found her."

Which meant that Melanie Sebastian was ready to be found. There was no hurry. She would wait for me wherever it was. She had lived up to her word. She had let me find her just when she had promised.

16

THERE WAS A LOT to do that Saturday. It was too early for the DQ, and Gwen's place was only open during the week. I drove through the McDonald's where 301 and Tamiami Trail meet across from the office of the *Sarasota Herald-Tribune*.

The blue Buick was behind me. It was hard for him to hide on a sleepy Saturday morning.

I got a small black coffee and two Egg McMuffins. I ate the sandwiches as I drove, and when I parked in front of the offices of Tycinker, Oliver and Schwartz I drank my coffee. The street was almost deserted. A handful of cars were parked on the street, which on weekdays was full.

When I finished my coffee, I went into the office building and up the elevator to the door, which was open. There was no receptionist on duty and I could hear no voices. I moved down the corridor past the desk of the chief secretary and to Harvey's open office.

"Lewis," he said.

Harvey was clean-shaven, his hair brushed.

He was wearing an Oberlin sweatshirt and working at his computers with a mug of coffee or tea steaming next to him.

"Harvey," I said. "What have we got?"

"The technology doesn't exist to find the Buga-Buga-Boo virus origin. At least I haven't found it yet. The information superhighway does not yet have speed traps."

"Sorry to hear that."

"I haven't given up yet. You want Melanie Sebastian. I have her. Credit card in her name used yesterday at the Barrington House in Holmes Beach, that's on Anna Maria Island."

Harvey handed me the phone as he kept working. I looked up the Barrington House. It was a bed-and-breakfast. I called. A woman answered. I told her I was in from Baltimore and looking for a place for my wife and I to spend a quiet weekend at the end of the year. I said I'd like to come see the accommodations sometime this weekend. She gave me directions. I hung up, thanked Harvey and went back out past the empty offices.

I wanted to get rid of the gun I was carrying. I also wanted to get rid of the eight thousand dollars in cash. I wasn't worried about being picked up by the police for speeding or making an illegal turn. I'm too careful a driver for that, but Detective Etienne Vivaise might be looking for me again.

I drove to Carl Sebastian's high-rise condo building. I thought I might wake him up. I didn't. He answered the buzzer in the lobby after a full minute and asked who I was. I told him. He buzzed me in. When the elevator doors opened, he was there in a white robe, freshly showered, a V8 in hand. He looked nervous, anxious.

"You could have called," he said, "but if you have information about Melanie...I was up at four this morning. I can't sleep. I can't do anything."

"Today," I said as the elevator closed behind me. "I'll find her today. I'll talk to her. After that, it's up to her. If she says no, the choice is yours."

He ushered me into his apartment and closed the door.

"You're sure you can find her today?"

"I'm sure."

"When?"

"Before the sun goes down," I said.

He took a sip of V8 and nodded. His hand shook just slightly.

"I suppose I can't persuade you to tell me where she is so I can..."

"We have an agreement," I said.

"You're right. You're right. Just tell her I love her, want her back. She can make the terms. If I've done something wrong—"

"I know what to say," I said. "I need another five hundred dollars to close out the case. I'll give you a fully itemized bill for expenses."

He looked at me and said,

"You really know where she is?"

"I really know."

"This isn't a con to get an additional five hundred out of me?"

"Keep the five hundred and I stop looking as of this minute," I said.

He drained the glass of juice, thought for a second and said,

"I'll write you a check."

"Cash would be better," I said.

He put down the glass on the living room table and plunged his hands into the pockets of his robe. He looked at the portrait of his wife over the mantelpiece. I looked too. Then he sighed and said,

"All right. Cash."

I stayed in the living room, standing, looking at the portrait of Melanie Sebastian, while he moved to his office.

He came back in about three minutes, a folded wad of bills in his hand.

"I'll write out a receipt," I said.

"No, that's not necessary. Find her today, please."

Sebastian was himself again. I didn't count the money. I placed the wad of bills in my pocket and left.

The sun was out. The clouds were white and billowy and moving slowly. I drove over to Sarasota High School to watch the baseball team work out and play an intersquad game. There were about two dozen parents, girlfriends and people like me with nothing else to do in the stands.

I didn't see my angel in the blue Buick. Maybe he wasn't a baseball fan. The coach stopped the game from time to time to point out some problem, show the shortstop the right move for a double-play ball going from first base to second base and back to first, demonstrate to the center fielder how to throw home from the outfield so the ball could be cut off by the pitcher.

It wasn't like sitting in the stands watching the Cubs on a weekday afternoon, but it helped keep me from thinking too consciously about the gun and the money in my pocket.

I left after an hour. I had a Chicago Bulls baseball cap in the dresser in my room, but I hadn't thought about bringing it. If I stayed out in the sun too much longer, the top of my head would be sunburned: one of the several disadvantages of being almost bald.

Time moved slowly. So did I and so did the blue Buick. By eleven-thirty I had killed as much time as I could. I headed for the post office on Ringling.

The lot was almost full. I parked. A hot-dog cart stood on the sidewalk doing minimal business. I bought a dog from the dark, deeply tanned woman who wore an apron and a smile. She was a tall, slim brunette about forty.

The dog wasn't kosher and the bun wasn't steamed. I put extra onions and mustard on it and stood eating while I watched the front of the post office.

The blue Buick waited at the end of the parking lot.

"How's business?" I asked.

"Saturday's not the best," she said. "During

the week, working people line up sometimes. On Saturdays, you know, I catch 'em coming out of the post office."

"Then why come on Saturday?"

"I've got three kids and a husband on disability," she said. "It gets me out of the house and brings in maybe fifty to a hundred and fifty clear."

"You want to double your business?" I asked as I worked on my hot dog and watched the door.

"No," she said. "I want to keep living just above the poverty level."

"Kosher hot dogs, fresh steamed buns, good buns."

"Cost too much," she said.

"Double your business," I said.

"You want to guarantee that?"

"Life's a risk," I said, finishing my hot dog and throwing my napkin into a garbage bag she had set up.

"I'll stick with what I know," she said. "High profit. Low maintenance. If I spend more on merchandise I'll need more volume and I'll have more customers than I can handle."

She had a point.

"See that car, the blue Buick at the end of the parking lot?"

"Yes," she said, shielding her eyes from the sun with her hand.

"Two dogs with everything, a bag of chips and a Coke," I said, taking out two fives and handing them to her. "No change."

"Thanks," she said.

"I'll watch the stand while you make the delivery. You can keep an eye on me."

She got the dogs together, wrapped them, pulled out a Coke and a bag of potato chips and put it all in a brown paper bag. I stood watching as she hurried across the lot and knocked at the window. The window came down. She handed him the package and pointed back at me. I waved. He took the bag and rolled up the window.

I had missed the arrival of the blonde, but there she was. She was wearing a white skirt and blouse and her long hair was in a single braid that hung over her left shoulder. She was carrying a red purse over her right shoulder and looking around.

A few people passed her going in and out while I stood watching and the hot-dog lady returned. All the men looked at her, pretending not to look. The women were more open in their glances.

I moved around a pair of parked cars and approached the waiting woman, who had spotted me. She was a beauty. She wore no makeup and was probably in her late twenties. Her eyes were blue, her skin clear. There was even a good chance that the color of her hair was natural.

I held out the envelope. She took it without a word, put it in her purse and walked away. So did I.

I got in the Metro, pulled out onto Ringling and headed east. The Buick was a tactful distance behind me. I imagined my angel working on his second hot dog, cheek full, dropping relish on his lap as we drove.

There is a definite advantage in being the one who is followed rather than the one who follows. A good driver with a lot of nerve who knows the city could have lost the Buick in ten minutes even if the pursuing driver was good at what he was doing. A decent driver with imagination could have lost him in fifteen minutes. Lewis Fonesca, who couldn't speed and was unable to take chances in a car, took a little longer.

I went down Ringling to Tuttle, turned right, drove to Bahia Vista and went back to the Trail, where I turned left and then right to get to the parking lot across from the medical office building. I drove up the ramp wondering if the Buick would follow me or just wait for me to come down. My guess was that he would have to follow. I could park and walk over the ramp to the hospital, but I needed the car. I could go out the other exit or try to sneak past him. I went to the top of the garage and then headed down, trying to decide what I should try. Worst case, I'd have to think of something else to do.

By this time he had to know I was trying to lose him. I went up and down for about five minutes till on my fourth or fifth pass by the front exit I saw four cars waiting to pull out. There was a slight space between the first and second cars. I forced my way into the open space. The Metro was small enough to do it with a little cooperation from the driver in the second car. The driver was a heavy old woman with glasses who had to strain her neck to see over the windshield. She didn't seem to notice what I had done. I was sure the blue angel knew. He was now four cars behind me waiting to get out. When it was my turn, I turned right and then right again and drove the half-block to Osprey. Instead of turning either way, I went into the parking lot of the medical complex on my right. The lot was full. I drove to the rear where I knew there was a driveway to the buildings in back, found a space, parked and got out. The Geo couldn't be seen from the street.

The Buick came to the corner and hesitated. Then he turned right and moved up Osprey looking for me.

When he was out of sight, I went back to the Metro and got out of the lot before he came back. When I was reasonably sure I had lost him, I drove behind the Southgate Mall to the large Dumpsters. I took the gun out of the plastic bag, removed the remaining bullets, wiped the weapon clean, dropped it in my McDonald's bag and, when I was sure I wasn't being watched, dropped the bag into the nearest Dumpster, acting as if I were simply a good citizen getting rid of his lunch garbage.

Eventually, I took the bridge across to St. Armand's, drove straight up Longboat Key, up Gulf of Mexico Drive and past both Pirannes's high-rise on my left and the Sunnyside Condos on my right, where he docked the *Fair Maiden*. I drove on, hoping I had put John Pirannes out of my life.

I drove over the short bridge at the end of the key and went through the far less upscale and often ramshackle small hotels and rental houses along the water in Bradenton Beach. Ten minutes later, I spotted the sign for Barrington House and pulled into the shaded driveway. I parked on the white-crushed-shell-and-white-pebble lot, which held only tow other cars.

Barrington House was a white three-floor 1920s stucco-over-cement-block building with green wooden shutters. There were flowers behind a low picket fence and a sign to the right of the house pointing toward the entrance. I walked up the brick path for about a dozen steps and came to a door. I found myself inside a very large lodge-style living room with a carpeted, dark wooden staircase leading up to a small landing and, I assumed, rooms. There were bookcases whose shelves were filled and a chess table with checkers lined up and ready to go. The big fireplace was probably used no more than a few days during the central Florida winter.

I hit the bell on a desk by the corner next to a basket of wrapped bars of soap with a sketch of the house on the wrapper. I smelled a bar and was doing so when a blond woman came bouncing in with a smile. She was about fifty and seemed to be full of an energy I didn't feel. I put down the soap.

"Yes, sir?" she asked. "You have a reservation?"

"No," I said. "I'm looking for Melanie Sebastian, a guest here."

Some of the bounce left the woman but there was still a smile when she said,

"No guest by that name is registered."

I pulled out the photograph Carl Sebastian had given me and showed it to her, the one of Carl and Melanie happy on the beach. She took it and looked long and hard.

"Are you a friend of hers?"

"I'm not an enemy."

She looked hard at the photograph again.

"I suppose you'll hang around even if I tell you I've never seen her?"

"Beach is public," I said. "And I like to look at birds and waves."

"That picture was taken three or four years ago, right out on the beach behind the house," she said. "You'll recognize some of the houses in the background if you go out there."

I went out there. There was a small, clear-blue swimming pool behind the house and a chest-high picket fence just beyond it. The waves were coming in low on the beach about thirty yards away, hitting the white sand with a moan, bringing in a new crop of broken shells and an occasional fossilized shark's tooth or dead fish.

I went through the gate to the beach and looked around. A toddler was chasing gulls and not even coming close, which was in the kid's best interest. A couple, probably the kid's parents, sat on a brightly colored beach towel watching the child and talking. Individuals, duos and quartets of all ages walked along the shoreline in bare feet or floppy sandals. Melanie Sebastian was easy to find. There were five aluminum beach loungers covered in strips of white vinyl. Melanie Sebastian sat in the middle lounger. The other four were empty.

She wore a wide-brimmed straw hat, dark sunglasses and a two-piece solid white bathing suit. She glistened from the bottle of lotion that sat next to her atop a fluffy towel. She was reading a book or acting as if she was, knowing I was on the way. I stood in front of her.

"*War and Peace,*" she said, holding up the thick paperback. "Always wanted to read it, never did. I plan to read as many of the so-called classics as I can. It's my impression that few people have really read them, though they claim to have. Please have a seat, Mr. Fonesca."

I sat on the lounger to her right and she moved a bookmark and laid *War and Peace* on her lap. She took off her sunglasses. Her face was beautiful, somber. Her body was lean and taut. Normally, I would have enjoyed looking at her. Normally.

"We spent two nights here after our honeymoon in Spain," she said. "You would think Carl might remember and at least call on the chance that I might return here, but..."

"I've been paid to find you and deliver a message," I said. "Will you talk to him?"

She sat for about thirty seconds and simply looked at me. I was decidedly uncomfortable and wished I had the sunglasses. I looked at the kid still chasing gulls. He was getting no closer.

"You're not here to kill me," she said conversationally. "You could have done that in your office, or at least tried. But that would have been awkward."

"Kill you?"

"I think Carl is planning to have me killed," she said, turning slightly toward me. "In fact, I'm sure he is. Considering that it's Carl, he doesn't have much choice. But I can see that you're not the one who's going to do it."

"Why does your husband want to kill you?"

"Money," she said, and then she smiled. "People thought I married Carl for his money. I didn't. Mr. Fonesca, I loved him. I would have gone on loving him. He was worth only about a hundred thousand when we married, give or take a percentage point or two in either direction. I, however, was worth close to eleven million dollars from an annuity, the sale of my father's business when he died, and a very high-yield insurance policy on both my parents."

"When you left, you cleared out all your joint bank accounts, credit cards. I checked. Your husband has almost nothing. I checked that too. His business is in debt and he's on the edge of bankrupt."

"How did you find out?"

"Computers are frightening things. Almost as frightening as people."

"I hope Carl paid you in cash."

"This morning. After I found out about

his situation. It still doesn't make sense, Mrs. Sebastian."

"Call me Melanie. Your first name is...?"

"Lewis. Lew."

"It makes perfect sense," she said. "I know Carl has been telling people I'm having an affair with Dr. Green. Lew, I've been faithful to my husband from the day we met. Unfortunately, I can't say the same about him. I have ample evidence, including almost interrupting a session between Carl and Caroline Wilkerson in the buff in our bed five weeks ago. I was supposed to be out of town. I came back a day early to surprise him. It seems the man almost old enough to be my grandfather married me for my money. After I carefully closed the door without Carl or Caroline seeing me, I went out, stayed in at the Hyatt, did a lot of thinking. On the way out, I took Caroline's driver's license. I wanted to give her something to think about."

"You have reasons for divorce," I said. "But..."

"My word against theirs," she said. "He'd drag it on, find a way to hold up my assets. I haven't the time, Lew. So I did a little digging and discovered that Caroline was far from the first. I don't know if he is an old man afraid of accepting his age or if he simply craves the chase and the sex. I know he had no great interest in me in that department for the past year."

"You waited five weeks after you knew all this and then suddenly walked out?"

"It took me five weeks to convert all my stocks and my life-insurance policy to cash and to withdraw almost every penny I have in bank accounts. I didn't want a scene and I didn't want Carl to know what I was doing, but, obviously, he has known for several days."

"And you think he wants to kill you?"

"Yes. I don't think he knows the extent of what I have done, nor that I've cashed in the insurance policy," she said. "Carl claims to be a real estate dealer. He has averaged a little over twenty thousand dollars on his real estate deals each of the years we've been married. As for his investments, he has consistently lost money. He thinks that when I'm dead he'll have millions when, in fact, he'll have only a few thousand dollars in his bank account, an apartment he won't be able to maintain, and a 1995 paid-for Lincoln Town Car. Not much for a nearly seventy-year-old man with an image to maintain."

"And he's trying to kill you before you hide your money?"

"Yes, but it's too late. I've put all the money, but what I've kept with me in cash, into boxes and I've sent the boxes to various charities, including the United Negro College Fund, the Salvation Army and many others."

"Why don't you just tell him?" I asked. "Or I can tell him."

The toddler's mother screamed at the boy, who had wandered too far away in pursuit of the gulls. The kid's name was Harry.

"Then he wouldn't have tried to have me killed," she said.

"You want to die?"

"No," she said, "but I'm going to whether he kills me or not. Within a few months. I'm dying, Lew. Dr. Green knows it. I started seeing him as a therapist when I first learned about the tumor more than a year ago. I didn't want Carl to know. I arranged for treatment and surgery in New York and told Carl I simply wanted a few weeks or more to visit old school friends, one of whom was getting married. He had no objections. I caught him and Caroline in bed the day I returned. I had hurried home a day early to be with my husband, break the news to him. Treatment and surgery proved to be relatively ineffective. The tumor is inoperable and getting bigger. I don't wish to die slowly in a hospital."

"So you set your husband up?"

"You can look at it that way," she said. "But I couldn't do it without his full cooperation."

Harry the toddler was back with his mother, who was standing and brushing sand from the boy, who was trying to pull away. There were gulls to chase and water to wade in.

"You disapprove."

"I don't know. It's your life. You know a short tank of a man, about as bald as I am? Drives a blue Buick."

"Catano," she said. "Luke Catano."

"He's been following me since your husband hired me. He saved my life at least twice."

"He wanted you to lead him to me," she said.

323

"He wouldn't want you dead. Carl is in a hurry. Luke is Carl's 'personal assistant.' He has a record, including a conviction for murder two. Don't ask me how he and Carl came together. The story I was told didn't make much sense. So it looks like Luke Catano is my designated assassin."

"What if I don't tell him where you are," I said.

"You don't plan to tell him?"

"No, even if you tell me to."

"Good," she said. "I want to finish a few books, classics, before Catano comes. He'll find me without your leading him here. It may take him awhile. If it takes too long, I'll find a reasonably subtle way to let Carl know. I plan to die right here on the beach if possible. I've left a letter with my lawyer, documents proving my husband's infidelity, misuse of my money, which I knew about and chose to ignore, and a statement that if I'm found dead under suspicious circumstances, a full investigation into the likelihood of my husband's being responsible will be conducted. Now that I know Luke Catano is involved I'll drive into Sarasota tomorrow with a new letter for my lawyer including Catano's name. Lew?"

I must have looked dazed. I came back to the beach, the world, the beautiful dying woman and the boy trying to get away from his mother.

"Sorry," I said.

I got up.

"That's it, then," I said.

"Almost," she answered. "Adele."

I sat again.

"Adele?"

"The file on your desk. The day I came to your office. I read it before you got there, remember I was just finishing it when you arrived."

"I remember" I said.

"Is she all right?"

"Yes, I think so," I said. "She's going to a foster home, a good one. Her father's dead."

"I know," she said, looking at me. "I killed him."

"Oh, Holy Mother," I said, closing my eyes.

"Did Carl tell you I took his gun, the one in his desk, when I left?"

"No."

"I can see why. It was not purchased legally. After I left your office I thought about Dwight Handford. I must have decided to kill him while I was reading the file. The idea of what he was doing to...I'm leaving a relatively evil world, Lew. I didn't want to leave it before a monster like Handford. Somehow it didn't seem right that I should die and he should go on living. I memorized his address and got up enough nerve to kill him. I'd never fired a gun before. He had no idea who I was or why I was killing him."

"Christ," I said.

"You're shocked?"

"Yes," I said.

"But you're not sorry Handford is dead?"

"No."

My eyes were open now. Her hand was out, waiting. I got up and took it.

"You're a good listener, Lew," she said.

"My job," I answered.

"Carl is not a good listener. He's a talker. If he listened, he'd know where I might be."

I let go of her hand and she put her sunglasses back on and returned to Tolstoy.

I headed back to Sarasota, considered making a stop for coffee, but I didn't want to be with people. I kept seeing Melanie Sebastian sitting on that lounger in her wide-brimmed straw hat, reading and waiting.

In my room, I popped *Prince of Foxes* into my VCR. Not enough Orson Welles. Too much Tyrone Power. In a few days I'd forgive Power and watch *Blood and Sand*.

The phone in my office rang on and off for more than an hour. I lay in bed watching the movie. I ignored the phone till the movie was over and then I answered. I didn't want Carl Sebastian coming to my door or sending Luke Catano. It was Sebastian.

"Well?" he asked, sounding like a concerned and ill-treated husband.

"I found her, lost her," I said. "I talked to her for a few minutes. All she said was she didn't want to talk to you. I'll keep looking for her, no charge. If you want your money back—"

"No, no. Work fast," he said earnestly. "I'm worried about Melanie."

"I'll work as fast as I can," I said.

When I hung up, I took out the photograph

of Melanie and Carl Sebastian on the beach. They still looked happy. To the extent you can tell such things, they seemed to be very much in love.

I decided to wait a few days, drive around, ask questions in all the wrong places, let Catano keep up with me and then I'd give up and tell Sebastian I had lost her trail. I would send him a report. A few days after that, maybe a week or two, Catano and Sebastian would find her. Melanie would be dead. I hoped it would be on the beach but it would probably be a hit-and-run.

I tried not to think about it, but trying didn't help.

EPILOGUE

SALLY AND I went to a movie, something at Burns Court, something in French set in the distant past, costumes, horses, palaces, love, tragedy. We ate popcorn. My mind was on a beach.

Both of us ate lightly at the Bangkok Restaurant. I couldn't finish my pad thai. I always finished pad thai.

"Lew, where are you?" she asked.

"Sorry," I said. "I'm coming back."

"Remember," she said. "I told you the kids are away for the weekend."

"I remember," I said.

She played with her food for a few seconds and looked at me.

"I'm not ready, Lew," she said.

"I'm not either."

The restaurant was Saturday-night crowded. No one was paying any attention to us. Sally had worn a blue dress with a wide belt. Her earrings dangled with blue stones that caught the light. Her dark hair looked different than it had the day before. It had been cut and brushed back off of her ears.

"Let's be friends for a while," she said. "See where it goes. See when we're ready. I don't even know if my body remembers how to do it."

"I've heard you never forget."

"Disappointed?"

"Yes and no. Relieved in a way. You want to talk about your husband?"

"Yes, if you want to listen."

"I want to listen."

"You want to talk about your wife?"

"I think so."

"You want to go first?" she asked.

The waiter brought us more tea and I said, "Catherine. Her name was Catherine."